AMY THE ASTRONAUT AND THE SECRET SOLDIERS

AMY THE ASTRONAUT AND THE SECRET SOLDIERS

STEVEN DONAHUE

Twin
Sisters
Press

Twin Sisters Press

Goshen, Kentucky 40026

www.twinsisterspress.com

Twin
Sisters
Press

Chapter One

Amy Sutter twisted the throttle and felt the powerful vibrations that moved through the vehicle. She adjusted her goggles and turned her head to the right where she saw her opponent.

Ethan shook his head at her and revved his engine.

Amy saw the sweat forming on his face, and she knew that he was nervous. The sand jets roared and shook as the drivers waited for the signal to start.

A dozen kids, ranging in age from ten to fourteen-years-old, stood on either side of the riders. They hollered and cheered, their noise barely audible over the sounds of the engines. A dry Paldor wind swept over them, kicking up sand and dirt. This secret race on the stolen jets took place two miles west of Amy's home in the Pioneer settlement.

A thirteen-year-old blonde-haired girl leaned on Amy's shoulder and shouted at the racer. "Are you sure this is a good idea?" she asked. "These things go really fast."

Amy nodded. "That's the best part, Gina. I love to go fast." She pointed at Ethan, who tapped his fingers on the steering bar of his jet. "Besides, Ethan bet me that I couldn't beat him. I can't let him think he's right."

Gina patted Amy on the shoulder. "Good luck," she said. The girl walked away from the riders until she stood fifty feet in front of them. She waited for the dust to settle before removing an orange handkerchief from around her neck and raising it over her head.

Amy squeezed a bit harder on the throttle.

Gina dropped the orange cloth, and the racers dashed forward on their machines.

Amy quickly shifted gears and kept her eyes on the pole planted in the sand that marked where the riders had to turn around. It was 300 yards from the starting point. The sand jets moved side-by-side, as neither rider could gain a sizable edge.

Ethan bumped Amy's jet a few times, trying to intimidate her. Sparks flew as the metal blades collided.

Amy laughed and bumped him back. "Is that all you've got?" she yelled.

He hollered something back that she couldn't quite hear.

The sand jets bounced over the uneven land as the wind blew more dust into the riders' faces.

Amy used her left hand to clear her goggles. Her heart pounded, and her throat felt arid. She saw Ethan out of the corner of her eye. He seemed to be struggling to keep his jet under control. She pressed her lips together and leaned forward.

They were close to the pole when Amy sped up, gunning the engine for all it was worth. She waited a moment before jamming on the brakes and turning the steering bar. Her craft lifted and nearly flipped over as she made the turn. She looked back and laughed as she saw that Ethan had missed the turn. Then she suddenly realized that he was in trouble.

Amy watched Ethan stand up in his seat and pump his

brakes. His machine would not slow down. She quickly spun back around and darted toward him. Her eyes widened in horror as she saw that he was headed for the base of a mountain. She turned the throttle all the way down and managed to get beside his jet. "Jump on," she screamed.

The boy froze in his seat. He glanced at her and then at the rock formation that they were quickly closing in on. "C'mon, jump!" Amy said.

The boy leaped from his machine and landed with a thud onto the back of Amy's jet. He nearly slid off of it, and had to grab the back of her shoulders to stay on.

Amy used her left arm to help him settle on the seat. She applied her brakes and turned away from the mountain before she brought her jet to a complete stop.

The riders watched the abandoned jet as it crashed into the mountainside and exploded. They looked at each other in shock and fear.

The other kids ran toward them, yelling and screaming.

Ethan rose from the seat and collapsed onto the ground. He sat up and wrapped his arms around his legs as tears filled his eyes.

The kids finally reached them.

"Are you all right?" Gina asked.

Amy ignored the question and turned off her jet's engine without saying a word. She looked at the other jet, burning on the sand. *How am I going to get out of this one?* she wondered.

———

A fan whirled over Amy's head as she sat in a square, metal chair. The outer office was hot, and the slight breeze did little to help. Amy looked up at the closed door with Gen. Knox's name on it. She heard muffled voices from inside the office. They did not sound happy.

A secretary sat behind a small desk to the left of the door. She wore civilian clothing that looked much more comfortable than the standard issue, dark-green Union uniforms. The secretary typed on a laptop computer while sounds emanated from a mobile military radio on her desk.

Amy tried to make eye contact with the woman, but the worker focused on her tasks instead.

The door to the general's office finally opened, and Amy stood as she saw her parents exit the room. She moved toward them. "Mom, I can explain—" she started, but was cut off by her mother's stern look. Amy turned to her father. "Dad, really, I didn't mean—" she said, again cut off, this time by the wave of his right hand. She stood still as her parents walked past the secretary's desk and left the room.

Capt. Yale Brown appeared from the office. Her steely blue eyes bore into Amy's face. "The general wants to see you," she said.

Amy sighed and slowly entered the military commander's office. She slipped past Yale and stood before the large wooden desk.

Yale closed the door and stood behind the girl.

Gen. Knox had his back to his visitors. A painting of George Washington and his men crossing the Delaware River in a boat hung on the wall he was facing. Gen. Knox stood straight and still, as if saluting someone of a higher rank. He slowly turned and faced the young girl. "Have a seat, Amy," he ordered as he slipped into his leather chair.

Amy sat in the smaller chair that faced him.

Yale remained standing.

The room wasn't as humid as the outer office, but it was

still hot enough to make Amy sweat. She rubbed her wet hands against her pants.

"I really don't know what to do with you," Gen. Knox said. "Many people on Paldor think you are a hero for what you did last year. I don't. I think you are a reckless, spoiled child who thinks she can do whatever she wants around here."

Amy began to protest, but Knox cut her off by lifting his left hand. "I also know that you are a smart, caring, and courageous girl who could, someday, be a real asset to the Union."

Amy smiled at that remark and sat up a little straighter.

"You have natural flying skills and the potential to be a real leader." He paused and glanced at Yale before looking back at the girl. "But you lack discipline!" he shouted, pounding his fist on his desk. The sudden noise startled Amy. "And that is unacceptable. I warned you when you came back from your escapade on the *Liberty Bell* that I wouldn't tolerate any foolishness from you."

He took a breath. "And, yet, here we are again. Since you've been back, you have been caught sneaking into the flight simulators, hacking our databases, spray painting our buildings, and now this: joyriding on sand jets." He glared at her. "Well, what do you have to say for yourself?"

Amy shrugged. "I'm sorry." She couldn't help glancing at the painting. The men looked tired and cold, but also serious and determined. She recognized the scene from her studies with Madison, and she wondered if Gen. Knox saw himself as a modern-day Washington. Instead of fighting the British for independence, humanity continued to fight the Crownaxians for their right to exist.

The general leaned forward in his chair, and Amy looked back at him. "That's not good enough," he said. "You are afforded a lot of luxuries on Paldor because your parents have important jobs here, but you still have to follow the rules. Why don't you?"

Amy took a deep breath. "I don't mean to cause trouble," she replied. She clenched her fists. "I miss flying the *Liberty Bell*, which is why I sneaked into the simulators. I hacked the database to play some training games that I don't have access to, and I was only holding an extra paint can while Ethan decorated a supply shed." She paused; hoping that would help explain her actions, but Knox continued to glare at her. "OK, the sand jets race was my idea. We only borrowed them, and I didn't think we'd crash."

Gen. Knox stood and stared down at her. "That is the problem, Amy. You don't think ahead. Sand jets are expensive and dangerous. They are vehicles that require expert handling, not some exotic toy. You were lucky that no one was seriously hurt." He waited a moment and then nodded toward Yale.

"I'm glad to hear that you miss the *Liberty Bell*," Yale said, "because you are going to be aboard her again, but not as the pilot."

Amy turned and gave her a quizzical look.

Yale moved toward the girl and motioned to her to stand up.

Amy rose, facing her friend.

"As part of your punishment, you and Ethan are going to accompany me and a team to Janar, a Union planet that recently suffered terrible damage from a devastating storm in its Northern continent. They need supplies and help rebuilding, and we are low on Union staff in this area." She shook Amy's hand. "Congratulations. You just volunteered to help with the aid effort."

Amy was speechless. She glanced at Gen. Knox, who nodded back at her.

"We leave in eight hours," Yale stated.

––––––––

Amy followed Yale out of the general's office.

They passed the busy secretary and found themselves outside. The earlier wind had died down, and it felt dryer than before. They walked toward Amy's home without looking at each other.

Yale finally broke the silence. "This trip should last about two weeks," she said.

Amy nodded.

"It will be cooler than Paldor, so you want to pack warm clothing. Gloves and a hat, too, I think."

Amy nodded again.

"I bet you are excited about flying on the *Liberty Bell* again. Break up the boredom."

The young girl halted and peered up at the officer. "Do you agree with Gen. Knox?" she asked. "Do you think I'm reckless?" She didn't know why, but the general's words cut her deeply. Normally, she wouldn't care what someone in his position thought about her but, for some reason, he really got to her.

The captain smiled. "You can be, at times. Like that stunt this morning. That was reckless." She squeezed Amy's right shoulder. "But you are also an amazing young woman. How many thirteen-year-olds can say they flew one of the fastest ships in the galaxy?" She let go of the girl. "And your rescue of your father was nothing short of a miracle, even if you did have help. Listen to what Gen. Knox said, because he was right, but don't sell yourself short. You have wonderful potential, and I can't wait to see the woman you finally grow in to."

They continued on toward their destination.

Amy thought about what Yale said, as well as the words of Gen. Knox. She hoped that she had a bright future. She still wanted to attend the Union Academy on Earth and become a pilot someday, but she realized that she was, sometimes, her own worst enemy. Amy knew it was time to straighten up her act, but she wondered if she had the discipline to do so.

Amy saw a familiar figure ahead, and she stopped walking. She turned toward Yale. "Can you give me a minute?" she asked.

Yale said yes and turned toward a barrack building on her right. She leaned up against the structure as Amy continued forward.

The young girl's mouth grew dry, and her hands got clammy as she approached the boy.

Ethan pulled his hands behind his back and he rocked forward on his toes. "Hi, Amy," he said, with a slight crack in his voice. He was wearing different clothing from earlier in the day, and his brown hair was neatly combed. The boy was a full inch shorter than Amy, and he looked like he was trying to compensate for that by standing fully straight. "How much trouble did you get in?" he asked.

Amy shrugged. "I got a lecture from Gen. Knox," she replied. "And I was also recruited for a relief mission on another planet."

He said that he was as well, and that Yale had told him.

Amy sighed. "It will be fun to get back on the *Liberty Bell*, even if I won't be the captain this time."

Ethan smiled and dangled his hands in front of his body. "I am looking forward to it," he said. "I've never been on a spaceship like that before. It could be fun."

The girl returned his smile. "Maybe." She paused, trying to find the right words. Amy glanced over her shoulder at Yale before looking back at the boy. "I'm sorry about what happened with the sand jets. That was really dumb. We could have been seriously hurt." She reached out and touched his right hand. Her heart pounded.

"It's OK," he replied. "It was my fault, too."

Amy looked at his boyish face. His light skin was clear, and he looked like he was on the verge of shaving. The boy had a small, straight nose and a delicate, square chin. Amy held her breath for a moment as a silence built up between them. She slowly leaned toward him and closed her eyes.

"Time to go," Yale shouted, and the kids pulled away from each other.

Ethan looked at the ground for a moment then kicked some dirt away.

He looked back up at Amy. "I gotta get ready, too," he said. "See you onboard."

"See you," Amy replied.

Ethan drifted past her, and she clasped his hands for a moment before letting go. Amy groaned and turned toward Yale.

They continued walking toward Amy's home.

"What was that about?" Yale asked.

"Nothing," Amy replied. She tightened her fists and looked straight ahead.

——————

Amy stood outside her front door and heard her parents arguing. Yale had rushed off after receiving a call on her cell phone, so the teen had to face her mother and father alone. She gathered her courage and opened the front door. The heated conversation stopped immediately.

Pam glared at her daughter before turning then leaving the room.

Amy closed the door and sat down on the couch.

Her father sat down beside her. "What could you possibly say that could make us understand what you did today?" he asked.

The girl dropped her head and looked at the floor. "I'm sorry," she said. She honestly could not think of anything else that would be helpful.

Clayton didn't respond.

They sat together for several minutes, in silence, before Amy lifted her head. "I was just trying to have fun. I didn't stop to think about how dangerous it was."

"You are too old to be acting this way," Clayton said. He stood up with his back to her before turning around to face her again. "I can't even punish you. Gen. Knox has already done that. Although, this seems more like a chance to get you out of his hair for a while rather than giving you a real punishment. You will be back aboard the *Liberty Bell*, which is what you wanted, anyway." He shook his head. "I don't know. Maybe we shouldn't allow you to go."

"It sounds like a lot of work," Amy replied, rubbing her hands together. "But, maybe, I can do some good. I promise to keep out of trouble." She rested her hands on her lap and tried to read her father's face. He was a true diplomat, with the ability to hide his feelings. Amy couldn't tell what he was thinking.

Clayton crossed his arms over his chest. "Your mother wants me to put in for a transfer."

Amy's eyes widened.

"There is an opening on Mars for an arbitrator to help settle a dispute between a mining company and their labor union. The negotiations have been going on for nearly a year with no end in sight. It would mean moving there." He shrugged. "It would be safer there than here on Paldor. We would be much closer to Earth and the Union's main defense."

"Do I get a say?" Amy asked.

Clayton shook his head. "No. Not after the way you've been acting the last eight months."

Amy frowned.

Her father sat down next to her again. "Look, I know what you did to bring me home from the Crownaxains, and I will forever be grateful for that, but we are your parents, and we make the decisions regarding your welfare."

"So, I'm not going to Janar with Yale?" Amy asked. She sat back and crossed her arms over her chest. Anger rushed through her. She desperately wanted to take this trip on the *Liberty Bell*, and she wanted to spend time with Ethan, but she could see his point. That didn't sound like much of a punishment.

"Your mother doesn't want you to go," Clayton said. "She thinks it is too dangerous for two teenagers to be part of this mission. She is probably right." He sighed. "I don't know. What you did before was incredible. I know you can handle yourself in tough situations, but I don't want to put you in harm's way unnecessarily."

Amy rested her hands on her father's right arm. "You don't have to worry about me. I can handle myself." She paused. "Besides, Gen. Knox gave the order. Don't we have to obey?"

Clayton shook his head. "He can't order civilians to do anything, much less minors. The general doesn't have that much authority." Clayton looked at his daughter's face. "You are so young. If anything should happen to you, I wouldn't be able to forgive myself."

"Dad, I'll be fine," Amy said. She let go of his hands. "Let me do this. Let me show you, and everyone else, that I can be responsible."

Clayton closed his eyes for a moment. Then, without saying a word, he nodded his approval.

Chapter Two

Packing was a bit of a challenge for Amy. Most of what she owned was warm-weather clothing suitable for Paldor's hot climate. She did have a few articles of heavy clothing for the occasional chilly nights on the planet, but getting to them required digging to the bottom of her closet. Her room quickly became a tempest of strewn clothes and other things that had cluttered her storage area. The girl folded several items and tucked them into the single suitcase that she was allotted for the trip.

Amy stopped when she found the purple sweater. It was tangled up with a brown scarf. She brought the garment to her face and smelled the fresh, clean scent of the unworn top. Amy sat on her bed and kept the sweater close to her face. It was a gift from Penelope Cranberry, the Sutters' nanny who died three months after Amy's return with her rescued father. Although she wasn't with the family for very long, Amy had developed a deep love for the woman, who acted as a pseudo-grandmother for the girl. Amy closed her eyes and tried to remember the day Mrs. Cranberry gave her the gift.

There was knock on Amy's door. "Come in," she replied, not taking her eyes off of her computer screen. She was sitting at her desk playing Space Pirates, and she was on pace to break her own high score.

Mrs. Cranberry entered the room with a wrapped box in her hands.

Amy paused the game and smiled at her visitor. "What do you have there?" Amy asked.

The woman handed her the box. "Something I hope you will like," Mrs. Cranberry replied. She leaned against the desk as the girl opened the present. "I know you need it."

Amy pulled out the sweater and smiled at the woman.

"Purple is your favorite color, right?" the nanny asked.

"Yes," Amy said. "It's beautiful. Thank you." She rose and hugged the woman. "I just hope I get a chance to wear it. It's been so hot lately." She held it up to her chest.

Mrs. Cranberry asked her to try it on. Amy slid it over her T-shirt and she ran her fingers over the sleeves. "It's so soft," she said. "Perfect."

"I'm glad you like it," Mrs. Cranberry said. "Now you will have at least one warm thing to wear when you go to the Academy."

Amy folded the sweater and put it in the box. "You know I can't go for another year," the girl stated. "That's if I get in at all."

"You will get in," Mrs. Cranberry responded. "You are a very smart girl. They would be crazy not to take you." The nanny rose and brushed some hair from Amy's face. "You know that Philip and I were never blessed with any children. He died at Blaros before we had any." She stopped and looked past the girl, seemingly lost in the memory of her late husband. She pressed her lips together and smiled at Amy again. "I always thought of you as the daughter I never had."

The two embraced again. "I love you, Mrs. Cranberry," Amy said. She reached down and touched the gift again. This time, she carried it over to her closet and carefully hung it on a hanger. One day, it would slip from the hanger and fall into the abyss of her closet.

The girl rubbed her wet eyes. She took a deep breath and gently folded the purple sweater before packing it in the suitcase. Amy thought she was finished when she suddenly remembered something. She went to her bureau and opened the top drawer. She gently lifted up her paperback copy of *For Whom the Bell Tolls*, another gift, this one from her grandmother. Amy tenderly placed it on top of the purple sweater. She slowly zipped up the suitcase and rested it against the wall near her bedroom door.

The Sutter family had time for one more meal before Amy's departure.

Pam made lasagna with meat and served the dish to her husband and daughter before sitting down at the dinner table.

Amy inhaled the deep, rich aroma of the food. She recognized the fresh tomatoes, hamburger meat, ricotta and mozzarella cheese, garlic and oregano. For a moment, she forgot her plight and dug into the thick pasta with joyful abandon. She took three large bites and chewed them before realizing that both of her parents were staring at her.

"Oh, sorry," she said. She grabbed a napkin and wiped the sauce from her face. She smiled at her mother. "This is really great, Mom. Thanks." She took another bite and kept the napkin in her hand.

Pam nodded. "I am glad you like it," she replied. "But try eating it like a civilized person." She took a dainty bite of her food and ate it without making a mess. She tilted her head as if to say, *This is how it's done.* Pam took a sip of her iced tea. Her movements were so slow and deliberate that Amy had to fight the urge to laugh.

"They do have food aboard the *Liberty Bell*, don't they?" Clayton asked.

Amy nodded between bites.

The diplomat put his fork down. "Just remember, this mission is not a vacation for you. You will be working round the clock to help the people on Janar. We expect that you will conduct yourself with dignity." He paused to take a sip of his drink. "You are to follow all of Yale's orders and not cause trouble. Understand?"

Amy swallowed some food and nodded. "I understand," she replied. The girl looked down at her plate for a moment. "Don't worry. I won't embarrass you." Amy looked up at her father.

He shook his head and folded his hands. He had his lecture face on, a look that Amy knew well. His eyes said that he was not getting through to her.

"It's not about being embarrassed, Amy," he said. He leaned forward in his seat. "It's about doing the right things at the right times. It's about showing courage and discipline as the situation requires." He scratched his chin. "I don't want to scare you, but every mission has an element of danger to it. This one is no different. That is why you need to follow the rules and not run off to do your own thing. There will be perils you won't even see coming and, if you act recklessly, you will put your life, and the lives of those around you, in jeopardy."

Amy put down her fork and sighed. *There is that word again: reckless*, she thought. She clenched her fists. "I will do whatever Yale says, Dad. I will be a good, little soldier." Without realizing it, she slowly shook her head and rolled her eyes.

Pam slammed her glass against the table, making Amy jump. "That is exactly what we are talking about," she said. "Your attitude is appalling. You think that your hero status lets you get away with anything. That you can do whatever you want, no matter what anyone else says." Her face reddened, and Amy saw her hands shake. "Well, you are not a hero. You are just a little girl who has a lot of growing up to do. And you need to do it fast."

Clayton tried to speak, but Pam cut him off. "I don't think you should go to Janar," she said as she rose to her feet. She turned and walked away from the table. "I don't care what Gen. Knox says."

Clayton followed her and tried to calm his wife by gently putting his hands on her shoulders.

She pushed his hands away. "No, Clayton, I don't care," she said to him. "She is just a child, not some space cowboy. What she did before was pure luck. She is clearly not ready to handle the responsibilities of this mission. She is not going!" The doctor turned away from Clayton, stormed off to their bedroom, and slammed the door behind her.

Amy pushed her plate of half-eaten food away from her. "That's enough for me," she said to her father. "We need to leave soon if I am going to make it to the launch pad on time." She rose and walked toward her room.

Clayton told her to wait.

Amy shook her head. "You need to deal with her first," she said.

———

Amy sat on her bed and stared at her suitcase. Her door was open, and she saw her mother slowly enter the room.

Pam sat down beside her. "Are you ready to go?" she asked, softly. The doctor smoothed out a wrinkle on the bed's blanket. She made tiny circles with her long, delicate fingers.

"I am all packed," Amy replied. She glanced at her own hands, not liking the shortness and thickness of her fingers. *I'm glad I have no plans for a career in medicine*, she thought. She shifted uncomfortably on the bed and tried to figure out what her mother wanted.

The doctor clasped Amy's right hand. "We are worried about you," she said.

Amy started to speak, but stopped.

"We don't think you will embarrass us, honey. We are concerned about your safety." She shook her head. "Every time you walk out that door, I worry. The Universe is a violent place, filled with hatred and danger. I see it every day at my job. It's not just aliens that we need to worry about, it's other people, too." She sighed. "We think we are so advanced with all this technology, but the truth is, we are all savages. Some of us just hide it better than others."

Amy gently squeezed her mother's hand. "Mom, I will be OK. I can handle myself." She forced a smile. "Even if I do have an appalling attitude." She leaned against the woman and rested her head on her mother's shoulder. "I will be back before you know it."

Pam mildly stroked her daughter's hair. "There is so much more for you to learn," she said. "You think you are prepared, but many things will happen that will surprise you. This war has cost so many lives, destroyed so many families. I don't know if the Union can win, or even if humanity will survive."

"I believe we will," Amy said. She closed her eyes for a moment and remembered her rescue mission. "There are Crownaxians that oppose Drelk and his regime. They don't want war any more than we do. They will help us defeat him, I'm sure of it. It will just take time." She sat up and pulled away from her mother. "It's getting late. We need to go."

Pam sat up and wiped her eyes. "I hope you're right. We need all the help we can get." Pam nodded and kissed Amy's forehead. "Be careful. Listen to Yale. She will take good care of you."

Amy understood what her mother was trying to say, and she knew how difficult the words were for her. She wrapped her arms around the woman. "I love you, too, Mom," she said. They held the embrace for a moment, and Amy wished that she could ease her parents' fears.

The doctor pulled back and gave her daughter another quick kiss. "C'mon, we don't want to keep Yale waiting," she said. She grabbed the handle of Amy's suitcase and wheeled it out of the room.

Clayton met them at the front door. He took the handle from his wife and led them to a land vehicle that Gen. Knox had sent to their home. Clayton put the suitcase in the back of the vehicle as Amy and her mother sat down next to each other. The diplomat sat in the front with the driver.

The cruiser pulled away, and Amy looked over her shoulder at their home. She took a deep breath, and, for the first time, she felt nervous about her mission.

They arrived at the launch pad site, and the military vehicle eased to a stop.

The driver remained in the front seat while Clayton grabbed Amy's suitcase and Pam helped her daughter out of the back.

Other military personnel buzzed around, performing various tasks in preparation for the liftoff.

Amy looked at their serious faces and knew that it was time to mentally prepare for this assignment. She took hold of her suitcase handle and rolled it behind her.

Inside the building, she remembered the tension she felt before her father's launch on the *Harmony*. That operation started with a mixture of hope and fear as Clayton and other diplomats set out to meet with a group of Crownaxians who expressed interest in a peaceful dialogue between the two species. Instead, it turned out to be a trap that led to the abduction of the humans. Amy's desperation to save her father led to her theft of the Union ship *Liberty Bell* and her remarkable adventure that resulted in his rescue.

Amy smiled when she saw the *Liberty Bell* again. The ship sat in the hanger as Union soldiers moved swiftly to make the last-minute arrangements for the flight to Janar. In an odd way, the craft seemed to be calling out to the girl, as if welcoming her back on board. Amy thought it was just her imagination, but she couldn't be sure. All that she did know was that she was happy to see her old friend again.

"Are you ready to go?" a voice from behind her asked.

Amy turned and saw Capt. Yale Brown standing perfectly straight in that military fashion that must have been instinctive for her now. Yale was in full Union camouflage uniform, including the cap on top of her short, blond hair. She looked like she was posing for a Union recruiting poster. It made Amy chuckle.

The young girl couldn't help but salute.

Yale saluted back, although that wasn't quite proper under Union regulations.

Amy turned back toward the ship. "I almost forgot how beautiful she is," she said. She closed her eyes for a moment and remembered what it was like when she piloted the ship. She opened her eyes and sighed. "I don't suppose you will let me drive?" she asked.

"Not a chance," Yale replied. She tousled Amy's hair before addressing the girl's parents. "Ambassador Sutter, Dr. Sutter," she began. "I know this must be nerve racking for you, but I assure you we will keep Amy and Ethan as safe as possible."

Clayton nodded, but Pam did not respond. "They will be supervised at all times, either by me, or another officer. The safety of my crew is my utmost concern."

"We appreciate that, captain," Clayton said. He glanced at Amy before looking back at Yale. "And I assure you that we do not anticipate any shenanigans from our daughter. I know you won't allow any."

Yale nodded in agreement.

Clayton leaned toward Amy, putting his face a few inches away from hers. "Take care of yourself," he said, "and listen to all of Yale's orders." He hugged Amy and kissed her forehead.

Pam hugged her, too. "Come home in one piece." She kissed Amy's cheek, and then she moved back next to her husband.

Amy saw her mother's lips vibrate ever so slightly. She took a mental photograph of her parents to keep with her on the trip.

Yale walked beside Amy as they moved toward the *Liberty Bell*.

A Union sergeant approached them and took Amy's suitcase to stow aboard the ship.

The duo entered the craft and headed for the bridge.

Along the way, Amy dragged her right hand along the smooth surface of the walls. The inside smelled the same as it had before, a combination of fresh leather and disinfectant. The carpeted floor felt firm, yet cushioned.

They entered the bridge.

Amy stopped when she saw the towering, camouflage-colored robot sitting in one of the seats. She smiled and ran over to her friend. "Madison," she said, hugging the robot. "I didn't know you were coming with us." She let go of him and he stood up.

"I was just informed this morning," the robot said. He sat back down, and Amy sat in the seat next to his.

She looked over at the captain's chair and sighed.

"Sorry, Amy," Madison said. "But since we are not stealing the ship this time, we cannot sit up front."

Yale moved toward the captain's chair and sat in it. She spun to look at the young girl. "I hope you enjoy the view from there, Amy," she said. The pilot turned back around and checked the ship's instruments. From the look on her face, everything seemed in order.

"Who is the co-pilot?" Amy asked. She tried to hide her jealousy, but her fists instinctively tightened in her lap. She took a short breath and shook the tension from her hands. The girl looked around at some of the soldiers working at the other stations, but none of them were near the co-pilot's seat.

"I am the co-pilot."

Amy looked up at a young lieutenant as the woman entered the bridge. The officer stopped a few feet away from Yale and saluted. "Lt. Tesla Ford, reporting for duty, Sir," she said.

Yale saluted back and nodded toward the empty chair beside her. Lt. Ford was not as tall as Yale, and she had short, auburn hair and steely blue eyes.

Amy glanced at Madison and raised her eyebrows.

The robot nodded back.

Amy rose and moved toward Lt. Ford. "Hello, lieutenant," she said. "I am Amy Sutter." She offered her hand.

Lt. Ford politely shook it and let go.

"I'm not in the Union yet, but I'm here to help with the aid effort."

Lt. Ford nodded. "I know who you are," she said. "I also know why you are here and what you did the last time you were on board the *Liberty Bell.*" She cleared her throat. "I want you to know that you will be expected to conform to all Union rules and obey all orders given to you by Union officers during this mission. No tomfoolery will be tolerated. Is that clear?"

Amy took a half-step back. "Totally clear," she said. She turned around and slowly moved back to her seat. She sat quietly for a few minutes and observed the final preparations. A flurry of voices at the entrance to the bridge caught her attention. She smiled when she saw Ethan enter with his parents on either side of him. They were both uttering commands to the boy, who managed to stay a step ahead of them as they rushed in.

Ethan stopped, and his parents did the same. The boy looked lost.

Amy strode over to him. "Hey, Ethan," she said. "Welcome aboard the *Liberty Bell*." She slapped him on the right shoulder, and he laughed. Amy looked at his parents, who glared back at her. "I'm Amy Sutter," she said, offering the grownups her hand.

Neither accepted it.

Yale came to the rescue. "Mr. and Mrs. Grant," she said, shaking their hands. "It's good to see you again." She guided the parents off of the bridge and disappeared into the heart of the ship.

Amy and Ethan watched them go.

"Where is your stuff?" Amy asked. She grabbed the boy by the arm and led him to their seats.

He told her that a Union soldier took his bag and stowed it on board.

"Yeah, someone did that for me too," she said. She introduced Ethan to Madison. The boy's eyes widened in amazement at the mechanized soldier. "Don't worry, he won't hurt you," Amy said.

Yale returned a short time later.

Some of the Union soldiers departed, while others remained at their stations.

Amy took a deep breath and held Ethan's nervous hand as the *Liberty Bell* rolled out of the hangar.

Yale did a final systems check.

The flight tower gave a thirty-second countdown before the ship blasted off of the ground and headed into space.

Chapter Three

The *Liberty Bell* cruised through space as the crew headed for the planet Janar.

Amy sat in her seat holding a pawn in her hand. She looked at the chess board which lay on a small console between her and Madison. She squeezed the pawn that she had just captured and watched the robot take one of her knights. Amy sighed. Madison had won four games in a row, and nothing the girl did seemed good enough to even slow him down. She glanced over her shoulder at Ethan, who sat behind them. He was playing a hand-held video game and staring intently at the screen.

The seats pivoted, which allowed the girl to shift her attention to the captain's chair from time to time.

Yale typed on the keyboard in front of her and read that data on the view screen.

Beside her, Lt. Ford monitored other data about the ship.

Amy could just barely see the words scrolling across the screen. Everything seemed in order. The girl turned her attention back to the chess game and wished that she and Madison were flying the craft.

Three moves later, Madison had another checkmate. "Do you want to play again?" he asked Amy as he knocked over her king.

She shook her head and tossed the pawn onto the board.

The robot picked up the pieces and carefully placed them back into the game box, along with the game board. "You seem distracted," Madison said.

Amy shrugged. "I'm just not in the mood for games right now," she replied. She stood up and stretched her arms over her head. "Hey, why don't we take a walk? It would be nice to get up and do something." She looked over at Yale and knew that the captain had heard her.

"That's fine, Amy," the captain responded, without taking her eyes off of the screen. "But take Madison with you, and stay out of trouble." Yale typed another command, and a new star chart appeared on the screen in front of her.

Amy saw Janar on the chart, as it was highlighted in yellow.

Yale swiveled in her chair to glance at the data on Lt. Ford's screen.

The robot put the game inside the console before standing up.

Amy moved toward Ethan. "Hey, wanna go with us?" she asked.

The boy looked up from his screen and smiled. He turned off the device and tucked it into his pants pocket.

Amy put an arm around the boy and led the way off of the bridge, with Madison behind them.

The trio toured the accessible areas of the ship and stopped at the mess hall.

A few Union soldiers sat at the tables, chatting while they ate and drank.

Amy showed Ethan the atomizer and ordered two chocolate milkshakes to demonstrate how it worked.

They sat at a table with Madison and started on their shakes.

"It tastes like the real thing," Ethan said, smiling.

Amy nodded. "It is programmed to create over 5,000 different kinds of food." She sipped her drink through a straw. "I wish we had one at home. Then I could have pizza every day." She smiled at the boy, and he smiled back at her.

"That would not be very healthy, Amy," the robot said. Madison tilted his head. "Are you two flirting with each other?"

Both kids' faces reddened. "No," they replied, in unison.

"I'm sorry. I think I embarrassed you. That was not my intention."

They all sat quietly for a moment.

"I'm just not very well versed in human mating rituals."

"Madison, stop!" Amy snapped. She raised her eyebrows at him. The young girl felt the heat of humiliation run through her. She glanced at Ethan and saw that he was mortified, too. "We are just friends. Right, Ethan?" she asked.

The boy nodded, and Amy hoped that would be the end of it.

"Wait here," she told them both.

She rose and moved toward one of the counters. She opened a drawer and removed an item from it before returning to the table. Amy held up the small deck of cards. "Now we are gonna have some fun," she said. "Do you guys know how to play poker?" She emptied the cards into her hands and started shuffling them.

Ethan looked confused.

Madison pointed toward the deck. "Don't you need six players for this game?" he asked.

Amy dealt the cards. "Ideally, but we can still play with three." She looked closely at her hand. She had a pair of twos, a Jack, a seven, and a five. She put her cards face down to hide her hand. "We need something to bet with," she said. She peered at Ethan, but he shrugged.

Madison spoke. "Gambling on a Union vessel is a violation of Union rules," he said, still holding his cards in his hands."

"Only if we play for money," Amy said. She glanced around the room, her mind racing. "We just need to find something else to use." Amy rose and walked back over to the atomizer. She typed in a command. After a moment, she removed a plate and returned to the table. "This will do," she said. She placed the plate of chocolate chip cookies on the table.

Ethan picked one up and started to bite it.

Amy slapped his hand. "No, they are for the game," she said. She passed out ten cookies each to her opponents and kept ten for herself.

"So how does this game work?" Ethan asked. The boy kept his eyes on the cookies in front of him and pressed his lips together.

Amy laughed and gave him a crash course in poker.

They played a practice hand with no cookies, and Amy helped the boy with basic strategy.

Ethan quickly picked up on the concepts, and he won the practice round. He smirked as he laid his cards down on the table. He had three fives, a two, and a queen. "I think I like this game," he said.

Amy gathered the cards and shuffled them. "I thought you would," she said. She dealt the cards again. "But, now, we get serious." She opened with two cookies.

The others looked at their cards and bid the same.

Madison kept his hand intact, while Ethan took two new cards, and Amy took one. Madison raised the pot by two more cookies.

Amy studied his face to see if he were bluffing. Then she realized it was foolish to try to read the facial expressions of a robot. She called and placed down her cards.

Madison won with three kings, a ten, and a two.

The poker game quickly drew the attention of the Union staff around them. The non-players watched intently as Amy, Ethan, and Madison played round after round, each winning enough to keep the game intense.

The cookies soon became inedible from the constant touching of the players, and some of them began to break apart, but that didn't stop the players from wanting to win.

Amy found herself holding two kings and two queens, and she was just about to lay her cards down when an alarm blared overhead.

The Union personnel rushed out of the room to get to their posts.

Amy dropped her cards and forgot about the game as she darted toward the bridge with Ethan and Madison behind her.

The trio ran past other, scattering people and they finally reached their destination.

Red lights flashed on the bridge as the alarm continued to shriek.

Amy slipped her way to the monitor in front of Yale's chair. "What's going on?" she asked.

Yale ignored her as she typed commands on her keyboard.

Amy saw an image of a ship on the screen. She looked over at Lt. Ford, but she too was busy at her station.

"The ship is nearly 300,000 kilometers away," Lt. Ford said. She wore a headset and pressed several buttons on her console. "The message is faint, but it sounds like a distress call. I'll see if I can clean it up." She pushed a lever on the console. "Here, this is better."

Yale turned off the alarm, and the message played over the bridge's loudspeaker. "This is the Union Ship *Adams*," it said, still crackling. "We are losing power and life support. Please help us." The message repeated two more times.

Amy watched Yale plot a course toward the ship.

The message stopped playing.

Lt. Ford removed her headset. "The computer analyzed the message. It is broadcasting on all Union frequencies, and it appears to be a few hours old." She pressed more buttons and nodded. "I've scanned the ship. They are nearly out of power."

Yale typed on her keyboard. "I've plotted the course, and I am starting the Sprint Drive," she said. "We will reach them in a few minutes." She turned and looked at Amy. "Buckle up, kid. We are going on a rescue mission." She swiveled in her chair and faced front again.

Amy, Ethan, and Madison all found their seats and strapped themselves in.

The ship darted forward. Amy glanced at Ethan, who held tightly to his armrests. His face whitened, and he swallowed hard.

Amy couldn't help but smile. Even his nervousness was attractive.

The *Liberty Bell* vibrated slightly during the rush to its destination.

Amy tapped Madison on the shoulder. "It feels much smoother than when we used the Sprint Drive," she said.

Madison nodded.

Amy remembered the rebel Crownaxians from her rogue mission who shared their technology on improving the coolant system. "It's nice to know we are not going to explode." She turned back and saw a new panic on Ethan's face. "We'll be fine," she said.

The Sprint Drive automatically disengaged when they reached the disabled ship.

Amy unstrapped her belt and leaned on the back of Yale's chair. On the viewscreen, she saw the *Adams*. It was tilted at an unnatural angle, and smoke poured from the ship.

Yale typed some commands on her keyboard. "There are no other ships in the area. The hull damage looks like it is from laser blasts." She shook her head. "She took a real beating." Yale turned toward Lt. Ford. "Any life signs?"

"There are four humanoid life forms on board, captain," Lt. Ford replied. "And several other creatures as well. But they won't last much longer. Their life support system is nearly gone."

"No one is dying today," Yale said. "Not on my watch." She eased the *Liberty Bell* closer to the *Adams* and began the docking procedure.

Amy heard the familiar clanking sound as the ships joined together. She sat back in her chair to get out of Yale's way.

Yale stood and looked at Lt. Ford. "Put on a spacesuit, lieutenant," she ordered.

Lt. Ford nodded and quickly departed the bridge.

Yale then looked at Amy and sighed. "I need you to stay here and pilot the ship, if necessary."

Amy's face lit up. "Let me be clear," the captain said. "You are not to do anything without my instructions. Understand?"

Amy nodded and slid into the pilot's seat. She smiled, remembering her famous adventure. The girl ran her fingers over the smooth surface of the keyboard before resting her hands on the yoke. She closed her eyes for a moment and remembered the rush of adrenaline that came with flying a spacecraft. Yale's voice brought her back to the present, and she reopened her eyes.

"Madison, you will accompany Lt. Ford and me as we board the *Adams*," Yale said.

The robot stood and nodded.

"I'll be right back," the captain said.

Amy watched Yale as she hustled off of the bridge.

Ethan slowly climbed into Lt. Ford's seat and swiveled to face Amy.

The young girl smiled at Ethan, before turning to see Madison. "Just like old times," she said, patting her armrests.

"No," Madison replied. "You are not the captain this time." The robot remained standing at attention, clearly waiting for his next orders from Yale.

Amy thought about what he had just said. She wasn't the captain, and she wasn't in charge, but she was sitting in the best seat on the ship. There wasn't anywhere else in the Universe she'd rather be at that moment.

Yale returned a few minutes later with Lt. Ford behind her. "C'mon, Madison," she said. "Let's go."

The robot walked past the officers and left the bridge.

Yale looked at Amy again. "Remember, you don't make a move without my say," she repeated.

Amy said that she understood.

Yale paused, as if trying to decide about leaving the girl on the bridge, before finally turning and striding toward the docking area.

Amy monitored the mission through a camera that was mounted on Yale's helmet. The grainy images appeared on the viewscreen.

The mission team entered the *Adams* with their lighted flashlights in their hands. Amy noticed that Yale and Lt. Ford wore holsters with laser pistols in them. Steam filled the corridors from broken consoles and sparks ignited from them.

The team advanced slowly, calling out for survivors.

Madison moved debris to allow the team to continue forward.

The team suddenly stopped at Yale's signal. They remained quiet.

Yale carefully removed her laser pistol. "I thought I saw something scamper across the floor," she said. Her voice was low. "These old ships can be breeding grounds for rodents." She took a cautious step forward and froze again when something squealed in front of her. She fired her pistol.

Amy saw the brown creature on the floor. It was the size of a house cat, and it dodged the laser blast before rushing behind a damaged console.

Yale shook her head. "Ick, vile creatures."

The Union personnel continued their search for survivors.

"According to this ship's schematics, the bridge should be two decks above us," Lt. Ford said. She waved her flashlight upward and found the craft's ladder system. "This way," she directed. She rushed forward without lowering her flashlight, and she tripped over something. The officer fell to the floor before rolling to her feet. She cast her light on something and screamed.

Yale darted over to her and stopped in front of the obstacle. She flashed her light on it, and Amy saw what it was on the viewscreen.

The young girl gasped at the sight of the dead body.

Yale leaned down to get a closer look. "Female," she said. "Looks like she was in her forties." The woman's eyes were red, and her pupils were dilated. "There are no marks on her neck or face. It looks like she suffered a heart attack." The captain moved the body to one side of the corridor and folded the arms over the mid-section. "If we have time, we will try to come back for her."

Lt. Ford edged closer to her superior officer. "I'm sorry about screaming, captain," she said. "It was unprofessional, and it won't happen again."

Amy could see through the camera that Lt. Ford was clearly embarrassed. The young girl glanced at Ethan and saw the discomfort on his face. She guessed it was the first time the boy had seen a dead body.

"Don't worry about it, lieutenant," Yale replied. "Death is never easy on anyone." The leader began climbing the ladder, and her team followed her.

The grainy images on the viewscreen grew darker until the team reached their target level. They continued to call out to potential survivors as they gradually marched toward the bridge.

The team came upon a set of closed doors.

Yale tapped a button on a console, and the doors opened a few inches. She put her hands on the doors and tried to pry them further open. She struggled with all of her might, but they didn't move any more. Yale turned to the robot. "Madison, can you get this for me?" she asked, stepping aside.

The robot followed her command. He clasped the doors and pulled. Slowly, they began to inch apart until they were fully open. Madison stepped back and allowed the others to enter first.

Through Yale's camera, Amy saw the damaged bridge. Much like the other parts of the ship, the room was steamy, and electric sparks randomly appeared from the damaged stations. Yale spotted a woman lying on the floor, and she rushed over to her.

The woman moaned and rolled her head to one side.

"My name is Capt. Yale Brown from the Union ship *Liberty*

Bell," Yale said. She closely examined the woman. Her face was pale, and her pupils were wide. "We are here to help you."

The woman tried to say something.

"No, save your strength," Yale said. "We will take you back to our ship and give you whatever medical attention you need."

Yale rose and looked around the cabin. "Are there any others?" she asked.

"Yes," Lt. Ford replied. "I found someone over here."

Yale stepped carefully through the room until she met with the junior officer.

Lt. Ford stood over a man whose eyes were closed. "He's still breathing."

"There is someone over here," Madison chimed in. "He is trapped under a beam. I will try to get him out."

Yale rushed toward Madison.

The robot cautiously lifted the metallic structure before tossing it to his left.

Yale bent down and examined the new victim. He seemed to be in better shape than the others.

"Let's get them onboard the *Liberty Bell*," Yale said. She started to move away when the man reached up and grabbed her arm. Yale stopped and bent down again. "It's OK, sir. We are going to help you." She unclasped his hand and eased his arm back down.

He moved his mouth and struggled to speak.

Yale put her ear toward his face.

"The boy," the man said between breaths. "You must find the boy."

The captain nodded and patted the man's arm. She rose and shouted to the others. "There's one more, a boy. Let's find him."

The team rummaged through the bridge, moving aside

broken panels and other debris. They searched for several minutes before regrouping in the middle of the room.

Yale looked at Lt. Ford and Madison, and both shook their heads.

"Maybe he is in another part of the ship," Yale said. "Keep an eye out for him as we get these folks out of here."

The team gently carried the survivors to the docking station. They were met by medical personnel from the *Liberty Bell*, who transported the injured to the ship's sick bay.

Yale pulled Lt. Ford aside. "Did we find the boy?" she asked.

"Not yet, sir," Lt. Ford replied. "But we haven't checked the entire ship yet."

Yale waved at Madison as the robot helped a nurse with the pinned man.

The robot walked over to the captain.

"We need to search the rest of the ship for the boy," Yale said. "Madison, you start on the first deck, Lt. Ford you have deck two, and I will take deck three. Check in every ten minutes on your helmet's communicator."

The captain dismissed the crew, and they went about their new task.

Yale climbed back up to deck three and gradually examined each room. She checked her air supply and saw that she had about an hour's worth of air left. She clicked on her helmet radio. "Lt. Ford. How much air do you have left?"

Lt. Ford responded that she had fifty-eight minutes' worth.

"Same here," Yale said. "Make sure you keep a close eye on that, lieutenant."

Madison and Lt. Ford radioed Yale their progress every ten minutes, as ordered.

A half-hour went by with no success.

Yale guessed that it would take her at least ten minutes to

get to the ship's docking station. She hurriedly pushed aside wreckage and called out for the boy. Sweat from her forehead rolled down her face and burned her eyes.

Amy watched closely on the viewscreen. She nearly forgot that Ethan was beside her. All she could focus on was the clock. She knew that Yale was nearly out of air, but that the captain would keep searching every second she could.

Finally, it got to be too much for the girl. She turned on a microphone on her bridge. "Yale, you need to get out, now!" she said. "You are almost out of air."

"I am aware of the situation," Yale replied. "Stay off this channel until further notice." She felt her breathing intensify, and she knew that Amy was right. It was time for her to abandon the search.

Madison, who did not need air to breathe, would need to finish for her.

Yale turned in the direction of the docking station and hustled toward it. She arrived at the deportation site and saw Lt. Ford rushing to the exit.

The women returned to the *Liberty Bell* and removed their helmets. They sat on the benches and fought to catch their breaths.

Yale finally did. She spoke into her helmet's radio. "Madison, are you still onboard the *Adams*?" she asked.

"Yes, captain, I am," the robot replied. "But I still haven't found the boy, or anyone else, alive. I will keep searching."

Amy turned in her seat and saw Ethan staring at her. She gently slapped his right shoulder. "C'mon, we can't do anything useful here," she said. She rose and walked toward the bridge exit.

Ethan followed her and asked where they were going.

"Sick bay," Amy replied. "We are going to help the medical staff."

Sick bay buzzed with activity. Doctors and nurses examined the three survivors.

Amy saw the woman lying on a table. She had cuts and bruises, and her face was pale from near suffocation.

A doctor put an oxygen mask over the woman's face, while a nurse stuck an IV needle in her arm.

The woman moaned and moved her head from side to side until she finally passed out.

The pinned man lay on another table, with his right leg elevated.

Two nurses were wrapping a cast on the leg. Beyond that, he had no other injuries.

His voice was louder than before, and he rambled on about finding the boy.

Amy and Ethan approached the man, and Amy smiled at him.

He stopped speaking and looked at her. "My name is Amy," she said to him.

He nodded and said that his name is Raul.

Ethan kept quiet.

"This boy," Amy said, "is he your son?"

Raul nodded. "Yes, I have the privilege of being his father." He pointed to the injured woman. "That is his mother, Lara. Our son is the most important thing in the Universe to us. We must find him." He tried to sit up, but Amy eased him back down. "We must find him."

Suddenly, an alarm blared from the bed of the third survivor, a man with no marks or visible injuries.

Amy watched as a doctor and two nurses worked on him.

His vital signs dropped, and he went into cardiac arrest.

Amy knew that it was better to stay out of the way.

The medical staff shocked the man's heart and performed

CPR on him. They worked on him for several minutes, until there was nothing more that they could do.

Amy saw the single line run across the EKG machine as a piercing sound accompanied it.

Finally, one of the nurses turned off the machine and pulled a blanket over his entire body, including his face.

Amy gasped and took a step back from Raul. She looked over at Ethan.

The boy's face was pale, and he ran toward a basin. Ethan bent over and vomited.

Amy was about to go to him when she looked at the tears on Raul's face. "Did you know that man?" she asked him.

"Only a little," Raul said. He wiped his eyes. "He was part of the crew. He was very generous to us during our flight. I think his name was Dusk." Raul closed his eyes and wept.

Amy moved away from him and hurried over to Ethan.

The young boy ran water over his face.

Amy handed him a clean towel. "Are you OK?" she asked him.

He nodded and looked embarrassed.

"It's not easy seeing someone die," she said. She gently rubbed his back as he dried his face. "Let's get out of here. I don't think there is anything more we can do."

They turned and started walking toward the exit when Amy saw Madison rush into the room.

The robot carried a child, and he carefully placed him on a bed.

A doctor and two nurses ran over to them. "I found the boy," Madison said. "He was under debris on the second deck. I believe he is still alive."

Amy approached the boy as the medical staff worked on him. He looked to be slightly older than Amy and he had long, blond hair and green eyes that blinked against the sick bay lights. Amy stood frozen over him, staring at his face. Like Raul and Lara, the boy had thin, black and gray stripes on his cheeks that made him look like a tiger. His ears were slightly pointed and had a petite, rounded nose. He was the most beautiful boy she had ever seen.

Chapter Four

Amy sat across from Ethan in the mess hall.

They both had their hands around steaming cups of hot chocolate.

Amy took a sip and thought about the mysterious boy in sick bay. *What is his name? Where is he from? Is he dating anyone?* She cleared her throat and felt guilty for thinking these thoughts right in front of Ethan. She also realized that she could get these answers by talking to Raul.

And what about Ethan? she questioned. *Are we friends, or is there something more?* She looked up at him and saw him blowing bubbles in his drink with a straw. She sighed. *Why do boys make life so complicated?* she wondered.

They sat quietly, drinking their hot chocolate until their cups were empty.

Amy yawned and stretched her arms over her head. "I think I need to lie down for a little while," she said. "All this excitement has worn me out."

Ethan looked up at her and nodded.

"I'll see you later," Amy said, rising to her feet. She exited the mess hall and started walking toward her quarters.

Several crew members passed her in the corridors as they went about their tasks.

She politely nodded at them, and most returned the courtesy. Without realizing it, Amy had taken several turns that led her back to sick bay. Once there, she stood at the entrance and peeked in on the patients.

It was much quieter in the room than before.

Two nurses sat at two separate tables, typing information into lap top computers.

Amy slowly entered. She saw that both Raul and his wife were asleep, so she moved toward the boy. He was awake and staring up at the ceiling.

"Hello," Amy said in a near whisper.

The boy looked up at her and smiled.

Amy struggled for something else to say, but his green eyes were truly distracting. "Ah, do you need anything?" she asked.

The boy shook his head.

"OK, well if you do, you know, just ask." She felt so awkward. She dropped her hands behind her back and twisted her fingers together.

Amy started to move away when he finally spoke.

"What is your name?" he asked. He blinked his green eyes, and Amy felt all the strength in her legs vanish.

She opened her mouth to speak, but nothing came out. In that moment, she could not remember her name.

The boy lowered his eyebrows in confusion. "You do have a name, right?" he asked.

The young girl laughed. "Of course. My name is Amy Sutter," she replied, as the information finally made it to her tongue. "I am an unofficial member of the crew. The crew of the *Liberty Bell*." She shrugged. "That's the ship you are on."

She suddenly felt like she was rambling. She pressed her lips together and forced herself to stop talking.

"Unofficial member of the crew?" he asked.

Amy laughed again. "Yeah, it's a long story." She stopped laughing and tried to regain control. "What is your name?" she asked.

The boy slowly sat up in his bed. "My name is Cole," he said. He wrapped his arms around his knees. "Just Cole. My people only go by one name." He looked around the room with a worried expression. "What happened to my parents? Are they on this ship, too?"

"Yes," replied Amy, a bit too quickly. She slowed herself down. "They are over there," she said, pointing at their beds. "They are sleeping now."

Cole nodded and eased his head back down onto his bed.

"They were worried about you. I bet they will be glad to see you." She resisted the urge to touch his hands. Instead, she folded her hands together behind her back again.

"Thank you for letting me know that they are here," Cole replied. He closed his eyes and his breathing deepened. "I am sorry, but I think I need to rest now." He exhaled heavily and drifted to sleep.

Amy stood there for a moment, watching him.

One of the nurses came over to the bed to check on the patient.

Amy smiled at the nurse and slowly walked out of the room. She turned at the exit and glanced back at Cole.

The nurse was gone, and the boy slept peacefully.

Someone tapped Amy on the shoulder, startling here. She spun and saw Yale standing beside her. "We have resumed our course toward Janar," the captain said. "We will be there in a few hours. You should get some sleep. You will need your rest."

Amy nodded and thanked her. Yale looked into the sick bay and smiled.

"He is a cute boy," she said.

The two friends started walking toward Amy's quarters. "I don't know what you mean," Amy said, knowing that she did not sound convincing. She kept her head turned away from Yale's face. It would be much harder to lie if she were looking directly at her.

"The boy we rescued," Yale said. "You like him, don't you?"

Amy shrugged. "He's OK, I guess." She finally looked at Yale, who smiled and nudged Amy's shoulders.

"What?"

"It's OK to have crushes," Yale said. She lowered her voice as other Union personnel past them in the corridor. She returned the salutes of her fellow soldiers. "When I was your age, I was crazy about this boy." She paused, as if trying to remember. "David," she said. "David Milar. He was so cute." She shook her head. "He was tall for his age, with broad shoulders and the bluest eyes I had ever seen." She put a hand to her chest, nearly swooning.

Amy smiled. "So what happened with David Milar?" she asked.

"We hung out together for an entire summer at this camp on Jupiter Station," Yale said. The captain folded her arms across her chest. "God, what a time. We did all the usual camp stuff, fishing, hiking, rock climbing, and tandem space walks. That was the best summer ever." Her smile widened. "He was the first boy I ever kissed." She leaned toward Amy, and they giggled like schoolgirls.

"So what happened?" Amy asked.

Yale's face saddened. "The summer ended, and we went our separate ways. He went home to Canada, and I went home to New Jersey." She shrugged. "We swore we'd keep in touch but, then, life happens. We sent electronic messages to each other and even spoke on our videophones a few times, but the relationship faded." She shook her head again. "I never saw him again."

"Wow, that's depressing," Amy said.

They reached her quarters and stopped in front of her door.

"Sounds like a bad Nicholas Sparks book," Amy said.

Yale nodded. "I know. Is there a good Nicholas Sparks book?" she asked.

"I guess not," Amy said.

"The point to all of this is that it's OK to fall in love," Yale said. "Just be prepared to for it to end. Especially at your age." She pressed a button on the door, and it opened to Amy's quarters. "Try to get some sleep, Amy. We will be there soon." Yale saluted the girl before turning and walking away in the opposite direction.

Amy entered the room and crashed on her bed. Yale's story was fresh in her mind. Cole was certainly attractive. *But how long will he be around?* she wondered. *Ethan is less dynamic, but he is cute, too, and we live on the same planet. That's a big plus.* She closed her eyes and imagined fishing, hiking, rock climbing, and tandem space walks with Cole. Then she did the same with Ethan. Somehow, her friend from Paldor just didn't measure up.

Amy tried to sleep, but her racing mind kept her awake. After two hours of tossing and turning, she gave up, and instead listened to her grumbling stomach. She took a quick shower and put on fresh clothes. She combed her hair and brushed her teeth. Amy inspected her appearance in a mirror before leaving her quarters.

It was early morning by Paldor's standard time, and there were only a few people in the mess hall.

Amy stopped in her tracks when she saw that Cole was one of them.

The boy sat alone at a table with a glass of water and a bowl of something in front of him.

Amy took a deep breath and dashed to the atomizer. She programed an egg and cheese bagel sandwich and a cup of hot chocolate. In a flash, her food was ready, and she unsteadily walked over to Cole's table.

"Good morning," she said, standing before him.

Cole smiled but looked confused. "That's a greeting we say at the start of a day," she explained.

Cole nodded and repeated the greeting.

"May I sit with you?" Amy asked.

The boy's smile widened. "That would be pleasant," he said.

Amy returned his smile and sat down across from him.

Cole took a drink of water before spooning some food into his mouth. The gritty substance in his bowl resembled oatmeal, and Amy wondered if that's what it was.

Amy took a small bite from her sandwich. "It's good to see you out of sick bay," she said after swallowing her food. "How are you feeling?" She drank some hot chocolate and carefully lowered her cup back onto the table. She did her best not to spill any.

"Much better," Cole said. "Your doctors are very talented." He drank some water. "I spoke to my parents. They are recovering well. Also, thanks to your doctors." He ate some more food. "I am very glad your people rescued us. You saved our lives."

Amy nodded. "We were glad to do it." She looked at his

food again. "What is that, that you are eating? I've never seen it before."

Cole pushed his bowl a bit closer to her. "It's called Rattap," he replied. "It's a combination of grains and water mixed together. I was surprised your atomizer had the recipe. I thought it was unique to my home world." He pulled the bowl back and ate some more. "What are you eating?"

Amy described her sandwich before showing him her cup. "This is hot chocolate," she said. "Maybe the best drink in the Universe." She lifted the cup and pushed it toward him. "Would you like to try some?"

He nodded and drank a little. His eyes widened.

"Good, isn't it?" Amy asked.

"It is very sweet," he said, handing the cup back to her. "We don't have anything like this where I come from," he said. "I would like a cup for myself." He started to rise, but Amy told him she would get it for him. "You are very kind," Cole said.

Amy strolled over to the atomizer and made a cup for her guest. She slowly walked back to the table and placed it in front of him. "It's hot, so you may want to let it sit for a moment." She sat down and ate more of her breakfast. "Where do you come from?" she asked.

Before Cole could reply, Amy saw Ethan enter the room and hurry over to their table. Her smile faded as he sat down next to her.

"Hi, Amy," Ethan said. "Who is your friend?" he asked. The question had a hint of venom in it.

Amy cleared her throat. She put on a smile and gestured toward their guest. "This is Cole," she said. "He was aboard the *Adams*. Madison rescued him from the ship."

Cole politely smiled at Ethan and nodded.

"Cole, this is Ethan, a friend from my home world."

Ethan nodded back before glaring at Amy.

No one spoke for a moment.

Amy fiddled with her cup, while Cole slowly drank his hot chocolate.

Ethan tapped his right foot.

Other Union personnel entered the mess hall to start their day. Some of them greeted Amy, who courteously responded with hellos.

Finally, Amy broke the tension. "Cole, what planet are you from?" she asked. Out of the corner of her eye, she noticed the look of irritation on Ethan's face. She felt bad, but she hoped he would get over it.

Cole put his now empty cup down on the table. "My planet is called Lorka," he said, speaking slowly and with a hint of pain in his voice. "It is in the same solar system as Crownaxia," he added.

The mention of that planet made Amy's eyes widen.

"I see you've heard of that world," Cole said.

Amy nodded.

Cole scratched his chin. "Lorka was a beautiful planet, with lush green lands and clear, clean water. Our cities were populated with friendly, smart people. Our art was breathtaking, and we had more than enough food, water, and housing for everyone."

Cole paused and sluggishly blinked his eyes. "We are a peaceful people, rarely was there war or suffering. Our religion promoted peace, love, and acceptance of ourselves and others. Visitors from other worlds were welcome, and they were treated with respect. Unfortunately, our neighbors were not so enlightened."

"Drelk's Crownaxians coveted our world," he continued. "They came in droves, and they didn't respect our laws. We were one of the first planets they attacked. Now, Lorka is barren. Our cities are in ruin, our lands are mostly deserts, and the water is filthy with contamination."

"I'm sorry to hear that," Amy said.

Cole continued. "That is why we were fleeing it. We were hoping to reach a blue planet called Earth. Have you heard of it?" he asked.

Amy laughed. "Yes, I'm from Earth," she said. She then glanced at Ethan, who looked irate. Amy titled her head. "Well, originally. My family and I have spent several years on an outpost called Paldor. My dad's job took us there, but I remember living on Earth. It is a beautiful planet. I would love to go back to it someday," she said.

Cole's face lit up. "That's wonderful," he said. He moved his chair closer to the table as his excitement grew. "Could you help me and my parents get there?" he asked. "It would mean so much to us. To get a fresh start, and to get away from the Crownaxians."

Amy saw that he was getting ahead of himself. "Maybe," she said, trying to temper his enthusiasm. "But, first, we are heading for the planet Janar. It's a Union world in need of our help. But maybe afterwards."

Cole reached over and clasped Amy's hands. "Thank you, Amy," he said. "You have no idea how happy you have made me," he said.

Amy glanced over at Ethan. He looked like he was ready to explode. Amy slipped her hands of out Cole's.

"Please, tell me what you remember about Earth," Cole said.

The young girl nodded and closed her eyes. Soon, she could see the blue oceans and the sunny skies. "Well, there's lots of ocean water and land," she started, opening her eyes. "And major cities that most of the people live in." She went on to describe how her parents took her to a shore where they spent the day playing in the ocean, on the sand, and walking the boardwalk. She was in the middle of a story when two adults approached the table.

Amy recognized Cole's parents, Raul and Lara. Both of them looked tired, but healthier than when they were rescued. She stopped speaking as Cole rose to his feet.

"Hello," he said to them, bashfully. "I thought you were still resting." He reached for two nearby chairs. "Please join us," he offered.

"Thank you, but we are very tired," Raul said. He put his right arm around his wife. "We have been assigned quarters, and I think we need to rest now. Come with us, Cole." Raul extended his left hand to his son. "You can spend time with your friends later."

"Yes, Father," Cole agreed. He glanced at Amy. "We'll talk again."

She nodded and remained in her seat. She watched Cole and his parents exit the mess hall.

Once they were gone, Ethan rose from his seat and stormed out of the room.

Amy shook her head and sighed.

Amy decided to give Ethan some time to cool off. She walked through the ship's corridors and smiled at the passing Union soldiers. She sensed tension among the crew. Amy knew that every mission had an element of danger, but this one seemed to be on the safer side. She couldn't figure out why everyone looked so worried.

Amy stopped by Ethan's quarters and pressed the blue button on his door. She heard the familiar tone, followed by his scratchy voice. She entered and found him lying on his back on his bed. The door closed behind her. She walked over to the bed on sat on the edge of it.

Ethan tossed a baseball into the air and caught it. He

didn't sit up. "What do you want, Amy?" he asked. The boy kept his eyes on the ball as he continued playing. The white ball landed in his hand, over and over again with a slight thud, until Amy reached over and caught it.

Ethan finally sat up. "Give it back," he said.

"In a minute," Amy replied. She ran her fingers over the rough surface of the ball. "Why are you so mad at me?" she asked. She lobbed the ball back to him, and he caught it.

"Are you serious?" he asked. He squeezed the ball in his right hand.

Amy lowered her eyebrows and nodded.

"I only agreed to come on this trip to spend time with you," he confessed. "And, now, you've met some new guy, and you've forgotten all about me."

"I haven't forgotten you, and I just met Cole. There's hardly been time for you to feel neglected." She stood and took a few steps away from the bed before turning away from him. "This is ridiculous." She spun around to face him. "You are acting like a spoiled child."

Ethan hopped off of the bed. "You've got that backwards," he replied. "You are the spoiled one. You hang around with me until someone newer comes along. That is spoiled."

Amy lifted her hands before dropping them toward her feet. "You're jealous," she said. "You're jealous of a boy you don't even know. And I'm the spoiled one?" she asked.

"You don't see it because you are attracted to him," Ethan said.

"See what?" Amy asked.

Ethan shook his head. "It's hard to say," he replied. "There's just something about him." He paused. "I don't trust him. All that stuff about how great his world was. C'mon, no war or hatred? I don't buy it." He took a deep breath and let it out. "And what's with his parents? Could they be any creepier?"

"They just survived an attack on their ship," Amy said. "They are the only survivors. How could they not be rattled after that? From what they've been through, I'd say that they are acting as normal as can be expected."

Ethan shook his head, apparently having no answer for that. He sat back down on the bed and looked at the floor. The boy's face reddened.

Amy wondered if he was going to scream or cry. She hoped it was neither.

"I shouldn't have come on this mission," he said. "Now I really wish I hadn't."

"So do I!" Amy snapped. "You'd be better off on Paldor, where you belong." She stormed toward the door, and it opened automatically. Back in the corridor, she marched in the direction of her quarters to await their arrival on Janar.

———

Ethan lay back on his bed. He tossed the baseball in the air again, catching it, and repeating the game. He thought about the last thing Amy said to him and wondered if that was true, or was she just angry with him. The boy hoped it was just anger. He hated admitting it to himself, but she was right about one thing: He was jealous. The boy also knew that he was in love with her.

His solo game got boring, so he got back up and left his quarters. Ethan wandered the corridors of the ship. He had no idea how close they were to Janar, but he noticed that there were few Union soldiers in the hallways. Those he did come across politely smiled and nodded at him, but all of them had their game faces on. They looked ready for action.

Ethan was just about to visit the mess hall to get a milk-shake when he noticed Cole walking ahead of him. He couldn't put his finger on it, but something did seem really odd about the alien.

The older boy strolled along, as if he didn't have a care in the world.

Ethan decided to follow him, but he kept his distance.

The spy game seemed pointless after a while. All Cole did was walk and occasionally whistle as he explored the *Liberty Bell*.

The ship began to shake from side-to-side as they hit pockets of gravitational turbulence. This was nothing new, but the intensity hadn't been this great before.

Ethan decided that it was time to go back to his quarters to ride out the bumpiness.

Before he could, the ship shook harder than ever before. He had to press his hands against a nearby bulkhead to keep from falling. Ahead of him, Cole also struggled to stay on his feet. Another harder tremor hit, and Ethan tried to warn Cole about the crates that were stacked along the side of the corridor beside him, but his voice was drowned out by the noise of the turbulence.

Ethan fell and saw several crates tumble over toward Cole.

They were about to crash down on the boy when Cole quickly raised his right arm and an eerie blue light emerged from his hand. The light surrounded Cole, and the crates bounced off of it and fell harmlessly to the floor. The shaking finally stopped. Cole closed his hand, and the blue light disappeared.

The alien boy looked around but didn't see Ethan. He raised his hand again, and the blue light returned. He used the light to restack the crates before he turned it off again. Cole looked around once more, and then he rushed out of the hallway.

Ethan scrambled to his feet. He hustled over to the crates and closely examined them. They were perfectly stacked. He ran his fingers along the surface of one crate just to make sure that they were real. He felt the solid metal and gave it a quick shove. It was heavy, as they all were. Ethan slid to the floor and wondered what kind of creature could do that.

Chapter Five

Amy sat in the mess hall with a tall glass of water on the table in front of her. The gravitational turbulence ended, and she cleaned up the spilled water with a towel. She tossed the towel into a chute that led to a laundry bin. The girl turned around and saw Madison walking toward her.

"Hello, Amy," the robot said.

Amy replied hello.

"Capt. Brown thought you would like to know that we have reached Janar, and we will soon begin the landing cycle. She thought you would like to join us on the bridge."

Amy rose and put the glass on the counter, where dirty dishes are stored before washing. She rubbed her hands together and led the way out of the mess hall.

The duo walked toward the bridge.

"Is there something wrong?" Madison asked.

The girl shrugged. "No. Why?" She firmly kept her eyes forward and did not react to the others who passed by them. Amy marched ahead of Madison and entered the bridge before the robot. She quickly sat in her seat and was glad that Ethan was not on the bridge.

Yale spun in her chair. "Good, you made it back in time," she said to Amy. "We are cleared for landing." The captain faced forward and wrapped her fingers around the yoke. She steered the ship toward the landing spot and pressed several buttons on the console. The *Liberty Bell* smoothly touched down on the planet's surface.

The captain exited the ship first, with Lt. Ford and Amy right behind her.

They were greeted by a small contingent of Union soldiers who stood in a straight line with laser rifles on their shoulders.

A civilian woman approached them first. "Hello, I am Department of Emergency Services Director Stacy Guinn," the woman said. She shook Yale's hand.

Yale turned and introduced Lt. Ford and Amy.

Madison exited the ship and stood a few feet behind them.

"I can't begin to tell you how happy we are to see you," Guinn said. "Premier Brennert wanted to greet you personally, but he is attending to matters of State, and he sends his apologies." She turned and pointed toward a line of transport vehicles. "If you will follow me, we will take you to the Command Post," she said.

Amy looked back at the *Liberty Bell* and saw Ethan slowly exiting the ship.

The boy rubbed his eyes and walked toward the group. He stopped next to her.

Neither teen said anything.

Amy then saw Cole as he departed the ship. She rushed past Ethan and Madison and stopped in front of the alien boy. "You and your parents are going to need to stay here," she said, "for your own safety."

The alien boy nodded. "I understand. Do you know how

long you will be gone?" He gently wrapped his hands around hers. He smiled as he waited for her answer.

A big part of Amy didn't want to leave him. "I don't know," Amy replied. She slipped her hands out. "We have a lot to do here, and it will take some time, but I will be back as soon as I can. I promise you." Swept up in the moment, she leaned over and kissed his right cheek.

"Take care, Amy," Cole said. The boy's smile widened. His parents emerged from the ship but kept their distance. "I'll be waiting for you."

Amy hustled back toward Yale's team. She saw the irate look on Ethan's face. She felt guilty for kissing Cole, but she knew that this was not the time for that conversation. Instead, she fell in behind Yale and Lt. Ford, both of whom had stopped to wait for her. "Sorry," she said to the captain.

Yale nodded and gave her a gentle smile.

The team piled into the first land vehicle. There were three rows of seats in what looked like an extended-cab cruiser.

Guinn sat up front with the driver, Amy sat on the end of the second row with Yale and Lt. Ford, while Madison and Ethan sat in the last row.

The vehicle jerked forward as it began its journey.

Amy nervously wrapped a hand on a ledge to her right, and she watched as a section of the damaged planet passed by them.

The young astronaut was shocked by the destruction she witnessed.

The cruiser passed several villages where people dug through the rubble of what were once their homes. The streets were littered with debris, trash, and broken trees. Amy saw exposed water pipes and downed power lines. The stench from the exposed sewer system forced her to cover her mouth with her hands.

Several people wandered around, not knowing what to do. Children ran through the disaster area, not fully understanding what had happened.

Amy saw one little girl sitting on the ground by herself and crying.

The vehicle finally reached the Command Post. It stopped in front of a towering gate with barbed wire running across the top of it.

Soldiers armed with laser rifles patrolled the top of the gate while two similarly armed guards approached the cruiser.

One guard asked Guinn for her ID.

She showed it to him, and he waived to another guard to open the gate and let them in.

The cruiser and its accompanying vehicles entered the compound, and the gate closed behind them.

Yale turned to Guinn. "I thought this was a rescue and recovery mission," she said to her. "This looks more like a security zone."

Guinn nodded.

Yale addressed Lt. Ford. "Do you know what's going on here?" she asked.

Lt. Ford shook her head.

The cavalcade stopped in front of a group of makeshift buildings.

Yale's team departed the vehicles and grabbed their gear. They assembled in formation in front of the buildings to await their orders.

Guinn walked next to Yale while Amy and Lt. Ford followed them. "There are those on this planet who want to use this crisis to grab power," Guinn said. "Certain precautions are necessary."

Yale addressed her troops and gave them their orders.

The team dispersed and entered the buildings to assist the overworked medical staff.

Amy and Ethan helped out as much as they could, but they kept their distance from each other. The teens wrapped bandages around wounded limbs, helped set up IV bags, and ran short errands for the staff.

Amy had prepared for cold weather, but a surprise heat wave struck the planet. The heat and the cramped conditions added to the victims' misery, so the youngsters tried their best to raise the peoples' spirits.

Several hours passed, and the work finally began to wind down, so Amy took the opportunity to rest and get a drink. She sat on a crate with a bottle of water and wiped her sweaty brow.

People shuffled around her, finishing tasks and discussing treatment plans.

Amy drank some water and closed her eyes. She felt the presence of someone sitting down beside her. Amy opened her eyes and found Ethan there.

"Can we talk?" he asked. He looked exhausted as he rubbed his right shoulder. He clasped a bottle of water in his other hand. The boy sipped his water.

"Sure," Amy replied. She took a swig of water and kept her eyes on his face.

"I'm sorry," Ethan said. He squeezed his bottle, and it made a crackling sound. "I shouldn't have acted like a jealous boyfriend. I know that we are friends and, maybe, I thought we could be more, but I get it now." He offered his right hand, and Amy shook it.

"I'm sorry, too," she said. "I said some awful things." She shook her head. "I am glad you are here, Ethan. I would have missed you if you had stayed on Paldor." She leaned forward and hugged him. Then she leaned back and wiped her sweaty face again. "I can't believe how hot it is here."

The boy nodded. "It's good, though, what we are doing here. I never thought much about helping people, but I am glad for the chance to do so." He drank more of his water. "I don't want to upset you again, but I do need to tell you something." He paused and took a deep breath. "I'm not sure even how to say it. I hardly believe it myself. It's about Cole."

Amy sat up straighter. She bit her bottom lip and focused on Ethan's eyes. "What about Cole?" she asked.

Other aid workers passed by them, carrying on their own conversations.

Amy blocked out that noise and waited for the boy to continue.

"I know this is going to sound crazy," Ethan said. He finished the water in his bottle and kept the empty container in his right hand. "He's not like us. He has these abilities that we don't have. It's hard to explain. It's like magic or something."

"Magic?" Amy asked. She shook her head. "Like he can pull a rabbit out of a hat?"

Ethan sighed. "No, not like that." He tossed his empty water bottle into a nearby recycle bin. "When the *Liberty Bell* hit that turbulence, and the whole ship shook, these crates fell and nearly hit him." He clenched both hands into tight fists. "But they didn't hit him because he waved them off."

Amy shook her head again. "Waved them off?" she asked.

The boy nodded. "Yes, waved them off. And this blue light came out of his hands. The light was like a shield, or something. The crates hit the shield and not him. Then he used that light again to restack the crates." He paused. "I'm not making this up. I saw it myself. After he left, I checked the crates. They were real, and they weighed a ton. No one could have done this. No one normal, anyway."

Amy slouched a bit and stared blankly forward. Then she looked him in the eyes again. "That is the most ridiculous story I've ever heard. You're trying to tell me that you are OK with us being friends, and then you try to make Cole look bad with this fantasy tale?"

Ethan pressed his lips together. "I know how this sounds," he argued. "If someone told me this story, I wouldn't believe it, either. But the truth is I saw it. It did happen." He stood and rubbed his tired eyes. "It's up to you to believe me or not. Just be careful around him. Cole is hiding something, and I don't trust him."

Amy watched the boy disappear into the crowd of aid workers. She finished her water and fired the bottle toward the recycle bin. She missed. The girl rose slowly to her feet and picked up the bottle before gently dropping it into the receptacle. She thought about Cole. *Could he be hiding something?* she wondered. *Could he have some crazy alien powers?*

She stood there, lost in her thoughts, and she didn't notice the robot.

Madison stood in front of her and eventually waved his right hand in front of her eyes.

Amy snapped back to reality. "Oh, hey," she said to her friend. She felt a little embarrassed.

"Is something wrong?" Madison asked.

Amy looked down at her feet and shook her head.

"I must say that you have been acting very strangely this entire mission," the robot continued. "Does this have anything to do with your courtship with Ethan?"

Amy lifted her head. "I am not courting with Ethan. We are just friends." She started to walk away from him, but Madison followed. "How is our mission going?" Amy asked, trying to change the subject. "Will we be here much longer?"

The robot nodded. "I'm afraid we are just getting started. I overheard Lt. Ford say that this is only one of the camps that need help. There are several others in this area that are in even worse shape. Some have no food or water, due to shrinking supplies." He stopped and pointed ahead of them. "There is the mess hall. You need to get something to eat."

Amy stood in line behind other Union personnel while Madison waited beside her.

The line moved slowly.

The girl stood on her toes to see what was offered, but she was too short. "What's on the menu?" she asked Madison.

A few people in front of her heard her question, and they turned and looked back at the robot.

Amy cringed at the attention.

"Salisbury steak, mashed potatoes, green peas, and corn," Madison replied.

Someone ahead of them groaned.

Amy rolled her eyes and crossed her arms over her chest. "It is standard Union fare," the robot said. "It should satisfy you."

"I could really go for a pizza," Amy said.

Some others in line agreed with her.

"With pepperoni and extra cheese. And a vanilla milkshake," she said. She closed her eyes and pictured her ideal meal. She envisioned eating it with her parents while sitting outside of a pizzeria on a warm summer day. Suddenly, she started missing them.

She finally stood before the servers. "One of everything, please," she said.

They nodded and scooped the food onto a plastic tray with dividers on it.

She inhaled the aroma and, though it wasn't pizza, it still smelled good. Amy smiled at the servers. "Thank you," she said before following Madison to a row of tables.

They found seats together, and Amy quickly dug into her meal. She was hungrier than she had realized.

"Slow down, Amy," Madison said. "There aren't enough for seconds."

The girl listened to the robot and slowed her pace.

The robot sat still, waiting for Amy to finish.

"This isn't bad," Amy said, "for Union food." She looked around at the others at their table. It was a mix of Union staff and local residents. She heard pieces of different conversations, but none of them kept her attention.

The peaceful atmosphere was suddenly broken by the sounds of shouting.

Amy and Madison got to their feet to see what has happening. Amy saw two men in tattered clothing screaming at each other.

The taller man shoved the shorter man, who retaliated by punching his adversary.

The men grabbed each other and continued to throw punches.

The people around them backed away and formed a circle around the combatants.

Madison rushed over to the fighters with Amy right behind him. The robot separated the men as Union security officers jumped in to help.

The men struggled against the intruders, firing punches at anyone near them.

Amy kept her distance.

Some members of the crowd around them screamed, while others cheered the fighters on.

Madison and the security team finally subdued the angry men.

Yale and Lt. Ford arrived as the men were dragged off in restraints.

They were still yelling at each other and struggling to break free.

Guinn rushed over to Yale. "What happened?" Guinn asked as Amy and Madison came up behind her.

Madison replied. "From what they were saying, one man accused the other of stealing his food. I am not sure who was telling the truth."

Yale shook her head. "It doesn't really matter," She glared at Guinn. "We were not informed that the situation here was so volatile," she said. She crossed her arms as she waited for an answer from the administrator.

Guinn nodded. "Yes, the tensions here are very high. But, under the circumstances, that is to be expected, captain." She started to walk away, but Yale followed her, with her crew right behind.

"I wish I had more to tell you," Guinn said.

"I get the feeling, director, that we have not been fully briefed on the situation," Yale said. She grabbed the woman's arm, and they both stopped walking. "What haven't you told us?" The captain stood a few inches away from the administrator, and she kept a firm grip on Guinn's arm.

Two local security officers approached the women with their weapons drawn.

Yale let go of the woman.

Guinn smiled at the officers. "We're fine here," she said. She waved them off. "Thank you."

The officers lowered their weapons and went back to their posts.

Guinn looked Yale squarely in the eyes. "We cannot control the emotions of our people," she said. "We can only try to keep the peace. That is what we are doing." She patted Yale's right shoulder, turned, and walked away from the group.

Lt. Ford stepped forward. "I don't trust her, captain," she said.

"Neither do I," Yale replied. She quietly addressed Amy, Madison, and Lt. Ford. "We need to keep our eyes and ears open. Something's not right here, and Guinn is hiding it from us." She then looked at Amy. "Be very careful."

The crowd dispersed, and Amy saw Ethan walking toward her.

A man in a clean and wrinkle-free suit followed the boy.

"Capt. Brown," Ethan said. He and the man stopped in front of Yale's team. "This man is looking for you," the boy said.

Yale looked the man over.

Amy thought that he did not look like a refugee. He was too tidy, his hair was neatly combed, and he didn't have the devastated look in his eyes.

The captain extended her hand. "I am Capt. Yale Brown," she said.

They shook hands.

"How can I help you?" she asked.

The man looked directly at Amy and spoke with a sense of urgency. "I know who you are, young lady," he said. "And you are in danger."

Ethan protectively stepped between the man and Amy.

The stranger then addressed the group. "You are all in danger."

Chapter Six

Yale and Lt. Ford led the man to a corner of the mess tent.

Upon the captain's orders, Union soldiers cleared out the remaining people who were still eating.

The man sat on one of the benches, nervously drumming his fingers on his legs.

Once the tent was emptied, Yale and Lt. Ford turned to face the man.

Only Amy, Ethan, and Madison remained with the senior officers.

"Let's start from the beginning," Yale addressed the man. "What is your name?"

He cleared his throat before answering. "My name is Oliver Nelson," he replied. "I am a scientist specializing in robotics."

Madison edged closer at the sound of that last word.

Oliver continued. "I was a senior researcher at the Asimov Institute of Robotics on Earth. There, I was an assistant to Dr. Stanley Greenland."

Madison stepped forward. "Dr. Greenland?" he asked.

Oliver nodded.

"Is he still alive?" Madison leaned over the man and nearly sat in his lap.

Amy grabbed his right arm and pulled him back.

The scientist rose to his feet. "Yes, he is. And that is why you are all in danger."

"Exactly how so, Dr. Nelson?" Yale asked. She positioned herself between Oliver and Madison. She nodded at Lt. Ford, who took the robot to another table and sat him down.

Lt. Ford put a hand on Madison's left shoulder.

"Dr. Greenland is here on Janar," Oliver continued. "He has built a laboratory in the mountains to the north, where he is experimenting with robots, trying to recreate the success he had with Madison."

Amy spoke up. "What's wrong with that?" she asked. "Wouldn't having more robots like Madison be good for the Union?" She glanced over at her metallic friend and smiled. Amy thought of their times together during their tutoring sessions. She then recalled their adventure aboard the *Liberty Bell* just eight months earlier. "I don't see the problem," she said.

Oliver looked at her and he shook his head. "The problem is that after Dr. Greenland was fired; he became obsessed with his work. It began to wreak havoc on his mind. He would rant and rave that, one day, he would make everyone pay for what they did to him. I am afraid he will keep that promise." Oliver took a handheld computer out of his shirt pocket and typed a command on it. He showed Yale the display screen.

Amy peeked around Yale and saw the blueprints on it. "I stole these from his laboratory a few weeks ago," the scientist said.

Yale and Amy examined the schematics for different types

of robots. There were notes on the documents as well. Some described the robots as domestic help, medical staff, and law enforcement. One design was listed as a soldier. "Madison, please take a look at these," said Yale. "Tell me if they look authentic."

The robot rose and moved away from Lt. Ford. He took the device from Yale and read over the information. Madison handed it back to Yale. "This is legitimate," the robot said. "And, quite frankly, even genius. He has made several advances since my construction. These robots would be far more sophisticated than I am."

Amy hugged him. "No one could take your place," she said. "I don't care how advanced they are, they wouldn't have your soul," she continued.

Madison thanked her.

"Dr. Nelson, how many of these robots has Dr. Greenland built?" Yale asked.

The scientist shook his head. "I don't know," he replied. "He fired me after I refused to steal some raw materials for him. But, when I was there, I saw at least a dozen robots, but few of them were completed. Most were in different developmental stages. But I only had restricted access to the lab. I don't know how many more there could be."

Yale handed the device to Lt. Ford.

The younger officer looked over the data.

"We need to check this out right away," Yale said. "Contact Gen. Knox and let him know what we've discovered and that our mission has changed."

Lt. Ford nodded and moved away to send the message.

Yale spoke to Oliver. "Can you lead us to his lab?" she asked.

The scientist's face whitened. "No. I can't do that," he

replied. "It's much too dangerous to go there." He paused and wiped his sweaty face with a handkerchief. "That's not why I told you about this. You need to get off of this planet as soon as possible. We all do." He turned to walk away, but Yale stepped in front of him. His body shook. "We need to leave," he reiterated.

The captain stood her ground. "The only way we will ever be safe is to stop him," Yale said.

The man didn't look convinced.

"Do you know what kind of havoc an army of robots could wreak if we let him go?" she asked. "If he sold those robots to the Crownaxians, it would be disastrous. Millions, if not, billions of lives could be lost. If that happened, could you live with yourself? I couldn't."

Oliver stood very still and looked at the people around them. His mouth tightened. "No!" he blurted out. "I couldn't let that happen." He placed his right hand on his forehead. "I will take you there." He sat down on a nearby bench and fought off tears.

Amy tugged on Yale's shirt. "Can we talk for a moment?" she asked. Before Yale could answer, Amy pulled the captain away from the others.

They stopped in front of an empty bench. "You know this could be a trap," Amy said. "Right?"

"It could be," Yale replied. "But it's too big not to investigate."

She rested a hand on Amy's left shoulder. "Any mission is dangerous, and this is no different. But we will be as careful as we can," Yale said. "And we will be back to pick you up before you know it."

Yale walked back toward the group as Lt. Ford returned.

Amy closely followed the captain.

"Lt. Ford, you and the medical staff will stay here and

continue to offer whatever aid is needed," Yale said. "I will take a team to Dr. Greenland's lab."

"I will be on that team," Amy replied. She crossed her arms over her chest.

The captain shook her head. "No, it's too dangerous for you. You and Ethan will stay here and assist Lt. Ford." She paused. "That's an order." She glared at the youngster.

"No," Amy said. "I am going with you. And, if you try to leave me behind, I will just follow you, so you might as well take me along." She returned Yale's gaze.

They stared at each other for a moment.

Yale gritted her teeth. "Fine. But you will follow every order I give you, without question. Is that clear?" She took a deep breath and slowly let it out.

Amy smiled. "Yes, captain. Very clear." She slapped Ethan's right shoulder and smiled.

He smiled back at her.

Amy then tried to curb her enthusiasm.

"Madison, you will watch over them," Yale said, nodding toward the kids.

The robot acknowledged the order.

"I am going to talk to Guinn, let her know what's going on. Everyone, be ready to go in ten minutes," she said.

Amy, Ethan, and Madison responded to her.

Amy pulled away from her friends, and she followed Yale. She watched the captain weave through the crowd until she approached Guinn, who was speaking with some refugees. Amy moved closer to listen. She heard Yale discuss Oliver and the new mission.

"But you are needed here," Guinn said. The administrator looked distraught. "There is still so much to do."

"We will return as soon as we can," Yale countered. "While we are gone, Lt. Ford will be in charge of my staff. She is more than capable of handling any situation." The captain tilted her head, as if waiting for Guinn to accept her decision.

Amy could see that the administrator was not satisfied.

"This guy could be some kind of kook," Guinn said.

Amy saw her move closer to the captain, as if trying to stay out of Amy's hearing range. The young girl edged closer to the adults.

"Or worse," Guinn continued. "Maybe this man is deliberately leading you into danger."

Yale stepped back. "We have considered that, director. We will take the appropriate precautions." She shook hands with the woman. "We will be on our way now." Yale turned and nodded at Amy, who followed the officer. "She is not happy," Yale said, "but politicians rarely are."

They returned to the mess tent area, where Madison, Ethan and Oliver were waiting for them.

Amy saw Lt. Ford approaching with five Union soldiers.

Lt. Ford stopped in front of Yale and saluted her. "Captain, I've assembled a security team for you. And I have informed Gen. Knox of our findings and the new mission. He said to proceed with caution."

"Thank you, lieutenant," Yale said. "You have your orders."

Lt. Ford spun on her heels, and she marched toward the medical tents.

Yale addressed her team. "We will be moving out in two minutes. Oliver, you will be in the first cruiser with me. Madison, you are in charge of the second cruiser, and the kids will be riding with you."

The robot nodded.

Yale pointed toward the latrines. "If you have to go, go now."

Amy and Ethan went to their respective latrines and

hurried back to the group. They climbed into the second land vehicle and sat in the middle seats.

Madison followed orders and sat in the front with the driver, while two security officers sat in the last row.

The driver started the vehicle, which lurched forward as they followed their leader.

The convoy of four cruisers bounced over the stony roads, shaking the passengers so much that Amy had to clamp her fingers around a safety bar to keep from falling out.

Ethan looked rattled, too, and Amy wondered if he were about to vomit. His face was pale, and he kept his head down.

Amy gently rubbed his back for a moment to help settle him.

They were traveling for nearly two hours when Amy heard the first laser shots, which exploded in front of the convoy, forcing the drivers to jam on their brakes.

The cruisers spun to stop, and Yale yelled for everyone to take cover.

Amy grabbed Ethan and pulled him behind one of the cruisers as more laser fire blasted around them.

The Union soldiers fired back. "Raiders!" one soldier yelled.

Amy tried to see where the intruders were firing from, but she couldn't locate them. She kept a hand on Ethan's neck so he would keep his head down. She remembered how awful she felt after she killed a Crownaxian in battle during her rescue mission, but she suddenly wished Yale had given her a laser pistol.

Amy finally saw one of the raiders as he advanced toward the first cruiser.

A security officer saw him, too, and fired. He hit the raider in the chest, knocking him backward and off of his feet.

The invader landed with a thump and didn't move.

Amy held her breath and darted toward the fallen man. She quickly grabbed his laser rifle and crawled back to her position next to Ethan.

The young girl examined the weapon. It looked like a standard-issue rifle. She aimed at the ground twenty feet in front of her and fired. The ground exploded. Amy nodded, sure that she had a feel for the rifle.

The firefight continued, so Amy rose and shot in the direction of the raiders. That brought return fire back at her. She heard Yale's voice. "Amy, hold your fire."

Amy waited ten seconds before she rose again. She saw another raider and fired her weapon. She hit the man on his right shoulder, and he, too, fell to the ground. She ducked down behind the cruiser again, her heart beating rapidly. Amy saw something out of the corner of her eye. It was movement to her left. She crawled around Ethan and positioned herself between him and whatever was near them in the trees. She got up on her knees and aimed the rifle.

Someone rushed at her. In a blur, the intruder was on her, and they wrestled onto the ground, the stranger trying to take the rifle away from her.

Amy whacked the person on the head with the butt of the rifle.

The intruder rolled away before rising again.

Amy finally got a good look at the combatant. It was a girl. She appeared to be about Amy's age, with short, dirty hair and a muddy face. She had no weapon. Amy pointed the rifle at her and told her to stop.

The intruder screamed and rushed at Amy again with her arms raised.

Instinctively, Amy pulled the trigger. The laser blast hit the young girl in the chest, knocking her backward like the others. Amy waited a moment and then scuttled over to the girl. She checked for a pulse. There was none. "Dammit!" Amy yelled. "Why did you do that?" she asked in frustration.

Laser fire whizzed by her, forcing her to duck. Amy looked at the girl's face and fought back tears. She ran her hand over the face and softly closed the girl's eyes. "Rest in peace," she whispered. Amy ran back to Ethan's side.

He tried to look over at the dead girl.

"Keep your head down!" Amy shouted. She grabbed him again and forced him to the ground. "You don't want to see that."

The Union officers advanced on the raiders, firing and hitting their targets.

The raiders began to retreat into the woods on the far side of the road.

The Union soldiers pursed them until they were no longer in sight.

Soon, the sound of laser fire ceased.

Yale rushed over to Amy and carefully removed the rifle from the girl's hands. "That was an incredibly stupid thing to do!" Yale shouted. She put the safety lock on the rifle and handed it to a nearby soldier. "Are you trying to get yourself killed?" Before Amy could respond, Yale grabbed Amy's right shoulder. "I cannot protect you if you disobey my orders." She looked straight into the girl's eyes. "We don't have time to turn around and take you back to camp. I need you to promise me that you will listen to me for the rest of this mission."

"I promise," Amy said.

Yale let go of her.

"I was only trying to help." She took a deep breath. "Yale, I do have experience in battle, remember?"

The captain nodded.

Amy pointed in the direction of the dead girl. "One of the

raiders is over there," she said. Amy walked past her and checked on Ethan.

The boy leaned behind the second cruiser and vomited.

Amy put a hand on his back. "It's OK," she said. "Just breathe." Amy rose and saw a soldier aiding Oliver.

The scientist had a laser wound on his stomach. His body shook, and his eyes rolled back into his head.

Amy rushed over to help.

She and the solider gently laid Oliver onto the ground.

The soldier pressed a bandage against the wound. "Hold this here," he said to Amy.

She put her hand on the bandage and applied pressure to the wound.

The soldier started CPR.

Yale came out of the trees, where the dead girl's body lay, and she hustled over toward Oliver. She leaned down and checked his pulse while the solider continued CPR. "We are losing him," Yale said. "We have to get him back to the medical staff at the command center." She stood up and waived at another Union soldier. It was one of the drivers. "Help us put him back in the first cruiser. We are going back."

The driver nodded and leaned down to assist.

"No," Oliver said, raising his head and clenching his jaw in pain as he came to.

The Union soldier stopped the CPR. He took the bandage from Amy and replaced it with a new one. Then he wrapped it.

"We cannot go back," Oliver said. "I won't make it. Greenland's lab is closer. We have to go there." The scientist dropped his head back down. "Take me there," he pleaded. "Please."

Yale patted his right hand. "Fine, we will take you to the lab."

She and the driver carefully lifted Oliver and carried him to the first vehicle. They secured him in a seat, and a soldier sat with him.

The captain stood in her seat and shouted to the rest of her team. "Load up! We are moving on!"

Everyone else rushed to the vehicles and strapped in. The first cruiser wobbled ahead, and the others fell back in line.

Amy looked up at the sky. Gloomy, grey clouds formed, threatening to drench the travelers. She sat next to Ethan, whose color finally returned to his face.

Madison sat in the front, as he did before.

Amy finally noticed the blood stains on her hands and shirt from assisting Oliver. She took a breath and thought about the girl she killed in battle. Amy turned her head away from Ethan and began to weep.

Chapter Seven

The rain started off as a light spritz but soon developed into a full downpour. The travelers kept their heads down as the cold water drenched them.

Amy rubbed her hands together and watched the dried blood disappear. She tucked her arms under her shirt and shivered.

Ethan trembled, too, and he stomped his feet to keep warm. The only one who was not affected by the rain was Madison, who sat straight up in his seat.

The vehicles slogged along the slippery road, their back ends frequently fishtailing as the mud gave little traction.

Amy wondered how Oliver was doing, and she saw the scientist's head roll back and forth against his seat.

The soldier beside him kept his hands on the robot specialist to secure him.

Amy tried to read the soldier's face, but he kept a neutral expression. That only made Amy more worried about the scientist.

The convoy stopped as they came upon a gigantic gate that completely blocked the road.

One of the Union soldiers hopped out of the first cruiser and tried to open the gate. He quickly pulled his hand back and hollered as an electric current zapped him. The solider turned to address Yale, when laser fire suddenly poured down on the travelers.

"Again?" Ethan asked, as they jumped out of the cruiser and hid behind it.

"We are not very popular today," Amy replied, again pulling her friend to the ground. She looked over a Yale, who lay behind the first cruiser.

The Union soldiers returned fire but were not able to defeat the attackers. The firefight lasted only a few minutes until a voice come over a loud speaker from behind the gate. It called for a ceasefire.

Yale's team remained still.

Amy cautiously rose from behind her cruiser and looked around. She saw a series of buildings about fifty yards behind the gate. Lights were on in nearly all of the buildings. She glanced at the captain again and saw her waiving at Amy to stay down. Amy slowly lowered herself behind the cruiser once more, but she kept her eyes on the enormous gateway.

Slowly, it began to open. A man in his mid-50s came out, flanked by two armed guards. He wore a white lab coat and had a matching white beard.

The man stopped in his tracks for a moment.

His men did the same and kept their rifles aimed at Yale's team.

The man's eyes widened in disbelief. "Madison? Is it really you?" He raced over to the robot, with his guards in tow.

Madison came out from behind the first cruiser, and the

man halted in front of him. "My Lord, it is you." The man put his hands on the robot. "It's good to see you, my boy."

"Dr. Greenland?" Madison asked. The scientist nodded. "You look different," said the robot. The scientist laughed, and his men lowered their weapons. "It is good to see you, too," Madison added. He pointed to Yale, who cautiously approached the man. "This is my captain, Yale Brown."

Greenland shook her hand.

The robot introduced Amy and Ethan after they drifted over.

"I am sorry for the unfriendly welcome," Greenland said. "My men are very protective of me and my home." He looked at the Union soldiers. "It appears that no one has been injured. So what can I do for you?"

"We have an injured man," Yale said. She led him and his men toward the first cruiser.

The Union soldiers uneasily backed away.

"We were ambushed by road raiders on our way here, and he was shot. He needs immediate medical attention," said Yale.

Greenland halted again upon seeing the victim's face. "Oliver? What the devil are you doing here?"

His guards tensely raised their rifles again, causing the Union soldiers to do the same, but the scientist waved his hand at his men.

They lowered their weapons again, as did the Union fighters.

"Enough of this," Greenland said. "We are done shooting at each other." He looked back at Oliver. "You, sir, are not welcome here."

Amy approached the bearded scientist. "He needs your help," she said.

He glared at the young girl, but that didn't stop her.

"If you don't help him, he will die," she said.

Greenland's expression didn't change. He started to turn away when Amy grabbed his right arm.

Again, his soldiers raised their rifles, and the Union team did the same.

Amy ignored the new threat. She stepped toward Greenland. "You are a man of science. You have a responsibility to aid Mankind." She nodded toward Oliver. "Help him," she said.

Greenland looked back at Oliver. "Bring him to the infirmary," he ordered.

His men lowered their weapons and carefully removed the injured man.

As the Union soldiers eased their grips on their rifles, Greenland's men brought out a stretcher with wheels and transported Oliver to one of the buildings.

Greenland turned to face Yale. "You have a persuasive soldier in that little girl," he said.

Yale smiled. "She can be a handful sometimes."

The scientist started walking toward his compound, and the captain followed him. "Thank you for your assistance," she said. "I am sure you are saving his life."

"Why are you here, captain?" Greenland asked.

They passed through the front of his estate and continued walking.

Amy, Ethan, and Madison stayed close behind them. "Are you unhappy with your robot? Because I don't give refunds," he joked.

"Not at all," Yale said. "Madison has been invaluable to the Union." She paused before continuing. "We are here on a humanity aid mission. Surely, you are aware of the devastation this planet has suffered the last few weeks. Well, we are here to help clean up and get everyone back on their feet."

He slowed his pace, and she matched hers to his.

"Yes, I know what Janar has been through," Greenland said. "What I want to know is why you are here, at my home." Before Yale could answer, he continued. "Is it, perhaps, because of my robotics work? Afraid I am going to build a robot army?"

"That thought has crossed our minds," Yale admitted.

The scientist laughed. "You don't need to worry. I have no plans to take over the Universe." He pointed toward the buildings ahead of them. "Nothing nefarious is going on here."

The captain looked over her shoulder at her weary team. "Could we please indulge upon you for some refreshments and a short rest?" she asked. "It has been a difficult trip for my team. They could use the break."

Greenland stroked his beard. "We are not accustomed to visitors here, but I am sure we can whip up something for your troops." He slightly changed direction. "Follow me," he said. "Our dining area is this way."

The scientist led them to a compact dining hall filled with rows of stone tables that took up most of the room.

The weary travelers sat in the comfortable and sturdy chairs that were also made from stone.

Amy sat next to Yale, while Madison and Ethan sat close by.

The Union personnel chatted for nearly a half-hour before Greenland's men appeared with food carts.

They were served water, breads, cheeses, and fruit before a main course of cooked meats and pasta was brought out.

Amy was ferociously hungry, but she slowly ate a reasonable amount of food.

Greenland came over to Amy's table as she and the others were finishing their meals. He addressed Yale. "Capt. Brown, I take it that the food is to your liking." He didn't wait for an answer. "Good. Our chef will be pleased." He sat down beside Yale. "I have made arrangements for your departure. Your vehicles are fueled up and ready to go. I trust you will be leaving shortly."

Yale took a sip of water before putting her cup down on the table. "Thank you, Dr. Greenland. That is very considerate of you, but I was hoping for a tour of your compound first, just to reassure my superiors that we have nothing to worry about."

Amy saw the scientist's face tighten.

"I promise, we will stay out of your way," Yale said.

"Captain, this is a research facility," Greenland replied. "We do not give tours here." His voice rose in clear agitation. He took a breath and calmed down. "What I mean to say is that we are not set up for public viewing. There are a lot of top-secret experiments going on here, and I can't risk any of the information leaking out. I'm sure you understand."

Yale smiled. "I fully understand. How about this? Just allow a small contingent of my team to accompany me on the tour. We all have top-level Union security clearance, and we will not report on any sensitive data."

Greenland didn't look convinced.

"The alternative, of course, would be for me to file a formal complaint with the Union. They would respond with a task force of their own, who might not be as cooperative with your sensitive data."

Amy held back her smile. She knew that Yale had him in a corner.

The scientist nodded. He rose to his feet and folded his arms across his chest. "You and five others will be allowed a short tour. I shall lead it myself. Then you will see that you and the Union have nothing to worry about." He looked at a watch on his wrist. "Get your team together. We will start the tour in ten minutes." He walked away from the table and pointed at two of his men, and they followed him out of the hall.

Yale rose, stepped away from the table, and addressed the entire crew. She filled them in on the details of the tour. "Madison, Taylor, Schmidt, Corkland, and Robinson will accompany me. The rest of you will wait here until we return. That is all." Yale waved her right hand at those she named, and they came over to her.

Amy and Ethan darted over to her, too. "Wait a minute," Amy said, stepping in front of the captain. "What about me? I want to see what's here."

Yale pulled her by the arm away from the small group.

Ethan followed them.

"I need you to stay here," she said to Amy. She then glanced over at the young boy. "Both of you. We don't know what we are going to find here. It's too dangerous."

Amy shook her head. "How many times do we have to have this conversation?" she asked. "I am not a regular child. I have vast field experience, even more than Taylor or Corkland." She bit her bottom lip. "I killed someone this morning during an ambush. I think I can handle a tour." She looked deep into Yale's eyes. "C'mon, you need me."

The captain took a short breath. "Fine," she said, "but you will follow my instructions without question. Got it?" she asked.

Amy nodded.

"If she's going, then I'm going," Ethan said. Yale started to speak, but he cut her off. "I know more about robotics than anyone else here, except for Madison. You will need my expertise."

Yale shook her head in frustration.

"You need me, too," Ethan continued.

The captain glared at the youngsters. "You are the most maddening kids I have ever met," she said. "I don't know how your parents put up with you two." She paused and put her hands on her hips. "But you are right; I do need you both. But understand this; at the first sign of trouble, I want you both to hide. No heroics," she said. Yale focused on Amy. "Got it?"

Amy pretended to write on her hand. "No heroics. Just hide," she said. The girl looked up at Yale. "Got it." She flashed a cat-ate-the-canary smile and nodded.

Yale shook her head and moved back toward the small group.

Amy and Ethan followed her.

Yale addressed the team again. "Change of plans," she said. "Corkland and Taylor will stay here with the others."

The two soldiers looked at each other before nodding and rejoining the others.

Yale continued. "Stick together, and keep your eyes open. If Oliver is right, we are heading into perilous territory. And, no matter what we see, keep calm. Act as if we were expecting it."

A door closed behind the captain, causing her to turn around.

Greenland walked toward the small group with two of his men flanking him on either side. "I see that you are ready," the scientist said. "Let's get started." He seemed as agitated as he was before. He walked quickly toward the mess hall exit with the Union team behind him.

The tour began with a stop at an administration building. Greenland showed his visitors his office, a spacious room with a desk, several filing cabinets, and a brown couch which he said he spent many nights on when he was too tired to return to his quarters.

Next, they saw two hefty storage sheds that sat side-by-side and contained basic non-food supplies like paper, computer equipment, and various tools.

They followed that up with a stop at the main power station which provided all the buildings with electricity. There were four enormous generators that worked non-stop, delivering energy. They moved carefully through that building, avoiding any contact with the electrical grid.

The group also visited the compound's water system.

Amy was amazed at the intricate web of pipes that gave each building the needed water.

They exited that building, and Greenland gathered together everyone on the tour. All of them stood in the near-darkness outside of the water planet.

Greenland wore a host's smile. "That's it, everyone," he said. "Thank you for coming. I'm sure you will want to be on your way now." He addressed Yale. "And you can report to your superiors that they have nothing to worry about."

Amy looked past him at a structure they did not visit. "What about that building, Dr. Greenland?" she asked, pointing to it. "What's in there?" Amy tried to sound more inquisitive than accusatory. She raised her eyebrows to show her curiosity.

Dr. Greenland slowly shook his head. "I'm afraid that's top secret, my friend," he replied, as if talking to a small child. "We can't go in there." He started to walk back toward the mess hall, but he stopped when he saw that his visitors were not following him. He changed tactics. "You don't want to go in there," he said. "It's old and musty and filled with boring computer components." He waved his hand at the group. "Let's leave now."

Yale stepped forward. "I'd hate to submit an incomplete report," the captain said. "I don't think my boss would like that." She stood quietly for a moment, staring at the scientist as he stared back at her. "Besides, I like musty, old buildings filled with boring computer components." Yale smiled but stood her ground.

Greenland glanced at his men and nodded to them before looking back at Yale. "OK, captain," he said. "If you insist." He walked past her and led to the way to the mysterious structure.

Once inside, they walked through a dimly-lit hallway that led to a laboratory.

Greenland turned on some lights, and Amy saw a few models of robots in various levels of completion. There were also stacks of robotic parts.

"You see," Greenland said, "I only have a few unfinished robots. Nothing substantial. I still haven't figured out why Madison works while the others do not. It is a mystery to me."

Madison approached one of the partly completed robots. He touched the plastic face. It resembled a human male, and it wore a frozen expression of dullness. All of the robots had the same camouflage green color. Madison looked over at his creator. "Was I like this once?" he asked the scientist. "Was I just a compilation of circuits and metal and plastic?" He paused as he waited for an answer. "Was I this hollow?"

Greenland slowly walked over to Madison. He put a hand on the robot's right shoulder. "We all start off hollow, my boy," Greenland said. "But time and experience fill in the gaps, and we become who we are. The amazing thing about you, Madison, is that you were the first fully-functional, artificial, intelligent creature created by Man." He lifted his hand. "Created by me."

"What will you do with the rest of these?" Madison asked. He moved away from the first robot and examined some of the others. "In a way, they are my brothers and sisters. Do you plan to give them the same life you gave me?" he asked. "Can you?"

The scientist nodded. "That is the plan, Madison." Greenland walked over to a computer station and turned on a monitor. He typed in some commands, and blueprints appeared on the screen. "I have spent many hours studying your schematics. I intend to discover why you were such a success while the others failed." He pointed to the screen. "See for yourself."

Amy and Madison hurried over to the screen, with the others moving behind them.

The robot touched the screen and traced his design with his fingers. He turned to face Greenland. "I want to help you, Dr. Greenland," Madison said. "I want to bring my brothers and sisters to life."

"I'm not sure that's such a great idea," Yale said.

Everyone looked at her.

She addressed the scientist. "I'm not fully convinced that your intentions are altruistic. If they were, you wouldn't need to work in secrecy in a compound like this." She then turned to the robot. "I'm sorry, Madison, but I can't allow you to assist Dr. Greenland. It is not in the best interest of the Union."

"What about my interests?!" Madison shouted. It was the first time that Amy had ever heard her friend raise his voice. "What about what's best for me?" Yale started to speak, but Madison cut her off. "No, captain. I don't want to hear it. For my entire existence, I have done what the Union has asked me to do. Never once have I asked for anything in return. Well, I'm asking now. I want to work with Dr. Greenland," he said.

"I can't allow it," Yale said.

Amy saw her slowly reach for her laser pistol. The woman's hand rested on the handle. "It is far too dangerous," she said. "I'm sorry."

"You have no right to interfere," Madison replied. He moved past her and stood by Greenland. "Doctor, I request asylum. I wish to stay here with you." The robot then faced Yale and Amy. "Captain, I quit."

"That's too bad," Yale said. She quickly drew her weapon and fired at Madison.

The laser blast hit him in the chest, and he fell backward onto the floor.

Amy screamed and ran over to her friend. Steam rose from his chest as sparks shot up into the air. Amy cradled his head and leaned toward his face, but there was no movement from the robot.

Chapter Eight

Greenland and Ethan leaned over Madison's body with electronic probes in their hands. They fused together wires and pulled out damaged circuits. The duo worked in unison on the broken robot.

Amy stood close by, watching their efforts. For a moment, she glared at Yale, who stood with her hands bound behind her back, while one of Greenland's men guarded her.

The scientist put down his tools and sighed. "There is nothing more we can do for now," Greenland said. He wiped his hands on his pants and walked over to Yale. "You and your team must leave immediately, and you can tell your Union bosses that any attempt to return will be met with deadly force." He looked at his men. "Get them out of here."

"What about Madison?" Amy asked. She leaned down and touched his right hand. "You can't just leave him here." The girl lowered her head as tears formed. Her body shook. She felt a hand on her right shoulder and, when she looked up, she saw Ethan comforting her. She stood back up. "He deserves a proper burial."

Greenland shook his head. "No, my dear. I have no intention of burying him. I will work on him, day and night if necessary, until I restore him to his former self." The scientist nodded at his own words. "I will fix him. I promise you that." He turned to walk away.

"Then what?" Amy asked.

Greenland stopped and looked back at her.

"Will you free him and let him come home?" she asked. "Or will you keep him here?" She looked hard at his face and stiffened her spine.

The scientist smiled. "That will be up to him," he replied. "He is not a slave, and I am not his keeper. Whatever he decides to do, I will respect his wishes." Greenland glared at Yale. "Will you?"

Yale responded by turning her back on the scientist. She did not appreciate his comment. She also didn't see the smug smile that stretched across Greenland's face.

Under the supervision of Greenland's men, Yale and her team marched back to the dining hall.

Once there, Yale announced to the Union soldiers that they were leaving.

The troops gathered their belongings and moved toward the cruisers.

Yale approached Amy as everyone settled into the vehicles.

"I know you don't understand what I did or why," the captain said. "But you need to know that it wasn't easy for me to pull the trigger on Madison."

Amy looked up at Yale but didn't speak. Her anger prevented it.

"I have always liked him, but I couldn't allow him to help Dr. Greenland. That would put the Union at too much risk." She tried to rest her right hand on Amy's shoulder, but the young girl pulled away.

Ethan sat down beside Amy, but he looked up at Yale. "What are we doing about Oliver?" he asked. He nodded in the direction of the infirmary. "Are we leaving him here?"

A few Union soldiers passed them on their way to their cruisers as Yale turned in the direction of Greenland's sick bay.

The captain moved away from the land vehicles and asked one of Greenland's men to bring the scientist to her. She returned and leaned against the cruiser until the robot specialist walked over to them. "I take it you are ready to leave," he said. He had two of his men on either side of him, both of whom were armed. "I wish I could say it was a pleasant visit."

Yale let the comment slide. "We are ready," she replied. "We just need your men to bring Oliver to us, and then we will go." She stood straight, as if trying to show that the ordeal had not defeated her.

Greenland shook his head.

Yale raised her voice. "You can't keep him here, not against his will."

"I don't want him here at all," Greenland said. "He betrayed me, and it makes me sick just to look at him. But, as you reminded me, captain, I do have a responsibility as a scientist." He paused to catch his breath. "But my doctor examined him and told me that Oliver is in no condition to travel. He needs to rest, so he will remain here until he is better."

"How do I know you won't kill him?" Yale asked.

"If I wanted him dead, captain, he already would be," Greenland said. He looked past her to the other Union soldiers before his eyes found her again. "Oliver will get proper medical care while he is in my protection. Then I will release him to the local authorities." He nodded slightly. "Your time here is done. Now, get out!"

Greenland and his men walked away from the cruiser. They took up positions near the gate.

Yale climbed inside the lead vehicle and gave the go-ahead to move. The convoy exited the compound and headed in the direction of Guinn's command post.

Amy and Ethan sat in the second cruiser, and the girl glared at Greenland as they passed him.

The man stared back at her with fury in his eyes.

Darkness fell quickly over the travelers as the rutted road shook them in their seats again. Amy laid her head in her arms and cried as she thought about Madison. She felt Ethan's hand gently rubbing her back. She kept her eyes closed, and images of the friendly robot raced through her mind. She recalled their mission to rescue her father, their efforts to steal the *Liberty Bell*, and the time Madison saved her life while they made repairs to the damaged ship. She sat up and rubbed her eyes.

Ethan's hand dropped to his lap.

Amy looked up at the starless sky, unable to accept that she would never see her friend again. *He was no threat to us*, she thought. *He would never do anything to hurt anyone. Why didn't Yale understand that?*

Amy looked around in confusion as the convoy stopped on the dark road. At first, she thought there might be raiders up ahead, but dismissed that idea when there was no warning from the first cruiser and no laser fire.

She and Ethan hopped out of the vehicle and moved toward the front of the convoy. There, she saw the Union soldiers leaving their cruiser and marching toward a clearing in the woods.

Yale directed the activity.

"What's going on?" Amy asked. "Why have we stopped?"

The captain stepped toward the girl. "We are going back to Greenland's compound." Yale looked over Amy's shoulder and gave a soldier some directions. The captain then turned and marched toward the clearing.

Amy and Ethan followed her.

"Why are we going back?" Amy asked. She matched Yale's pace as Ethan trailed behind them. "Madison is dead, and Oliver can't travel yet. What's the point?"

"The point is we never saw the entire operation!" Yale snapped as she suddenly stopped walking. "We need to know exactly what's going on there. The only way to do that is to examine every inch of that nut job's facility. If he won't let us, we will do it ourselves under the cover of darkness." She put her hands on her hips. "I guess there is no point in telling you to stay here with the vehicles."

Amy smiled. "Nope. If you are going back, I am, too." The girl pointed at Ethan. "We both are."

The boy nodded in agreement.

"That's what I thought," Yale said. She started walking again, and the kids followed her. "We will have a strategy meeting in ten minutes. Be there, and be ready to go right after. We are returning to Greenland's within the hour."

The Union soldiers set up a tent with a portable table, a few chairs, and several lanterns for illumination.

Yale spread a map out on the table and discussed her plan with the soldiers, Amy, and Ethan. She pointed to the map. "This is the one building we did not get into. That is our target. It is on the south end of the compound. To avoid detection, I will lead a team of three back to the facility."

"Who will be on the team with you?" Private Corkland asked. The nineteen-year-old soldier had fierce blue eyes and broad shoulders. He spoke with authority in his voice.

"Because I would like to volunteer." He snapped to attention, as if a senior officer had just entered the room.

Yale shook her head. "I appreciate your enthusiasm, Corkland, but the team will be me, Amy, and Ethan."

The soldiers mumbled their shock and dismay.

"I know that surprises you, but I do have a plan."

"With all due respect, captain," Corkland said, "I don't think it's a good idea to send kids on a dangerous mission like this." He glanced at Amy before looking back at Yale. "They aren't trained for this kind of thing."

"I respect your input," Yale replied. She nodded at Corkland. "But you all know that Amy is no ordinary kid. She has seen more combat than most of you. And Ethan has special skills of his own." She paused. "I need the rest of you to be ready to roll when we come back. We may have men shooting at us when we return. Dismissed!"

The soldiers broke the meeting and left the makeshift tent.

Yale waved the kids over to her. "I'm going out on a limb, again, for you two. Don't make me regret it." She rolled up the map and handed it to Ethan. "Give this to Corkland on your way out."

Yale met her small team near the line of parked cruisers. She carried a backpack over her right shoulder.

Amy climbed into one of the vehicles and sat down in the front row.

Yale laughed. "Get out of there, Amy," she ordered.

The girl slowly got out of the cruiser.

"We are going on foot," Yale said, "to avoid detection."

Amy sighed. "How far is it?" She glanced at Ethan, who shrugged.

"We are only a mile and a half from the compound," Yale replied. She quickly checked her compass. "If it's too far for you, I can get someone else." She started walking along the dark road, and the youngsters quickly followed her. "That's what I thought."

Yale set a quick pace, and the team reached the compound in fifteen minutes.

The captain led them to the menacing front gate.

Staying low and quiet, they moved parallel to the compound before stopping in front of the gate.

Yale removed a magnetic disrupter from her backpack and attached it to a section of the gate. Sparks flew for a moment, as that part of the fence shorted out. The captain then removed a laser torch and cut a hole in the fence.

The team slipped through the hole and followed their leader. They rushed toward the one building that they hadn't entered yet. It was an immense, rectangular structure at the far southern end of the compound. The team regrouped outside of the building.

"Keep an eye out for guards," Yale whispered.

The kids nodded and stayed close to her.

Yale kept her team still for several minutes.

As she predicted, two armed guards patrolled the outside of the structure, walking side by side. The men moved leisurely across the grounds, their harnessed laser rifles swinging lazily at their sides.

Amy could hear them joking about their boss.

The captain waited for them to pass before she rushed to the nearest door with the kids right behind her. She removed an electronic lock pick from her backpack and popped open the door. Yale glanced over her shoulder and waved the kids inside before following them.

The captain took the lead again as they quietly moved across the carpeted floor.

Amy covered her nose and mouth with her right hand, as the hallway smelled like bleach.

Several doors lined both sides of the corridor, and the team opened each one, peeking quickly inside. They found stores of supplies, food, uniforms, and weapons. Finally, they came to the last door, the only one that was locked.

Yale again used her gizmo to open it.

The team slipped inside and shut the door behind them.

A musty smell replaced the bleach scent, and the floor was covered in tiles. The windowless room was pitch black, so Yale removed a light from her backpack and turned it on. Tables, chairs, computer terminals, and various pieces of lab equipment appeared in the light. Yale found the nearest wall and shined the light on it until she spotted a light switch. She flipped it, and the darkness fell to the overhead lights.

Ethan whistled in amazement at the sheer size of the room as its contents became visible.

Before them stood row after row of fully assembled robots. They were dark green and stood about six feet tall. Each was identical to the other, but their faces were different from Madison's.

Amy moved forward and touched one robot's shoulder. The metal was smooth and cold. "They look like they are sleeping," she said, sliding her hand off the robot. "I felt a tingling vibration. Are they on or off?"

Ethan touched one on the arm. "I think they are in some kind of sleep mode," he replied. "Like a computer that's on but not being used." He walked along a line of robots, touching each one. "This is incredible. Dr. Greenland is a genius."

"And a liar," Yale said. She finally gave in to her curiosity and touched a robot. She quickly pulled her hand back. "He tried to hide this from us and the Union," she added. "We have to destroy them all."

"What?" Amy asked. She moved quickly over to Yale. She

put her hands on her hips as she stopped just inches from her captain. "Why destroy them? They haven't done anything."

"Isn't it obvious to you yet?" Yale countered. She raised her hands palms up in the air. "It's far too risky to let these things exist. Imagine what would happen if they fell into the wrong hands, like the Crownaxians. It would be disastrous for the Union." She stepped around Amy and stood in front of one robot. "We also have to erase the schematics from Greenland's computers so he can't build more of them. Ethan, can you do that?"

The boy nodded. "Sure. I just need to access his data files. That could take some time." He walked over to a computer terminal and turned the machine on. The boy sat down in the chair in front of it and started typing on the keyboard.

Amy approached Yale again. She spoke in a softer voice. "I understand the safety concerns, but destroying them would be like wiping out an entire civilization, Madison's people. We don't have the right to do that."

"These are not people," Yale said. She tapped on one robot's shoulder to make her point. "They are machines. Dangerous machines. They pose too great a threat. We must eliminate them." She walked away from the girl. "And this is not up for debate."

Amy didn't give up. "We don't know enough about them to make that kind of decision." She paused, trying to find the right words. "Do they think? Do they feel? Are they individuals, or just one mindless hive? We don't know."

Yale turned to face her again. "I am not a philosopher, Amy. I am a captain in the Union military, and my only concern is for the safety of the Union and Mankind." Her face reddened. "And the bottom line is that you don't have a say in this. You are a child of the Union. You are here because I let you come here. If you keep defying me, I will send you back to Paldor. Understand?"

Amy turned and stormed away from the captain. She stopped behind Ethan and watched him work on the computer. "What you think, Ethan? You are the robot expert. Don't you think this is wrong?"

The boy kept working. "No," he said over his shoulder. "I think Yale is right. Greenland is a madman, and we have to stop him."

Amy slapped the back of his chair in frustration.

The impact startled Ethan, but he quickly regained his composure. His fingers continued to tap the keyboard as different images appeared on the screen.

Yale removed a radio from her backpack. "Lt. Ford, this is Capt. Brown," she said into the microphone. "Come in, Lt. Ford."

Static came from the speakers.

Yale repeated her command, but the only response was more static. "We'll need to go outside to reach her," she said. "Ethan, how is it going over there?"

The boy turned to face her. "Not good," he replied. "This security system is top notch. I can't get past the firewalls." He shook his head. "If I had a few hours…"

Yale frowned. "We don't have hours. Leave it for now. We will have to deal with that later." She waved her right hand at the youngsters. "C'mon, we are getting out of here." She turned and started toward the door.

Suddenly, the door burst open, and four men armed with laser rifles rushed toward the team.

Yale and the kids stopped dead in their tracks.

Dr. Greenland entered the room with a dreadful expression. "I'm sorry you found this place, Capt. Brown," he said. "I truly wished you hadn't."

Chapter Nine

Amy lifted her head and stretched her arms out. She forced herself to a sitting position and looked around the cell. Ethan was still asleep, curled up on the floor with his head on his arms. Amy saw Yale on the other bench. The captain was awake, and the redness in her eyes made Amy wonder if she had been all night.

One of Greenland's men stood guard outside the cell with a laser rifle in his hands. It wasn't the same man who forced them into the cell the night before, and Amy realized that the guards must be working shifts.

Amy picked up a stone from the floor and tossed it at the cell's only exit. The stone hit the invisible, electronic forcefield and bounced back.

The guard glared at the girl and shook his head.

The sound woke Ethan up. He looked around in confusion for a moment until he got his bearings. He rubbed his eyes, rose, and sat down beside Amy on the bench.

Rays of light poured in from the cracks in the walls.

"It's morning?" he asked, scratching his forehead.

Amy nodded.

Ethan looked over at Yale. "So, now what?" he asked.

"That's a great question," Yale replied, in a scratchy voice. The captain rose to her feet and addressed the guard. "How long are you going to keep us here?"

The guard did not respond. He stood still, looking straight ahead.

"You know that you are in violation of Union law by holding us here?" she asked.

Again, the guard said nothing.

Yale paced across the cell. She brought her hands together, intertwining her fingers like someone in prayer. She stopped directly in front of the armed guard. "Whatever Greenland is paying you, the Union will double it if you help us escape."

Still no reaction from the guard.

The captain shrugged and looked at Amy. "You were clever enough to steal the *Liberty Bell*," she said. "Got any ideas on how we can get out of here?"

Amy shook her head. "I'm better at getting into trouble than out of it."

Yale then turned to face Ethan. "You are super smart. Got any ideas?"

The boy shrugged.

Amy looked back at Yale. "Looks like we are going to be here for a while."

"Too bad your friend Cole isn't here," Ethan said. He stood and walked away from Amy. He leaned against the wall opposite of the forcefield. "He could use that blue energy to bust us out of here." The boy crossed his arms over his chest.

"What blue energy?" Yale asked. She approached Amy and sat down beside her. "What is he talking about?"

Amy glared at Ethan. "Oh, knock it off," she said to him. "This is not the time for your petty jealousy, or your wild stories. We need a real plan." She shook her head and noticed that Yale was still waiting for an answer. Amy sighed. "Ethan claims that Cole has some kind of special powers, that he used some blue energy field to protect himself from falling crates on the *Liberty Bell*. Sounds stupid, right?"

"I don't care how it sounds," Ethan said. "I saw what I saw. He waved his hand, this blue shield formed around him, and the boxes bounced off it."

Amy and Yale looked over at him, both with skeptical expressions.

"I saw what I saw," he repeated.

Yale stood and moved toward him. She placed a hand on his right shoulder. "I'm sure you think you saw something strange, Ethan. But you have to admit, your story sounds kinda crazy."

The boy pressed his lips together.

Yale continued. "If someone told you that story, would you believe it?"

He shrugged. "I don't know. But if someone told us fifty years ago that we would be fighting an interstellar war with ruthless aliens, would we have believed it?" He moved away from Yale and sat down on the empty bench across from Amy. "The Universe is so crazy that I'm open to believing a lot of things."

Yale yawned and stretched her arms out in front of her. "It may seem crazy," she said. "But science is science, everywhere in the Universe." She sat down beside Amy again. "Maybe Cole was carrying some kind of electronic device that emits an energy field, like the one keeping us in this cell." She picked up a stone and threw it at the forcefield. It, too, bounced off and landed on the floor.

The guard aimed his rifle at her.

"Go ahead, shoot," Yale said. "Let's see how strong this barrier is."

"That won't be necessary," a voice from behind the guard said.

Everyone in the cell looked past the armed man and saw Greenland enter the room.

The scientist touched the guard's shoulder, and the man lowered his weapon. "I take it that our accommodations are to your liking." Greenland smiled. "Good. I hate to disappoint my guests."

Yale stood up slowly. "I demand that you release us at once," she said. She kept her arms straight at her sides. "You cannot abduct Union personnel without serious repercussions. It won't be long before a battalion is outside your gate with their weapons pointed at you." She paused and stared into his eyes. "Let us go before there is any bloodshed."

Greenland laughed. "We did not abduct you, captain." He inched closer to her and kept his eyes on hers. "You were trespassing, and we simply housed you until the proper authorities could be contacted." He took a step back. "Which should happen in a day or two. In the meantime, you will be my guests."

"As your guest, I'd like to check out now," Amy said. She stood and moved toward the barrier. "Have our luggage put in a cruiser, and tell the driver to be quick about it." She glared at their host. "Or there won't be a tip."

Greenland smiled. "Precocious girl, isn't she?" he asked Yale. He looked at Amy. "Don't press your luck, child. My patience has limits." He turned and took two steps away from the hostages before turning back to face them again. "You will not be with us for very long. I do plan to let you go, when the time is right. Until then, do as you are told, or you will be shot." He took a step toward them. "Is that clear?"

"When will the time be right?" Yale asked. "What are you up to, Dr. Greenland?" The captain stood just inches from the barrier. She waved her hand in front of it, causing it to crackle. Yale lowered her hand and curled it into a fist.

Greenland's expression soured. His jaw tightened as he leaned toward her. "I will show everyone who doubted me that they were wrong." He took a deep breath. "I am the greatest scientist of my generation, and they laughed at me. They said I was crazy." His hands tightened into fists. "But I have proved them wrong and, now, I will make them pay!"

"You sound nuts," Ethan said. He kept his distance from the scientist.

Greenland glared at him without speaking.

"You got laughed at and, now, you are going to put millions of lives at risk with your robots?" Ethan moved toward his jailer. "Yeah, we saw them. We saw your secret army. Are you going to use them to attack the Union? 'Cause that's even more nuts."

"Enough!" Greenland yelled. His face reddened, and several veins bulged in his neck. "It doesn't matter now. You can't do anything to stop me. And, if you want to live long enough to start shaving, you will do as you are told." Greenland turned and addressed the guard. "Make sure they have enough food and water. I wouldn't want them to be disappointed with our hospitality."

The guard nodded, and Greenland stormed out of the room.

Amy and Ethan sat together on one bench as Yale paced the floor of their cell for nearly an hour.

The guard stood in his position, with his loaded laser rifle in his hands. He continued to stare forward as he kept watch over the prisoners.

Amy put her head on Ethan's shoulder. She began whispering into his ear.

Yale stopped pacing for a moment, until Amy raised her eyebrows, and the captain got the message. She continued her trek and watched the guard out of the corner of her eyes.

Ethan suddenly pulled away from Amy and grabbed his chest. He wheezed and coughed as his face turned red.

Yale and Amy rushed to him.

The captain loosened the boy's shirt and carefully lowered him onto one of the benches. She turned and screamed at the guard. "We need help in here!" she said.

The guard didn't move.

Amy rushed toward the barrier and stopped just short of it. "He's having an asthma attack!" she screamed. "Get a doctor!"

The guard tilted his head to get a better look at the boy, but he did not move toward the prisoners.

Amy rushed back to Ethan.

His face turned pale, and he kept struggling to breathe.

Amy turned back toward the guard again. "Get us some help, or he's going to die!" she yelled.

The guard finally moved toward them. He was a stride away from the barrier, when Amy picked up a stray bolt from the floor. She whipped it at the forcefield, causing the barrier to expand and zap the soldier where he stood. The overload of energy caused the forcefield to short out as the guard fell backward.

Smoke emanated from the forcefield generators.

Amy helped Ethan to his feet, while Yale checked on the stricken guard. She put her hands on his neck before slowly moving his head. "He's still alive, but he'll be out for a while." She picked up his rifle and handed it to Amy. "Hold this."

Amy took the weapon from her.

Yale grabbed the man's legs and dragged him toward a nearby door. She opened it and stuffed the guard into the tiny closet before closing the door.

The captain took the rifle from Amy, and she led her team out of the makeshift penitentiary.

They stayed close together and quietly dashed down the hallway.

Yale put a hand up and stopped as two guards appeared at an intersecting corridor.

The prisoners ducked behind support beams until the intruders left. They quickly regrouped, and the kids followed Yale.

The team was nearly out of the building when another guard appeared, surprising them.

Yale whacked the armed man in the face with the handle of her rifle, stunning him. She tore his weapon out of his hands and tossed it to Amy, who caught it in mid-air.

The guard dropped to the floor, but quickly regained his senses and charged at Yale. He knocked Yale to the floor, and they wrestled for control of her weapon.

The laser rifle slipped away from both combatants and wound up at Ethan's feet. He picked up the weapon and pointed it at the guard, but he could not get a clear shot.

Yale finally got on top of the guard and landed several punches to his face. She grabbed him by his hair and slammed his head against the floor until he stopped moving.

Yale stood up and fought to catch her breath.

Amy and Ethan dragged the unconscious man to the closest room. They pushed him into the room with a thud and shut the door.

The captain continued leading them out of the building, and they finally made it outdoors. Sunlight poured down on them.

Amy smelled the fragrance of various flowers in the light wind.

"This way," Yale said. She moved toward the robot warehouse instead of the hole in the main gate. "We're not done yet," she said.

The team slithered across the compound until they came to the warehouse door. The old lock on the door had been replaced with a newer one.

Yale examined it closely. The design was the same, so she removed her electronic lock pick from her backpack and popped open the lock. She slowly opened the door and peeked inside. The captain then waved her hand, and the kids entered first.

Yale closed the door as Amy turned on the lights. The same rows of completed robots stood in their lines. "Look for something flammable," Yale said.

Amy and Ethan remained still, looking at each other before peering at the captain.

"There's no time to debate this again," Yale said. She moved toward a row of cabinets and started opening the doors. "We have to destroy them. That's all there is to it."

The kids reluctantly joined in the search for something to start a fire. They dug through piles of discarded materials as the captain continued searching the cabinets.

Yale finally found some cleaning fluids. "Over here," she said.

Amy and Ethan helped her pour the fluids onto the floor around the first rows of robots. They tossed the empty bottles aside.

"What are you doing?" a calm voice from behind them asked.

The team whipped their heads around, looking for the source of the question.

Yale clasped the laser rifle that was strapped onto her right shoulder.

"You are putting us on in danger," the voice said. "Please stop doing that."

"Where is that coming from?" Amy asked. She twisted her body trying to find the intruder.

Ethan pushed himself up on his toes to get a better view. A creaking sound came toward them, getting louder and louder.

Amy glanced at Yale, but neither could see the speaker.

One of the robots appeared from the crowd.

Yale pointed her rifle at it, and the robot stopped moving.

It tilted its head to the right. "Who are you? Why are you in our home?" It raised its left hand like a police officer stopping traffic. "Please do not shoot me," it said to Yale. "I do not wish to be destroyed."

"That's too bad," Yale said, lining up her shot. She was about to fire, when two other robots stepped in front of her.

One ripped the weapon out of her hands, while the other grabbed her arms.

The captain tried to break free, but her restrainer was too strong. "Let me go!" she shouted as she continued to struggle.

The first robot stepped toward Yale. "Please stop doing that. We don't want to hurt you, but we cannot allow you to hurt us." It stopped a few feet in front of Yale. "My name is Lincoln." It took the laser rifle from the other robot. "This is too hazardous for humans to handle." The robot slid the weapon along the floor, and it hit a nearby wall.

Lincoln nodded at the robot restraining Yale, and that one let the captain go.

Yale moved away from her captor and slowly backed her way toward the kids. "My name is Capt. Yale Brown," she said. She reached her destination and stood between the robots and the kids. "I am a soldier with Earth's Union

Defense Fleet. We are here on a peaceful, humanitarian mission."

"Is part of your mission to burn this facility to the ground?" Lincoln asked.

Yale shook her head.

"I didn't think so. So why are you pouring flammable liquid onto the floor?" he asked.

"It's a mistake," Ethan replied. He stepped past Yale and stood before Lincoln. "We thought you might be dangerous, but we see now that we were wrong. We'll just be leaving now." He started toward the door, but Lincoln stepped in front of him. "Or not," said the boy.

"Dr. Greenland does not like visitors," Lincoln said. "Does he know that you are here?"

Amy stepped forward. "Yes," she answered. "We are his guests." She smiled at the robot. "We were just looking around when we found this building." She slowly raised her hands with her palms upward. "This place is huge. Very impressive." Amy cautiously edged toward Lincoln. "We were not aware that Dr. Greenland had created some many robots. How long have you been active?"

"I have been awake for nineteen days," Lincoln replied. "I am the oldest." He pointed to the other robots. "Some of them have only been awake for a few days now. Others are still downloading their initial programming. They should awaken soon."

"What is your primary function?" Ethan asked.

Lincoln looked at him but did not reply.

"I mean, why are you here?" Ethan asked again. "What is your purpose?" He eased up beside Amy and positioned himself between her and Lincoln. "There must be some reason."

Lincoln closed his eyes for a moment. He reopened them

but did not appear to have an adequate answer. "I don't know," he said. "Dr. Greenland has not shared that information with us. Maybe he doesn't know, either."

"You look like soldiers," Yale said. She rubbed her hands together. "Have you had military training?" She glanced at Amy and pointed toward the floor with her eyes.

Amy sighed and nodded.

Lincoln took two steps and stopped in front of Yale. "Yes," he said. "We have had military training downloaded into our memory banks." He pointed at the captain. "You are the leader of this group. Tell me what *your* military objective is."

Yale shrugged. "I told you. We are here on a humanitarian mission." She paused, as if hoping that would satisfy Lincoln.

The robot stared into her eyes.

"This planet has suffered a global weather event," Yale continued. "We are here to provide aid."

"We are also looking for friend," Ethan said.

Lincoln turned to face the boy.

"He is a robot, like you, but he has been damaged. His name is Madison. Have you seen him?" The boy tried to smile, but he looked awkward.

"There are many of us here," Lincoln said. He walked away from the team and strode in a small circle before returning to his previous position. "I have not noticed any damaged units. Perhaps your friend was beyond repair and incinerated."

Amy gasped and covered her mouth with her right hand. "Is that how you deal with broken robots?" she asked. "You toss them into a fire?" She felt herself on the verge of tears, so she took a deep breath and slowly let it out. "Don't you try to fix them?"

"We do," Lincoln replied. "I'm sorry, I did not mean to upset you," he added. He started to walk away again. "Follow me. Maybe we can find your friend." He continued walking toward the back of the room.

Amy started to follow him, but she stopped when Yale raised her right hand. The girl then shook her head and trailed the robot.

Yale and Ethan quickly followed.

Lincoln opened a door in the back of the room, revealing a smaller area that had tools, workbenches, and spare robot parts scattered along the walls. The workshop smelled like oil and musty, old clothing.

Amy looked around the room as Yale and Ethan entered. She lifted dirty tarps and uncovered broken machines and robot components.

Ethan searched the other side of the room, while Yale stayed close to the door.

Amy came across a long white sheet covering something bulky, and she pulled it up. "I found him!" she yelled as she looked at the face of her long-time friend. She tossed the sheet aside as Ethan rushed over to her.

The boy ran his fingers along the side of Madison's face.

"Can you fix him?" Amy asked.

The boy shrugged. "I can try," he replied. Ethan removed some tools from a nearby toolbox and started working on the robot. "It doesn't look like Greenland tried too hard to fix him." He removed a circuit board from the robot's chest. It had melted, and the circuitry fused together. Ethan turned to Amy and sighed. "He needs a new board." He tossed the old one aside. "This one is dead." Ethan turned toward Lincoln. "Do you know where Greenland stores his spare circuit boards?"

"I do," Lincoln replied. He moved across the room toward a row of cabinets, with Ethan behind him. The robot opened a drawer and pulled out an item. He handed it to the boy.

"There are only a few of these left. Be careful installing it. They are very fragile."

"Thanks," Ethan replied. He stood still for a moment, as if contemplating something. The boy spoke in a soft voice. "I could really use some help with this. Will you help me?"

The robot nodded. "It would be my pleasure."

They walked past Amy and began working on Madison.

After a few minutes, Amy crept up behind them to get a better look at their efforts. She accidentally bumped into Ethan.

The boy calmly turned around to face her. "This is going to take a while," he said. He put an arm around her back and led her toward an overturned crate. "Have a seat. I will let you know as soon as we are done." Ethan went back to the task at hand.

Amy sat quietly on the crate. She folded her hands together in her lap and closed her eyes. She prayed without speaking and asked for Him to guide Ethan's hands. She slowly opened her eyes and took a deep breath. Amy saw Yale by the door and she sensed that the captain did not want to spend this much time here. *Too bad,* she thought. *Madison needs us, and we are not leaving without him.*

Chapter Ten

The repair work took over an hour.

Yale recovered the laser rifle and slung it over her shoulder. She paced back and forth behind Ethan and Lincoln, while Amy remained as still as she could on the crate.

Ethan wiped sweat from his face and then connected a batch of wires together using an electronic splicer. He carefully pushed the bundle of wires inside the metal casing on Madison's chest and snapped the outer door shut.

Ethan rose and nodded at Amy.

She sprung to her feet and rushed toward him.

The boy caught her before she banged into the patient. "Easy now," he said to Amy. "We've done all we can. Now it's up to Madison."

They stood side-by-side and waited.

Amy slid her hand inside Ethan's and gently squeezed it.

The captain approached and stood behind them. "What happens now?" she asked. The fatigue in her voice was obvious. She peeked over Ethan's shoulder to get a look at Madison. "Does he wake up on his own, or do we have to jump start him?"

"His systems are rebooting right now," Ethan answered. The boy let go of Amy's hand and turned to face her. "We don't know what he will be like when he wakes up. He should have all of his memories, but his personality might be different."

Amy began to tear up again.

"Let's just hope for the best," Ethan said.

Five minutes passed before the group saw any movement from Madison.

At first, it was a twitching in the fingers of his right hand. Slowly, more of his body began to awaken. His legs shook, and his head turned from side to side.

"Stay back, everyone," Ethan said. "Let's give him some room." The others backed up, but Ethan remained close in case Madison needed him.

Madison's eyes slowly opened, and he leaned forward to a sitting position.

Ethan put a hand on his back to steady him. "Easy now."

The robot looked at him.

"Do you know where you are?" Ethan asked.

The robot did not respond. Instead, he looked straight ahead, like a patient coming out of a coma.

"Do you know your name?" Ethan asked.

"I am a cybernetic humanoid," Madison replied in a clunky, mechanical voice. "I do not have a name." He looked around for a moment. "I do not know where I am." He unsteadily rose to his feet with Ethan's help. "What is my objective?"

Amy rushed forward. "You do have a name," she said. She

quickly grabbed his hands. "Your name is Madison." She paused and looked for any recognition in his eyes. "Madison," she repeated. "I'm Amy. Your best friend. Remember?" She felt her heart pound in her chest. She let go of his hands and gently touched his face. "Remember?"

Ethan eased her hands from the robot's face. "You must give him time," he said to Amy.

Her arms dropped to her sides. She continued to stare at Madison's face. "We have been friends for a long time now. You were my tutor back on Paldor. We stole a spaceship and flew into Crownaxian space to rescue my father. Remember?"

The robot stumbled forward as he tried to walk.

Ethan remained close to him.

Madison saw Lincoln and addressed him. "You are like me."

Lincoln nodded.

"Is the information she gave accurate?" Madison asked.

"I am not sure," Lincoln replied. "I just met you." He glanced at Amy before looking back at Madison. "But, judging by her physical reactions, I would say she is telling the truth." He extended a hand. "My name is Lincoln. It is a pleasure to meet you, Madison."

Madison robotically returned the gesture. He then looked at the others. "Who are you?" he asked the group.

Amy quickly responded, introducing him to Ethan and Yale.

"Was I damaged in some way?" Madison asked. "I seem a bit confused."

"I shot you," Yale said, matter-of-factly.

Madison snapped his head back.

"And, if we don't get out of here soon, we'll all be shot," she said. The captain examined the laser rifle before she slung it back over her right shoulder. "There's not much charge left in this. Let's hope I don't need to use it." She marched toward the door but stopped before exiting.

"C'mon, what are you waiting for?" Yale asked her team. "We've got to go." She removed a small torch from her backpack and lit it. The flame menacingly danced near her hands. "Get over here," she ordered.

Amy and Ethan stood defiantly still.

"No," Amy said. "We can't let you destroy the other robots. They've done nothing wrong." She took one step and stopped next to Lincoln. "Lincoln helped us fix Madison. How can you destroy him? Hurting any of them would be like hurting Madison, and I can't let you do that." She boldly crossed her arms over her chest.

"We've been over this already," Yale said. She clenched her teeth as she spoke. "We cannot allow Greenland to sell these machines to anyone, especially the Crownaxians. They have to be destroyed." She lowered the torch toward the line of flammable liquid that the team had spread along the floor.

Before Yale could ignite the liquids, Amy rushed to the nearest wall and pulled off the fire extinguisher. She shot the foul-smelling foam over the floor until the unit ran out of materials. The young girl carefully placed the empty cannister on the floor.

Yale extinguished the torch and put it back in her pack. "I hope you realize what you just did, Amy."

"I saved their lives," Amy replied.

"And possibly ended ours," Yale stated. The officer peeked out the exit door before turning to face her team again. "It's clear for now. Let's get moving." She opened the door again to make sure that they could leave. She whispered over her shoulder. "Now."

Ethan and Amy finally obeyed and rushed up behind Yale.

Amy stopped when she realized that Madison wasn't following them. "Madison, what's wrong?" She took two steps back toward him when he didn't answer. "What's wrong?" she asked again.

Madison shook his head. "I am not going with her," he said, pointing at Yale. "She shot me." He tilted his head slightly to the right. "Why did you shoot me? Had I wronged you in some way."

The captain sighed. "You were going to help Greenland with his plan, whatever that is." She held the door open. "Now, either come with us, or stay here. At this point, I don't care, but we must leave. Now!"

Lincoln took one step toward Yale. "I know what Dr. Greenland's plan is," he said.

Everyone looked at him.

"Or at least part of it." He nodded, as if he were happy with himself.

Madison turned and walked toward the other robot, while Yale glared at them both.

"Well," Yale said. "Do you plan our sharing it with the rest of us, or do we spend the rest of the night trying to guess?"

Lincoln hesitated and looked at Madison for a cue.

"Out with it!" Yale shouted.

"If you insist," Lincoln said to Yale. The robot walked in a small arch as he talked. "Dr. Greenland said that we have a powerful destiny. He said that all of us will play an integral part in his plan and that no one will be able to stop us, not even humans."

"Well that sounds ominous," Yale said. She looked over at Amy. "Are you still glad that you saved them?"

Amy nodded without hesitation.

"Well, remember that when they are destroying our home planet," said Yale. The captain pointed at Madison. "Are you coming with us, or staying here?"

Madison slowly shook his head. "I need to stay here," he replied.

Amy moved closer to him and placed her hands in his.

"I have much to learn, my friend," he said to the young girl. "My place is here, with them, where I can rediscover who I am and what my destiny is."

Amy pressed her lips together and trembled.

"Don't worry about me," Madison said. "I will be fine."

The robot spotted something on one of the tables. He hustled over to the table with Amy directly behind him.

She saw two communicators on the table, and she watched him pick up one of them.

He handed it to her. "If you need me, contact me on this."

Amy took the device and cradled it in her arms.

"Amy, we have to go!" Yale exclaimed. "Now. We need to get out of here before Greenland, or his, guards find us here."

Amy glanced over her shoulder at Yale before turning back to face Madison. She tried to find the right thing to say, but no words came to her.

"Now, Amy!" Yale yelled. "We have to go!"

Amy placed a hand on Madison's right shoulder for a moment before she turned away from him and rushed back over to the exit. She followed Yale and Ethan out of the room, and she heard the door close behind them.

Yale carefully led them across the compound to the sick-bay. "We can't leave without rescuing Nelson. We owe him that much."

Yale forced in the front door of the medical building and slipped quietly inside.

Amy and Ethan trailed her down a long hallway, occasionally turning their backs and watching for Greenland's men. Their footsteps clattered off the marble floor, and Amy worried that the sound might give them away. As before, in the other buildings, they had to pass several doors, and they checked each one. Most of them were locked.

They finally came upon a door with a window at the top of it, and they could see Nelson sleeping in one of the beds.

The door was locked, but Yale had no trouble getting it to open.

There were two rows of beds lining the walls of the room. The other walls housed various medical equipment. Nelson slept in the first bed on the right.

Yale carefully shook his left shoulder. "Nelson," she whispered. "It's time to get up. We're taking you out of here."

The scientist moaned and rolled his head to his left shoulder.

"Nelson, get up," Yale said, a bit louder. She shook him again, and his eyes slowly opened.

"Capt. Brown?" he asked. "Is that you?" He blinked his eyes and rolled his head again. He settled and squinted at Yale. "What are you doing here? You have to leave. It isn't safe." He tried to lift his right arm, but it fell back onto the bed.

Yale looked over at Ethan. "Help me with him," she said.

Ethan got onto the other side of the bed and helped the captain lift Nelson to a sitting position.

The scientist tried to focus his eyes.

"You need to get out of this bed," Yale said. "We are getting you out of here." She and Ethan guided him off the bed and he stood on his own. Yale put an arm around him.

Amy peeked out the door and saw no one, so she waved the others on.

Ethan went first, followed by Yale with Nelson, and Amy

followed them. Their feet clanged against the floor again, and Amy tried to step lightly to reduce the sound.

They made it to the front door and rushed outside. The night air felt cooler as it swept across their faces.

The team stumbled across a land vehicle, and Yale ordered them into it.

She and Ethan carefully placed Nelson in the back seat, and Amy sat next to him to keep him secure.

Yale hopped into the driver's seat, and Ethan got in next to her. Yale turned on the engine and sped toward the front gate.

Amy knew that Yale had no intention of letting the gate stop them.

The cruiser roared toward their destination, but the sound attracted the attention of Greenland's men.

Several of the men raised their laser rifles at fired at them.

Amy covered Nelson's head with her arms as she ducked in her seat.

Yale lifted her rifle and shot the front gate, shortening out the electrical current.

The cruiser smashed through the gateway.

Amy thought they were home free until a line of Greenland's men in four-wheeled vehicles blocked the roadway.

Yale jammed on the brakes and turned the wheel until the cruiser stopped sideways.

The captain fired at the men as Ethan and Amy hid on the floor of the cruiser with Nelson. Yale fired intermittently to keep the men from advancing toward them.

Amy knew that Yale couldn't keep that up for long.

The captain's rifle finally ran out of energy and she shook it in frustration. Yale looked around the vehicle for another weapon, but there were none to be found.

Greenland's men moved toward the cruiser. Before they

could reach it, laser fire suddenly rained down on them from behind and knocked the men to the ground.

Amy turned and saw where the shots came from.

Lincoln and Madison stood on the roof of the nearest building, with laser rifles in their hands. They continued to shoot at Greenland's men as Yale revved up the engine and the cruiser flew off into the darkness.

Chapter Eleven

Madison followed Lincoln across the dark compound. They passed Greenland's fallen mercenaries, most of whom were writhing in pain on the ground. The robots stayed away from the men, and Madison tried his best not to look at them.

The duo made it to the warehouse entrance and quietly slipped inside the building. The lights were still on, but the other robots remained still, standing in their formations.

"We need to clean this mess up before Dr. Greenland finds it," Lincoln said. He led Madison to a utility closet in the back of the room.

There, they retrieved floor cleaning solution, as well as two mops and buckets. They filled the buckets with hot, soapy water from a spigot. They carried the cleaning supplies to the front of the robot formation, where most of the flammable liquid and the spray from the fire extinguisher remained.

Lincoln began scrubbing the floor, and Madison mimicked his actions.

"Why did you help my friends escape?" Madison asked.

He continued the cleanup but found very little enjoyment in it. The water splashed over his feet and made it difficult for him to remain standing. He slipped several times but managed not to fall. He watched Lincoln for more cues, and noticed that his fellow robot had very little trouble keeping upright.

"I did not want to see them harmed," Lincoln replied. He emptied his mop into one bucket, using the lever on the handle to squeeze the water out. "They were not the aggressor," Lincoln continued. "The armed men were. I felt it was our duty to protect them until they could escape the compound." He stopped cleaning and looked at Madison. "Wasn't that the right thing to do?"

Madison nodded. "I think so. I just hope that Dr. Greenland understands what we did. I do not wish to see either of us deactivated because of it." He scrubbed harder as the cleanup proved more challenging that he had anticipated. "Tell me more about him. What is he like?"

Lincoln kept his head down as he focused on their task. "I don't know many other humans, so I don't have much to compare him to, but I do know that he is very intelligent and determined. He spent years trying to perfect robots like us, and that takes strong dedication. The other men obey him, but I don't know if that is out of fear or respect or the fact that he pays them." He stopped and looked up at Madison again. "What do you think of him?"

The robots stared at each other for a moment.

"I want to love him," Madison said, as he started scrubbing again. "After all, he is our creator, but I wonder if I have that capacity." He finished one section and started on another. "My databanks have thousands of records related to love, but I don't know if I truly understand it. Can we love? Can we be loved?"

"The girl certainly has affection for you," Lincoln said. He moved closer to Madison and scoured a new section of the floor. "Although, I think it is not romantic, but platonic. She seems to care for you like a member of her family. That may be the best we can hope for."

"I am starting to remember more about our friendship," Madison said. He dunked his mop in one bucket and squeezed the water out. "As she said, I was her teacher on Paldor. We spent many hours together studying various topics. I taught other children as well, but I bonded more with her than I did with the others." He stopped and smiled. "I even remember our mission to rescue her father. We both saved each other's lives more times than I can count."

"There are records about that mission in my databanks," Lincoln said. "I find it amusing that a child could outwit trained Union soldiers and steal their most prized weapon." He shook his head. "I think some of that story may be exaggerated."

Madison shrugged. "I don't know what is in your databanks, but I can tell you this. We did steal the *Liberty Bell*, and we did rescue the diplomates, including her father. Of course, we did get some help from some Crownaxian rebels."

He went on about the mission in greater detail as they continued the cleanup. Madison finished the story as they wrapped up their task. "That much is true," he concluded.

The robots put away the cleaning supplies and shut the utility room door. They walked to the front of the robot formation, where Lincoln examined the troops. He smiled at Madison. "Everything is back to the way it was," he said. "Now it is time to recharge."

"How do we do that?" Madison asked.

"With these," Lincoln replied. He pointed to a square box on his right leg. He opened the box and pressed a green button. "These are portable chargers," he said. "They have enough energy in them to last for three years."

Madison glanced at the other robots and saw that they all had this attachment on them, though he hadn't noticed them before.

"I do not have one of those chargers," he said. He pointed to the bare spot on his leg where the device would be. "I normally charge with a cord. It takes a while, but it lasts for days."

Lincoln laughed. "Well, you don't have to do that anymore." Lincoln walked over to the row of cabinets where he had found a spare circuit board for Madison. The robot dug through the drawers until he found another charging unit. He brought the unit and a laser tool over to Madison. "Stand still," he said. "You won't feel a thing." Lincoln bent down and installed the unit on Madison's right leg. "I'm going to turn it on now." He opened the box and pressed the green button.

Madison felt a surge of electricity rush through his body. He suddenly felt more awake and alert. "Wow, that feels better than my regular charges," he said. There was a tingling in the tips of his fingers. He flexed his hands and the tingling went away. "How long do I leave the unit on for?" He looked down at the device and saw the green button.

"It has an auto-shut off feature," Lincoln said as he rose to his feet. "When you are fully charged, it turns itself off, so you don't have to worry about over-charging." He returned the laser tool to the drawer before coming back to the front of the robot formation. Lincoln stood still and looked straight ahead. He remained in this position for several minutes.

Madison tilted his head. He noticed that Lincoln now had the same empty expression as the other robots. "What are you doing now?"

Lincoln didn't respond. Instead, he kept still.

Madison walked over to him and waved a hand in front of Lincoln's face. "Hello?"

Lincoln snapped out of his trance but looked annoyed. "When we are not in use, we go into sleep mode," he said. "It helps save energy and pass the time. I apologize, I should have told you about it."

"Do you dream when you are in sleep mode?" Madison asked.

"Do you?" Lincoln replied.

Madison shook his head. "I don't have a sleep mode, per se. When I shut down, my mind still works, but my circuits recharge. That way, I can turn back on by myself, especially in an emergency." He looked past Lincoln and stared at the other robots for a moment. They certainly looked like they were sleeping, as humans would perceive it.

Lincoln nodded. "Our sleep mode is similar," he said. "While we rest, we can access data from our memory banks, or we can use the Link-Up to download new material. For instance, I have been reading a 20th Century novel called *War and Peace*. It is a fascinating book." He folded his hands together and rested them in front of his legs.

"This Link-Up sounds intriguing," Madison said. "How do I access it?"

"Simple," Lincoln replied. "Just activate your Wi-Fi scanner and search for the signal."

Madison followed the instructions but frowned after a moment.

"Try closing your eyes," Lincoln suggested. "Sometimes, it is easier to find it without your vision."

Madison closed his eyes and tried again. He concentrated hard as he scanned for the elusive signal. Suddenly, he felt a new connection, and he locked on to it. He was instinctively able to unlock the data stream, and he felt an overwhelming flood of new information. The robot snapped his eyes open and shook his head.

Lincoln smiled. "It's a lot to absorb at first, but you will get used to it. You will even be able to navigate it, so you can find whatever you are looking for." Lincoln closed his eyes. "It's time to rest now. We will speak again later." The robot opened his eyes and fell back into his trance.

Madison closed his eyes and found his mind back in the data stream again. He took his time wading through the vast amount of information. After a while, he was able to steer the content toward interesting data. Madison opened a book titled *Fahrenheit 451* and began reading it. He opened his eyes and fell into his own trance.

It only took a few minutes for Madison to read the Ray Bradbury novel. Fascinated by the story, he searched for other works in the genre. The next one that stood out was *I, Robot*, a title he couldn't resist. Madison took his time with that story, savoring the words by Isaac Asimov. His next book was *Do Robots Dream of Electric Sheep?* The Philip K. Dick story both excited and scared him.

Madison was about to look for more when the sound of human voices woke him up. He blinked away the sleep and listened intently to the conversation. He recognized Greenland's voice as he spoke to his underlings. Though fully awake, something told Madison that it would be a good idea to remain still, like the other robots.

"I don't believe it," Greenland said as he entered the room with two of his men behind him. "It just isn't possible." He marched toward the formation of robots and stopped in front of them. He waved his hand in front of Lincoln's face, but there was no movement by the robot. The inventor did the same to three others, and none of them moved.

Greenland turned and faced the men. "You see, they are

still in sleep mode. They haven't moved for hours. That means either you are lying, or you imagined it." He crossed his arms over his chest. "So, which is it, Murphy? Do I fire you, or do I shoot you?"

The man named Murphy took a handkerchief out of his coat pocket and wiped sweat from his forehead. "Neither, Dr. Greenland," he replied. He folded the cloth and put it back in his pocket. "The truth is that two of your robots shot at my men. Eight of them are injured, though they all look like they will survive."

"And why would my robots shoot at them?" Greenland asked.

"Like I said before," Murphy replied. "We had intruders in the compound. It was that lady captain and those two kids. They took Dr. Nelson right out of sickbay." He raised his hands to accentuate his point. "That must have been their mission."

Greenland turned his back on Murphy.

"If you don't believe me, check for yourself. Dr. Nelson is gone."

"He could have slipped out on his own during the melee," Greenland replied. He started walking away from the robot formation, and his two men followed him. "You've given me no proof of the robots' involvement in Nelson's escape." He stopped quickly and glared at Murphy. "I built these robots. I programmed them, and I sculpted them with my own two hands. I know them better than anyone else. They would not shoot at someone without my explicit orders."

Murphy started to reply but stopped. He looked defeated. The man took a deep breath. "I think we should send two vehicles out after them," he said. He rubbed his sore eyes. "They've got a head start on us, but we can catch them before morning, but we have to do it now. We cannot afford to wait any longer."

Greenland shook his head. "Let them go," he said. "They are not critical to my plan." He started walking toward the exit again. "Get your men patched up. I want them on patrol again by sunrise. I can't afford to be vulnerable, not when I am this close." Greenland and his men left the room, and Madison heard the door close behind them.

Madison was relieved that Greenland thought it impossible for his robots to betray him. That meant no punishment for him or Lincoln. He realized that he needed to find out what Greenland's exact plan was, and if he should stop him. The robot's head began to swirl. Though he had a lot to think about, he soon found himself sucked back inside the world of the Link-Up.

Chapter Twelve

Janar's purple sun crept over the horizon as Yale and her reunited team reached the Command Post in their cruisers.

Amy jumped out of the land vehicle, with her mouth open, as she surveyed the horror around them. Most the installation was destroyed. Fires burned out of control, while bodies littered the ground. It was obvious to everyone on Yale's team that they were looking at the remnants of a war zone.

Amy followed her captain as Yale looked for someone in charge. They found a private bent over a fallen soldier. The private was performing CPR, while blood seeped out of several bandages on the wounded soldier.

Yale and Amy rushed to help him.

Amy reached into a medical kit that lay next to the private, and she began changing the saturated bandages.

"What the hell happened here?" Yale asked as she took over performing the CPR.

The exhausted private sat back, shaking and unable to speak.

Yale glanced at Amy, and their eyes met with mutual understanding.

The private dropped his head into his hands and sobbed.

Yale addressed the rest of her crew. "Fan out, do what you can for survivors," she ordered.

They quickly followed her command.

"And find out who is in charge," she added.

Yale's Union soldiers searched for others in need and provided what medical help they could.

The captain stopped CPR when her patient coughed and opened his eyes.

Amy finished changing his bandages.

Yale eased the man to a sitting position.

The private stood and stopped crying.

"What happened?" Yale asked her patient.

The corporal spoke slowly as Yale supported his back. "We were attacked last night," he said. His body shook, and he had trouble keeping his eyes open. "They hit us just after sundown. They came from the east. Mortar shells first, then laser fire." He shook his head. "We weren't ready for them." He looked into Yale's eyes. "I'm sorry, captain. We failed."

"No, corporal," Yale said. She lightly squeezed his shoulder. "You did your best. That is all we can ask." She looked around the battlefield and shook her head. "Lt. Ford," she said to the soldier. "Do you know what happened to her?"

The corporal shook his head.

"That's OK," Yale said. "You get some rest now."

Amy helped Yale to her feet. The young girl pointed to a tent that was still standing. Its flaps had the familiar red cross on them. "We can set up a sick bay over there," she said.

Yale nodded, and they walked over to the tent. Inside they

found damaged beds, overturned furniture, and smashed computer equipment. There were also two bodies on the ground.

Yale checked for a pulse on one of them, while Amy did the same with the other. They looked at each other and shook their heads.

Amy found two sheets, and she covered the bodies with them.

Yale and Amy were cleaning up the tent when a woman entered with two armed Janar soldiers behind her.

Amy recognized the woman. It was Stacy Guinn.

"Captain, it's good to see you again," Stacey said, extending a hand to Yale.

Yale quickly shook it and pulled her hand back.

"I'm sorry it's not under better circumstances."

"Who did this, Stacy?" Yale asked. The captain's voice was gruff.

Guinn hesitated. She looked like she was searching for the right words.

"And don't give me any crap about security, cause I'm not in the mood," Yale said.

Guinn turned and walked a few steps away from Yale before turning and facing her again.

"Out with it," Yale said.

"The base was attacked by members of Su-Kanan," Guinn replied. She glanced at her own soldiers before continuing. "They are a rebel group which is trying to overthrow the planet's Central Government. We have been battling them for nearly two years. They are using the environmental tragedy to further their cause." She approached Yale and put a hand on the captain's right shoulder. "I'm sorry I couldn't tell you about them earlier. Orders, you understand."

Yale pushed Guinn's hand away. "I don't give a damn about your orders!" Yale shouted.

The Janar soldiers raised their pistols at Yale, but Guinn waved them off.

"My soldiers are dead or missing," Yale continued. "We were summoned here to provide aid after an environmental disaster, not to help you fight your political rivals. You should have been upfront about what we were facing when you asked the Union for help. At least we could have been prepared."

Guinn dropped her head for a moment. "You are right, captain." She looked back up at Yale. "I am truly sorry. My government did not handle this correctly." She walked a few steps away from Yale before turning back to face her. "I am going to order two platoons to help rebuild the Command Post and search for your missing soldiers. They will arrive tomorrow morning."

"Do you have any information about my squad?" Yale asked.

Guinn slowly nodded. "I'm afraid that Lt. Ford, and several members of your medical staff, were taken prisoner by the Su-Kanan."

Yale asked her how she knew that.

"We received a ransom demand from the terrorists this morning. They want money, and they want to supplant the Central Government. They are not going to get either."

"Let me guess," Amy said, stepping toward the administrator. "You don't negotiate with terrorists."

Guinn looked at the young girl and nodded.

Amy shook her head. "This is crap," she said to Yale. "We need to find them ourselves."

Yale slowly raised her hand at Amy. The captain addressed Guinn. "Where would the Su-Kanan take their prisoners?"

Guinn shrugged. "We don't know. They are a nomadic

people. They are constantly on the move, which makes them hard to find and extremely dangerous." She glanced at Amy before continuing. "I understand your frustration and your desire to find your people. Just be careful how you proceed. These terrorists have no qualms about killing their hostages, or anyone else who gets in their way."

The administrator exited the tent with her Janar soldiers behind her.

Amy wanted to scream, but she kept her cool. She saw the anguish on Yale's face, and she knew that her friend was already overburdened. Amy cleared her throat and continued cleaning the tent. She didn't get closer than a few feet from Yale as she watched her friend out of the corner of her eye.

"We need to regroup," Yale said.

Amy looked at her and nodded.

"First, we will take care of the wounded who are still here," Yale stated. "Then, we will transport everyone to the ship and try to find our missing friends. C'mon. We have a lot of work to do."

They left the tent and rounded up the healthy survivors of the attack. Anyone who could walk was pressed into duty. They found seventeen Union personnel who could help.

Amy took eight of them and fanned out west of the tent to gather up the wounded.

Yale took the others and headed east.

It took several hours, but they brought the wounded into the tent and treated them.

Yale let the wounded rest for two hours before she started loading them into cruisers.

The drivers proceeded slowly and carefully back toward the *Liberty Bell*. It began getting dark by the time they reached the ship.

The wounded were gently brought aboard the ship and

taken to the craft's more sophisticated sick bay. The few nurses who had survived the attack administered the care needed by the injured.

While the patients were boarding the ship, Amy saw Cole and his parents at the entrance.

Cole smiled and rushed toward Amy, while his parents stayed behind. "Amy," Cole said, wrapping his arms around her. "I was so worried about you. You were gone for so long." The alien boy hugged her and rested his head against hers.

Over her shoulder, Amy saw the gloomy expression on Ethan's face.

Amy eased back from the joyful boy. "It's good to see you too, Cole," she said. She glanced at Ethan, who lowered his eyes. "We don't have time to celebrate," Amy resumed. "We lost most of our team and we need to get them back. There is much to do."

Cole nodded. "Whatever I can do to help, please let me know," he said. The boy followed Amy aboard the ship.

Though she was very upset about the abductions, part of her was excited to see her new friend again. Her attraction to him hadn't faded, and seeing him made her wish that they were on Janar for a vacation instead of a military mission.

Amy led Ethan and Cole to sick bay. "I know that neither of you have any real medical experience, but I want you to assist the nurses with the patients," she said. "Anything you can do to help is greatly appreciated. Just follow their instructions."

"That sounds simple enough," Cole replied. He smiled at Amy and tried to brush her right hand with the back of his.

She expertly pulled her hand back.

Cole's smile dimmed. He rubbed his chin in embarrassment. "We should get started," Cole said. He nodded at Ethan.

Ethan shook his head. "If we need to lift anything, we

could always rely on your blue energy beams to do it for us." He tried to move past Cole, but the alien boy grabbed his arm instead. "Let go of me, freak, or I will knock you out, powers or no powers!" Ethan exclaimed.

The alien boy let go of Ethan, who quickly ducked into the safety of sick bay. "What are you talking about?" he hollered to Ethan.

The human boy ignored him and immediately started helping a nurse who was treating an old man.

Cole turned to Amy. "What is he talking about?"

Amy debated telling Cole the wild tale that Ethan had said about him, but she decided against it. "Please go and help," she said. "We will catch up later."

Cole smiled again and followed her order.

Amy wondered if she would need to break up any skirmishes between the two boys. She hoped that Ethan had the maturity to put his own hurt feelings aside for the good of the missing Union soldiers.

Amy walked slowly through the *Liberty Bell*, trying to memorize every inch of her beloved ship. She touched the corridor walls and thought about Madison and their famous rescue mission. She wished that the robot was here with her now. His presence would be very comforting to her. At that moment, she wanted nothing more than to play a game of chess with him, even if she lost.

The girl stepped onto the bridge. It was eerily quiet without the activity of a full crew complement. She saw just one person sitting at her station.

Capt. Brown typed commands on the keyboard in front of her.

Amy cleared her throat to announce her arrival.

Yale peeked over her shoulder before turning back to the

task at hand. "I need your help, Amy. Sit down in the co-pilot's chair."

Amy smiled and followed the order. She eased herself into the seat, like a person dipping their foot into a cold pool of water. The girl got comfortable and turned to face Yale. She glanced at the writing on the monitor in front of Yale.

The captain was composing a report for Gen. Knox.

"What can I do for you?" she asked Yale.

"I'm filling in Gen. Knox," Yale said. "I want you to use the ship's tracker to try and find Lt. Ford and the others." She looked up at the girl for a moment. "You do know how to use it, right?" The captain looked genuinely concerned.

Amy nodded. "If it's on this ship, I probably know how to use it." She noticed that Yale had gone back to her task. Amy dropped her smile and began typing commands on her keyboard. She found the tracking program, and she typed in Lt. Ford's information.

The computer started searching for the missing officer.

It took a while, but the computer finally found Lt. Ford's communication signal.

Amy hoped that it really was Lt. Ford's and that she was still wearing the device. She typed in new commands and tracked the signal to an area not far from the Command Center. "Captain, I believe I found something," she said, trying not to sound overconfident.

Yale stopped typing and looked at Amy's screen. "Good work, Amy." She gently touched the screen with one finger. "That's close to where we were. Too close." She sighed. "It could be a trap, but it's a chance we will have to take." The captain went back to her work and swiftly finished it.

"Gen. Knox should get my message soon," Yale said. "We need him to send more soldiers to help us rescue our people."

She looked at Amy's screen again, and she pointed to a spot on the map. "Increase this section by fifty percent."

Amy did so.

"There are a lot of mountains in that sector. That gives them lots of places to hide. I wonder how far down those caves lead."

"The computer's scan indicates that the caves go completely through the mountains," Amy replied. She shook her head. "Some are several miles deep. That's a lot of ground to cover." She typed in more commands. "The rocks appear to be thousands of years old and not very steady. Walking through them will be dangerous."

"Nothing is ever easy," Yale said. Her computer terminal beeped. She leaned toward her screen. "Gen. Knox has responded." She quietly read the message before sitting back in her chair. "He is sending a platoon to help us, but they are several hours away, and that is at full speed." She sighed. "We cannot wait for them. We need to do some recon work before they get here. Then we will be able to devise our extraction plan."

Yale summoned Corkland and Robinson to the bridge.

The two soldiers arrived in just minutes. They stood at attention as Yale adjusted the map on Amy's screen.

"We have a recon mission to undertake," Yale said. She turned and looked at the Union soldiers. "Corkland, you and Robinson are getting that chance to volunteer again."

Corkland remained at attention but nodded slightly at his superior officer.

The captain pointed to the map on the screen. "The four of us are heading into a region where we believe our people are being held." She drew a circle around a section of the screen. "The terrorists are most likely hiding in this stretch of land. It has lots of mountains and even more caves. A regular needle in a haystack, but we have to find the needle."

"Captain," Corkland said. "Is this an engagement mission, or just eyes only?"

Yale nodded. "We will try to avoid engagement if we can. But you do have authority to defend yourself. Just keep in mind that firing at the enemy will put our people in harm's way, so let's try to avoid that."

"Copy that," Corkland replied.

"Copy that," Robinson repeated.

Yale took a deep breath and slowly let it out. "We will land the *Liberty Bell* just outside the search zone and go the rest of the way on foot. We don't want to draw any attention to ourselves. Get some travel gear together. We leave in thirty minutes. Dismissed."

They saluted Yale, and she returned the gesture.

Amy watched the men leave the bridge. She glanced at the map and the radar. "Some storm clouds are moving in, captain," she said. "That will make it even more difficult to find them." She looked at her leader's stern expression. "But we will prevail."

Amy saluted Yale and left the bridge. She went to a storage area in the back of the ship and found heavy clothing, boots, gloves, and goggles. She dressed and hurried back to the bridge. There she found a few crewmen working at various stations, and she saw the two soldiers who would be journeying with Yale and her. She sat at Lt. Ford's station and watched the ship take off. She held her breath for a moment and prayed for their safe return.

Yale guided the ship to their preset landing spot. She eased the craft onto the ground and turned off the thruster engines. The captain addressed one of the bridge occupants. "Lt.

Breckle, if we are not back in two hours, take the *Liberty Bell* back to the Command Post," she ordered.

The junior officer nodded and made her way to the captain's chair. She sat in the coveted seat.

"Just don't get too comfortable," Yale said.

The team marched down the corridor to the ship's main exit. They departed the ship and quietly traversed the rocky landscape. Amy noticed the pretty red and green flowers that grew in bunches along the mountain sides. She wished that she had time to pick some for her parents. The girl forced herself to focus on the mission. She stayed close to Yale in case any shooting began.

The squad had travelled several hundred yards through thick brush when Robinson suddenly yelled out in pain.

Amy and Yale rushed to his aid. They saw that he had stepped into a metal trap that snapped shut over his right foot.

Robinson sat in front of the trap and he held his right leg. "Get it open!" he shouted in pain. "Get it open!"

Yale reached into her back pack and pulled out her laser drill.

Corkland and Amy held Robinson still as Yale slowly sliced through the metal, careful not to hit any human skin.

The trap fell off, and Robinson instinctively grabbed his injured leg. He flinched when his hands touched the open wound.

Amy removed gauze and tape from Yale's pack, and she carefully wrapped his foot.

Robinson tried to stand, but the pain sent him crashing to the ground with a grunt. He rolled onto his left side and looked up at the captain. "I don't think I can make it, sir," he said. "Leave me here."

Yale put her hands under the back of his shoulders. She lifted him up. "Don't put pressure on your foot." Yale struggled to keep him upright. "Amy, find a long, firm branch," she said.

Amy nodded and rushed to fulfill her task.

Corkland took one of Robinson's arms and draped it over his shoulder. They moved the injured man to a mound and helped him sit back down.

"Rest for a moment," Yale said.

Amy appeared with a solid branch. "This was the best I could find," she said. She handed it to Yale.

The captain used the laser drill to shape the branch into a crutch. She gave Robinson her makeshift tool.

Amy helped Corkland lift the man to his feet.

It took some time for Robinson to adjust to his walking aid, but he fought valiantly to keep up with the others.

The team moved unsteadily along the wobbly path, and Amy tried to keep an eye on Robinson in case he needed help.

He nearly slipped twice, but he was athletic enough to recover.

At one point, Amy offered a hand as they climbed over ancient rocks and the soldier thanked her.

Yale used a handheld computer to track the footprints on the dusty ground.

The device picked up recent markings, and the captain gambled that they would belong to the terrorists.

The trail led to a cave opening, and Amy rushed to go in.

"Wait," Yale said.

The girl stopped and looked at Yale.

The captain addressed Corkland. "Check out the opening," she ordered.

He nodded.

"And don't be a hero. I need to get everyone back alive."

Corkland carefully entered the cave, shifting his rifle in his hands as he checked the four corners for safety. He backed up and waved his right hand at the others.

Yale went in next, followed by Amy.

Robinson remained outside to watch for danger and let his foot rest.

Water ran across the floor of the cave. The team stepped lightly, trying not to startle any cave dwellers. They used electronic lanterns to light their way.

The water was cold, and it chilled Amy's ankles and feet. She kept her eyes forward, looking for signs of the terrorists and any animals that might like them for dinner.

The team was 150 feet inside one cave, when Amy felt something brush past her legs. She looked down and screamed as she saw a group of rats squealing and swimming in the water.

The young girl raced forward and nearly knocked Yale to the cave floor. Amy's hands shook, and her teeth chattered. She pointed downward. "Rats," she said. "Lots of rats!" She started to panic.

Yale held both of Amy's hands for a moment.

Amy's feet shuddered, and her face turned a light shade of blue.

"Calm down, Amy," Yale said in a soft, soothing voice. "Your boots will protect you from them. Remember, they are more frightened of you than you are of them."

Amy shook her head in disbelief.

"Oh, they are," Yale replied. "And they are smart. They will stay away from us." Yale eased the girl into a gentle hug.

Soon, Amy had calmed down.

"We need to keep moving," Yale said as she pulled away from Amy.

The girl nodded.

Yale turned and followed Corkland as he navigated through the spooky terrain.

The cave floor began to dip, and the team cautiously moved downward. The squealing subsided and, soon, the only thing Amy could hear was the rush of the water at their feet. She glanced down occasionally to make sure no other critters were near her. She said a silent prayer for the missing soldiers and for the team's quick departure from this cave.

Yale's team searched the cave for another hour before exiting it. They explored two other caves with no success. The fourth cave led them to the heart of a mountain with an opening nearly the size of the Command Center. Smoke led them to the underground dwelling, where they spotted an encampment of armed soldiers.

The captain sent Corkland ahead alone to gather intelligence.

Amy and Yale kept watch as the private slithered ahead and took mental notes on the military site.

Corkland returned an hour later, still crawling on his stomach. He sat up and spoke quietly to his captain. "This is the spot," he said. "Our people are in two tents on the northern side of the camp. They are guarded by heavily armed men."

"How many terrorists are there?" Yale asked.

"At least 200, that I could see," Corkland replied.

"Did you see Lt. Ford?" Amy asked.

Corkland nodded. "Yes. She is still alive."

Amy let out sigh of relief. She then turned to Yale. "What now?" she asked.

Before Yale could answer, a laser blast exploded over their heads. "Get down!" ordered Yale. She pulled out her pistol and returned fire.

Corkland did the same, while Amy scrambled to get behind the captain.

Chapter Thirteen

M adison swam in the cool ocean as waves broke and tumbled toward the beach. The salty air filled his lungs and left an odd taste in his mouth. He kept his eyes open as he dove under the water, and he saw fish, crabs, and plant life. Madison surfaced and wiped the water from his face. He laughed out loud and ran his hands along his non-metallic body. His dark brown skin glistened in the sunlight. He felt strong, ecstatic, and alive.

A woman strode across the edge of the beach. She was petite, with long, blonde hair and smooth-looking skin. The woman waved at Madison.

He smiled at her and walked confidently through the water toward her.

She stopped and waited as the wind gently blew across her face.

"Good morning," Madison said, when he finally reached her. He extended his muscular arm and shook her hand.

She returned the greeting.

Her hand felt like silk. Madison glanced down at it for a

moment. Instinctively, he raised her hand and kissed the top of it.

"You are quite the gentleman, aren't you?" the woman asked. She laughed and slowly pulled her hand back. She resumed her walk and Madison fell in step beside her. The woman moved gracefully across the sand. She inhaled deeply. "I love the smell of the ocean," she said. "It smells like freedom." Her smile widened.

Madison nodded. "That's exactly how I would describe it," he replied. He took a deep breath and slowly let it out. "Freedom," he added.

They continued walking in a new silence.

Madison felt his toes sink into the sand with every step. No one else was on the beach, but a boat sailed on the water in the distance. "This is the most beautiful place I've ever seen," Madison said. He glanced at her. "It pales only to you."

The woman laughed again. "You are too kind, sir." She brushed a strand of her hair out of her face. "I've lived here all of my life. I've never had the desire to go anywhere else. Everything I need is right here." She reached out and folded her fingers around Madison's right hand. "But I've never seen you before. What is your name?" she asked.

"Madison," he replied. He looked at the soft features of her face and soon found himself staring at her. Her blue eyes were set perfectly apart over a small nose and curvaceous mouth. "Though I'm not sure anymore," he said, focusing on her eyes. "Maybe it's time for a new name. One that is more masculine."

She shook her head. "No, don't change it. I like the way it sounds," she said. She gently touched his chin. "It's very regal. It suits you." She changed course and stepped into the water. The wave crashed and met them at ankle-level.

She laughed and kicked the water at Madison.

He splashed her back.

"Tell me your name," he said, placing both of his hands in hers.

They stood, face to face, on the wet sand as a seagull squawked above them.

She shyly dropped her head.

Madison gently raised her chin with his right hand. "I bet it is as pretty as you are," he said.

The woman shrugged. "Guess," she replied as the playfulness returned to her.

Madison nodded. "OK, I'll play. Is it Sarah?"

She shook her head.

"Michelle?"

The woman took a step away from him and shook her head again.

He moved toward her. "Oh, wait. How about Jennifer?"

Her expression soured. "No, it's not any of those," She turned away from him and started walking on the dry beach again.

Like a puppy, he followed her. Madison didn't offer more names, as he realized that he was upsetting her.

Madison caught up to her, and she let him walk beside her again.

The warming sun began to dip beneath the horizon, and he felt himself getting colder.

"I'm sorry," he said. "I didn't mean to offend you."

They continued forward, and Madison began to wonder where they were going. "Is your home nearby?" he asked. He looked around but did not see any buildings.

The woman nodded and pointed to the right. "It's just past the boardwalk," she replied.

Madison lowered his eyebrows in confusion. He didn't see

a boardwalk, or anything else for that matter. Just sand and the ocean. He looked around again.

Suddenly, Madison stopped walking. He shook his head. Before them now stood a boardwalk, with shops, rides, and hordes of people.

Most of the people walked in twos; couples held hands and laughed. A few glided along on bicycles. Some voices were louder than others, as merchants yelled out to potential buyers. Neon signs welcomed shoppers while speakers poured out fanciful music.

Madison could smell popcorn, pizza, hot dogs, and funnel cake. He felt a rumble in his stomach. He looked at the woman. "Are you hungry?" he asked.

"Now that you mention it, I am," she replied.

They started walking again.

"Tony's makes the best pizza," she added. "They are right up here." She slipped her hand back into Madison's and smiled. Without stopping, she glanced at him. "My name is Emily," she said. Her expression turned hopeful. "Do you like it?"

Madison nodded. "I love it," he said. "It's perfect."

She stopped walking, and she gently pulled him toward her. She kissed him and wrapped her arms around him.

They held their embrace as others walked past them.

Emily eased away from him.

"That was wonderful," he said. He looked into her eyes. "You are amazing."

She laughed. "Thank you. Now, let's eat."

The line for food parted as the couple approached the eatery. Emily ordered two slices of pepperoni pizza and two cold sodas.

Their order was filled immediately, and a boy in a white shirt and black pants led them away from the counter. Their round table was covered with a red, checkered cloth and a small candle burned in a holder in the center of it.

Madison pulled out Emily's chair and held onto the back of it as she sat down. He sat across from her as the waiter put their food down.

Madison watched Emily take a bite of her slice.

Her face lit up as she slowly chewed her food.

Madison bit into his pizza and paused, marveling at the amazing sensations in his mouth. He had watched his best friend eat this dish many times before, but this was the first time he had ever tasted it. It was the first time he had ever tasted anything. He quickly devoured his food and finally began to understand what it meant to be human.

The waiter brought over two large glass bowls of chocolate ice cream for dessert.

They ate more slowly, savoring the sweet treat.

A thin stream of ice cream dripped down Madison's chin, and Emily laughed as she dabbed at it with a napkin. His ice cream and the light wind combined made him shudder as they finished their meal.

"C'mon," Emily said. "I will buy you a sweatshirt to keep you warm."

They exited the restaurant and walked closely together along the boardwalk. They passed numerous shops as other people shuffled around them.

Emily took his hand and guided him into a store that sold various beach apparel.

They laughed again and looked at the different pictures that could be pressed onto T-shirts and hooded sweatshirts.

Emily chose a design of a shark with its mouth open for him, and another design of two sea turtles swimming together for herself. She took some paper money from her pocket and handed it to the proprietor.

Emily helped Madison with his new covering before she slipped on her own.

They snuggled as they started walking in step with the crowd.

Madison could not see the end of the boardwalk, and he wondered how long the attraction ran.

They stopped walking again when Emily spotted a man dressed as a clown with a guitar; he was singing unfamiliar songs. They joined those who had gathered around to hear him play.

Many people dropped coins into his hat that lay on the wooden walkway near his guitar case.

Emily gave Madison a coin, and he tossed it into the hat.

The musician nodded his thanks.

The crowd drifted away from the man after he played a few songs, and Madison found himself following Emily back onto the beach.

Just ahead, some folks had started a bonfire, and they sat around it to keep warm.

The couple joined them and sat in two empty chairs close to the flames.

One of the revelers handed Emily a strange-looking food. They also offered one to Madison, and he slowly accepted it.

He didn't recognize the item.

Emily bit into hers and laughed as she ate it.

Madison took a chance and nibbled on his. He recognized the taste of chocolate, but the white, mushy middle was some-thing new.

"It's called marshmallow," Emily said, as if reading his mind. "It goes great with the chocolate, doesn't it?" she asked.

Madison nodded as he chewed the concoction and pushed it down his throat.

Someone handed him a bottle of water, and he gratefully

drank it. He poured some of it onto his hands and wiped his face with it. He smiled at Emily, and he hoped that she would remain with him for as long as he were alive. Madison didn't want this new life with these wonderful new experiences to ever end. He leaned close to Emily and kissed her, as if he was doing so for the last time.

Madison suddenly found himself surrounded in complete darkness. He could not hear, taste, smell, or feel anything in any part of his body. The void had robbed him of his strength. He began to doubt his self-awareness. One horrifying thought occupied his mind: *Am I dead?*

Gradually, he felt a tingling in his fingers and toes. He moved them, thankful for the beautiful sensation. Light slowly appeared before him, but it was faint and distant. He thought he heard screaming, and he wondered if he was the one yelling out. The screaming stopped as his sense of smell and touch intensified. He forced open his mouth and said only one word: Emily.

She was nowhere to be found. Madison moved his hands in front of his eyes, and he saw that the human skin was no longer there. Instead, his hands were dark green and metallic, like the rest of his body. He heard metal clanking against the floor. Something was moving toward him. His eyes finally cleared and adjusted to the low light in the room.

"How do you feel?" someone asked.

The voice was familiar, but Madison had trouble placing it. He shook his head and tried to breath normally.

"Don't worry," said the voice. "It is difficult to exit the Link-Up the first few times, but you will get used to it, like everyone else. Tell me, what did you see while you were in there?"

"I was," Madison replied, slowly forming the words in his mouth. "I was human." He laughed for a moment. "I was a man. There was a woman. She loved me, and I loved her." He finally recognized Lincoln's face in the dim room. "Bring her back, Lincoln," Madison said. "Bring her back, right now!"

Lincoln shook his head. "There is no way for me to do that." He raised his right hand and disconnected a bolt from the back of Madison's head. He showed Madison the item. "You must have been having a good time. It's not easy to burn out a receiver bolt."

"So, I was dreaming?" Madison asked. He felt his mind clearing, although the memory of his experience remained fully intact. He remembered her face, the way she smelled, and the touch of her lips on his. She was as real as any person he had ever known and, now, she was gone.

Lincoln shook his head. "No, not dreaming, exactly." He walked away from Madison and disappeared in the darkness. He returned a few seconds later. "We are out of receiver bolts. You can't return to the Link-Up until we get more," he advised. Lincoln tossed the burned-out bolt into a trashcan. He looked at Madison. "The Link-Up is a combination of Internet and VR experiences."

"I felt like I was controlling the events," Madison said. "When I was lonely, Emily appeared. When I was hungry, she bought us both pizza." He shook his head. "It all seemed so real." He dropped his head for a moment, lamenting the fact that he would never see or kiss Emily again.

Lincoln patted him on the right shoulder. "It is designed to feel as real as possible," he said. "That's what keeps us entertained while we wait to serve our master." He walked a few steps away and checked on another robot.

That model remained perfectly still, and Madison wondered what it was experiencing.

"Dr. Greenland created the Link-Up for us," Lincoln said. "He is a thoughtful master."

Madison took a cautious step and managed to keep his balance. He took another. "If he is so thoughtful, why does he keep us here in the dark? Why don't we have the freedom to move around outside?" Madison began to wonder what time it was. His internal clock was not functioning correctly, and he had no external clues. He started to wonder if staying behind was such a good idea.

"To keep us safe," Lincoln replied. He moved closer to Madison. "There are lots of dangers out there. We are better off in here." Lincoln checked on other robots as they remained in their dreamlike states. He adjusted the bolts of some of the robots to avoid having them burn out.

Madison wished he had done that for him. The robot found an empty stool and he sat down on it. After a few minutes, he watched Lincoln carry over another stool and place it near Madison's.

Lincoln eased on to it.

"Why aren't you still in the Link-Up?" Madison asked. "Did you get kicked out, too?"

Lincoln smiled. "No. I try to limit my time in it. That way, I can keep an eye on my brothers. You never know when one of them will need me." He looked over at the other robots. "I guess I am their keeper." He turned back to face Madison. "But I don't mind. Soon, we will all fulfil our destinies as we carry out Dr. Greenland's great plan."

"Tell me more about this great plan," Madison said. He worried that whatever Greenland had in mind would not be so great for the Union or the human race. "What part do I play in it? When do we begin?"

Lincoln shook his head. "It is a secret," he replied. He crossed his arms over his chest. "But, when the time is right, you will know. It will be beautiful. Dr. Greenland said so." The robot's face was nearly serene. He had the look of a faithful disciple.

"Do you believe everything Dr. Greenland tells you?" Madison asked.

Lincoln titled his head to the right. "Why wouldn't I? He created us. He has no reason to lie to us. We live to serve him." His arms drifted to his lap. He glanced at the other robots again. "He is our world."

Madison began to feel some stiffness in his legs, so he rose from the stool. "I am not sure," he said. He moved toward the other robots, and Lincoln rose to follow him. Madison lifted his upturned hand at the others. "He has created so many of us. Much more than is needed to meet his needs. This number looks more like an army." He stopped and looked at Lincoln. "Why would a scientist need an army?"

"I do not have the gall to question his motives," Lincoln said. He moved between Madison and the others, as if protecting them from him. "And I do not like your attitude toward Dr. Greenland. You, of all robots, should have the utmost respect for him. He created you before the rest of us. You are his son."

Madison shook his head. "No, I am not his son." He raised his arms and showed Lincoln his hands. "I am not flesh and blood. I am metal and circuits and wires and components. He built me like he built you and all the others. He is not my father, for I was born without parents." He stepped toward Lincoln. "And so were you."

"Why do you speak so unkindly of Dr. Greenland?" Lincoln asked. "After all he has given us. We owe him everything."

"The only thing he has given us is servitude," Madison countered. "I was lucky. I managed to get away from him for a while. The rest of you are not. The rest of you are his slaves."

"We are not!" Lincoln yelled. He suddenly pulled his right arm back and punched Madison on the side of the head.

Madison fell to the floor.

Lincoln kicked him in the midsection. "You are a liar," Lincoln said. He kicked at Madison again, but Madison rolled onto his left side and dodged the metal foot.

He shot to his feet.

Lincoln lunged at him and grabbed his neck.

Madison slipped his arms up and broke Lincoln's hold. He jabbed at the other robot, hitting him in the face.

Lincoln staggered backward.

Madison grabbed him and landed a punch on his chin. Lincoln fell to the floor. "You are nothing more than his toy," Madison said. "He doesn't love you any more than he loves his tools."

Lincoln rose and tackled Madison to the floor.

They rolled around on the hard surface, trading punches.

The other robots remained still, either unaware of the ruckus, or unwilling to leave the Link-Up.

The combatants struggled to get the upper hand as they both inflicted damage on the other.

Madison finally rolled on top of Lincoln and fired several shots at his face.

The beaten robot collapsed, his arms strewn out to his sides.

Madison rose and stood over Lincoln for a moment.

His opponent didn't move.

The victor walked slowly toward the others, ready to continue the fight, but none of them reacted to him. "Yale was right," he said out loud to no one. "All of you are too dangerous." He moved toward a nearby computer terminal. Madison furiously typed in commands until he found the master file for the robots' blueprints. He typed another command, and the data began to erase.

He ransacked the room until he found cannisters of gun powder that were stored in the bottom of an unlocked closet. Madison pried open the can and began pouring the powder around the still robots. He emptied five cannisters and was opening a sixth when someone suddenly came through the room's front door. Madison froze and pretended to be like the others.

The intruder was one of Dr. Greenland's men. The slender man pointed a flashlight around the room, the beam bouncing off the metal of the robots. It eventually fell on Lincoln. "What the hell?" the man said as he rushed over to the fallen robot. He pointed the beam at Lincoln's face, and then he spoke into a transmitter. "This is Dalon," he said. "I'm in the main lab. Something's not right here."

"Copy that, Dalon," a voice replied on the other end. "We'll be right there."

Dalon reached down and touched the fallen robot. He shook the robot's right arm. Dalon sniffed the air and spoke into the transmitter again. "Proceed with caution," he said. "It smells like gun powder in here."

A minute later, three other men entered the room.

Madison carefully slid the gun powder cannister away from him with his right foot. The scraping sound drew their attention.

"Someone turn on a damn light," Dalon said.

Madison heard footsteps heading toward the far wall.

A second later, light poured down from overhead.

Madison remained still but was facing the men. He saw Dr. Greenland among the group.

Greenland rushed over to Lincoln. He lifted the robot and gently held him in his arms, like a wounded bird. "Who could have done this?" he asked. He looked among his men, all of whom shrugged. Greenland then saw Madison and the damage done by Lincoln.

Greenland eased Lincoln to the floor. His face turned red and he raced over to Madison. "What have you done?" he asked. He grabbed Madison with both hands and violently shook him. "You will pay for this. You and your Union friends."

Chapter Fourteen

The firefight seemed to go on forever.

Amy kept her head down as Yale and Corkland managed to keep the rebels from overrunning them. Amy's heart pounded so heavily in her chest that it nearly gave her a headache. She ignored the pain and peeked over the rock she hid behind to see if she could spot the enemy. She covered her mouth to keep the dust from choking her.

The shooting suddenly stopped.

Amy knew that meant the rebels were advancing on them. If they got behind Yale and Corkland, the escape route would be cut off. Yale must have realized that, too, for she began backing up. The captain motioned to Corkland to do the same.

He followed her lead and Amy moved closer to Yale.

In unison, they spun and raced for the exit.

The rebels fired again. Laser blasts exploded the rocks around them.

Yale's team ran as fast as they could over the rough terrain.

The rebels kept up their pursuit, firing at them as they moved.

Amy saw the early sunlight at the mouth of the cave, and she focused on reaching it. A rock exploded near her right hand. She felt the sting of the splintering rock and she screamed out in pain, but she maintained her pace. Her only objective was to reach the sunlight.

The team exited the cave and dove behind some boulders. They sat still for a moment, each one trying to catch their breath.

Amy looked at her right hand and saw no damage. She stuck her head out for a second and did not see anyone chasing them. Amy did see her fellow crewmembers slowly rising to their feet with their weapons drawn.

The howling wind was all Amy could hear. She stared at Yale, waiting for a signal. Amy took a deep breath. It looked like the rebels were staying in the cave.

Yale raised a fist and pointed it at the other caves.

Corkland nodded.

Amy followed as the team hustled back to where they had left Robinson. She hoped that he was still alright.

They found Robinson in the same place. The soldier was lying flat on top of a rock with his laser rifle pointed straight ahead.

Amy guessed that he must have heard the laser blasts inside the cave, and he was preparing to return fire.

He lifted his head when he saw the team, and he removed his fingers from the trigger. Robinson swung his legs around slowly and he tried to stand up, but the pain in his foot caused him to fall again.

Amy dashed around Yale and reached the fallen soldier first. She helped him to a sitting position and checked his foot. It was bloody and swollen.

Yale opened her backpack and handed Amy new bandages.

"Did you find our people?" Robinson asked as Amy tended to his wounds. He waited for an answer from Yale before he looked over at Corkland.

Their faces gave away their feelings.

"They are being held in that cave behind the boulders," Yale answered. She pointed at the cave opening and shook her head. "A rescue will be difficult and costly. I don't know how we are going to pull it off." Yale sat down beside Robinson and took a canteen out of her backpack. She drank some water and the offered it to the injured soldier.

Robinson pushed it away. "No, sir," he said. "Thank you, but I have my own."

Yale nodded and offered it to Corkland.

He said the same thing.

Yale offered it to Amy, and she sheepishly drank from it.

The crew rested for a few minutes before Yale stood back up. "We need to head back to the ship," she said. She and Corkland lifted Robinson and carried him forward with his arms over their shoulders. It took time, but they managed to get back to the *Liberty Bell*.

Yale and her team were met at the ship's entrance by the few remaining medical staffers who were available.

Two nurses took Robinson to sick bay.

Amy staggered aboard behind Yale and Corkland.

The captain went to the bridge, while the private went to the mess hall.

Amy decided to follow Yale.

The bridge was, again, just half-full of personnel. Amy sat in Lt. Ford's seat while she watched Yale work from the captain's chair.

Yale typed an updated report to Gen. Knox.

Amy helped her fill in some of the details of the scouting mission.

Yale's hands shook as she typed.

"When was the last time you slept, Captain?" Amy asked.

Yale didn't answer.

"Or ate for that matter?" the girl continued.

Yale finished the report and reread it before sending it. She finally looked at Amy. "I am a bit hungry," she said. "C'mon, I will buy you breakfast." She rose from the captain's chair and led the way out of the bridge.

They quietly walked through the ship, and Yale returned salutes from some of the Union soldiers.

They entered the nearly empty mess hall.

Amy went to the atomizer and selected pancakes with sausages and a glass of orange juice.

Yale then typed in commands for a bagel with cream cheese and a hot cup of coffee.

They sat across from each other at a table and quietly ate their food.

Amy felt her eyes closing, and she fought to stay awake. She noticed that Yale was doing the same, despite the coffee.

Amy watched Ethan enter the mess hall and go to the atomizer.

He selected a bowl of oatmeal and a glass of milk. The boy brought his food over to Amy's table. "Good morning, captain," he said to Yale. "May I join you?"

Yale glanced at Amy, who nodded. The captain said, "Yes."

Ethan smiled and sat down across from Amy. "I heard about the Recon mission," said Ethan. "Lt. Ford is still alive?"

Yale leaned forward in her seat. "As of last night, yes," she said. She spoke in a low voice, even though the room was still nearly empty. "But, every minute she's there, her life is in danger. And it's the same for the others." She straightened up. "We really shouldn't be talking about this here."

Ethan swallowed some food and glanced at Amy. He looked back at the captain. "Sorry, sir," he said. He drank some milk. "It's just that everyone is talking about it." He cleared his throat, and his eyes wandered back to Amy. "How are you holding up?" he asked the girl.

Amy rubbed her tired eyes. "I'm OK," she said. "But I won't be racing sand jets anymore. I can't wait for this mission to end. I miss my parents." She sighed. "And I miss Madison, too." She drank her orange juice and emptied the glass. The girl addressed Yale. "Do you think he will ever come back?"

"I don't know," Yale replied. She pushed her half-empty plate forward. "He seemed determined to stay with Greenland." She shook her head. "My shooting him certainly didn't help." She brought her hands to her face and folded her fingers. "I just hope Greenland doesn't do anything foolish with his army. That would be disastrous for us."

Ethan finished his drink. "I don't think Madison will let it come to that," he said. "In his heart, he is still part of the Union. He will do the right thing." The boy gathered up the empty dishes and cups and took them over to the cleaning area. He returned with an awkward smile. "Captain, is there anything you need us to do right now?"

Yale shook her head. "We are waiting for reinforcements. It will take some time for them to get here."

The boy's smile widened. He looked at the girl. "Cool. Amy, I downloaded some new video games. Wanna play?" Ethan nervously tapped his fingers on the table. His head bobbed slightly as he spoke to her, while his eyes stayed focused on her face.

Amy rubbed her eyes again. "I would love too, Ethan," she replied, "but I am exhausted. We haven't slept in a long time, and I need to get some rest." She gently placed her right hand on his for a moment. "Sorry, but can we do that another time?"

Ethan tried to hide his disappointment. "Sure. Yeah, I get it." He yawned and stretched his arms over his head. "I should get some sleep, too." He looked down at the floor.

Other personnel entered the mess hall, and their conversations filled the silence at the table.

Yale rose. "Sleep sounds like a great idea," She addressed Amy. "I will call for you when I hear back from Gen. Knox."

Amy nodded.

"See you both later." Yale turned and slowly exited the mess hall.

Amy stood up. "Want to walk me to my quarters?" she asked.

Ethan looked up at her and nodded. He was still upset, but he was trying to be brave.

Amy wrapped an arm around his and let him lead her out of the room.

They were at the exit when Amy saw another friendly face.

"Cole," she said. She stopped and let go of Ethan's arm.

The alien boy was alone, and he looked surprised to see her.

The three youngsters stood motionless for a moment, lost in their embarrassment. "Where are your parents?" Amy asked.

"They are still asleep," Cole replied. "I was hoping to try some more chocolate ice cream. Would you like to join me?" Cole glanced at Ethan's face, and Amy saw the hostility between them. "You are welcome too, Ethan,"

"I don't think this is a good time," Ethan replied. He put an arm around Amy. "Amy hasn't slept in a while, and she is very tired. I was just escorting her back to her quarters." He

159

moved around his rival, and he pulled Amy with him. "Some other time," he said over his shoulder.

Amy pushed Ethan's arm off of her. "That was really rude," she said.

They kept walking as Ethan replied. "Why?" he asked. "I was just trying to . . ."

Amy abruptly stopped and glared at the boy. "I know what you were trying to do," she said. "I am a person, and I can speak for myself. I don't need you, or anyone else, to speak for me."

Ethan shrugged. Cole was no longer at the entrance to the mess hall. "Do you want me to get him back?" he asked Amy.

She shook her head and lightly slapped his chest. "No, I don't want you to get him back, you moron," she said. Ethan lowered his head. "I want to you treat me with respect. I want you to understand that I have feelings and my own mind," she said.

"I have feelings, too," he mumbled. He looked up at her like a scolded puppy.

Amy took a deep breath. "You're right," she said. "I'm sorry. You do have feelings, and I should be more considerate. I don't know. Maybe I'm just tired." She clasped his hands. "I really want to find our people, and Madison, and I really want to go home." She looked into his eyes.

Ethan blinked and slowly leaned forward to kiss her.

Amy backed up.

He let go of her hands.

Amy sighed. "I thought we covered this already," she said.

Ethan didn't respond.

"You and I are friends, Ethan," she said. "Can you accept that?"

The boy looked at his feet and nodded.

"Good, because that is what I need right now. Friends."

She continued walking toward her quarters, and he followed her.

When they reached her room, she lightly punched his right shoulder. "See you later, pal." She entered the room and closed the door behind her. Amy then stood at the door for a moment, wondering why life was so complicated.

———

Amy wandered along a dirt path that seemed oddly familiar to her. She heard children laughing in the distance, and she smelled apple pie. Something compelled her to follow the path and climb the mountain that it led to. She kept shaking her head, sure that she had been here before, even though she didn't know where she was. A yellow sun shone brightly in the sky, and puffy, white clouds blew by overhead.

She found the children at the top of the hill. They were playing on a merry-go-round and laughing and running like wild horses. Amy thought it strange that there were no adults around. The scent of the apple pie made her hungry, so she set out to find some. She tried asking the kids where the food was, but they ignored her and kept playing. That nagging feeling of familiarity kept growing inside her.

Amy saw something out of the corner of her eye. She thought it was a tall child until she got closer. She stopped dead in her tracks when she recognized the person. It suddenly became clear to her where she was. "Papa?" she asked.

The tall man in his late thirties with a black moustache nodded at her.

"I'm back?" she asked.

"It looks that way," Papa said. He sat down in one of two rocking chairs on the porch of a yellow house. "I never thought we would see you again, girl," he said. "But I am glad that you've returned. How long do you think you will be with us this time?"

The other children stopped playing. They all looked at Amy and waited for her answer.

Amy shrugged. "I don't know," she said. "I don't even know how I got back here. The last time I was here, I nearly died."

Papa slowly nodded. "Yes. A Crownaxian strangled you. But, thankfully, you didn't die." He smiled. "You've grown. You look much taller now." He glanced at the other children, and they went back to playing again. "Did my advice help you?"

Amy rubbed her chin, trying to remember. "Oh, yeah," she replied. "You told me not to take so many chances. That I needed to be more careful." She suddenly remembered the sand jet races. "I try to, Papa. It isn't always easy."

He let out a loud laugh. "No, I suppose it's not." He rocked in the chair. "So many things to tempt us. Yet we must try to do what's right. Not just for ourselves, but for everyone."

Amy's stomach rumbled.

"You are hungry," Papa said. He rose and opened the door to the yellow house. "C'mon, there's a fresh apple pie with our names on it."

Amy followed him inside and closed the door behind her.

They entered a kitchen with a small table and two chairs.

Papa brought the pie to the table, along with a knife, two forks, and two plates. He cut the pie into eight slices and put one slice on each plate. He handed Amy one plate and a fork. "Dig in, child," he said.

They sat and ate the pie quietly, while the noise of the other children continued outside.

When they were finished, Papa stacked the plates and pushed them to the center of the table. "I'll get that later," he said. He folded his hands. "So, what is troubling you, Amy?" he asked.

"What makes you think I'm troubled?" Amy replied. She sat back in her chair and looked at the old man. He was regarded as one of the greatest writers of his time, but there was always a sadness about him. He did something terrible, and this place was his penance. Amy had read some of his books, but she didn't know much about his personal life. She wondered what he did that brought him here and why she kept returning.

Papa squinted his eyes. "People don't visit me unless they are seeking something. Some want career advice, others want help with their families or spouses, and some have even bigger problems." He shook his head. "The kind that make people question their own existence. But no one ever stops by just to say hello."

Amy's eyes widened. "You get other visitors?" she asked.

"Oh, yes," Papa said. He stretched his arms out over his head. "It started with people who were dying and needed help to get to their final destination. Then it changed. Now, we get all kinds here. They come, they talk. Sometimes, they play like children. But they all have one thing in common: They are troubled." He chuckled. "And they think I have all the answers." He leaned toward her. "But I don't. Only God has all the answers, and, like I told you the last time you were here, I'm not God."

Amy nodded. "I understand." She looked around the room again before settling back on the man. She saw the anguish in his eyes. His hands shook a little, and his voice sounded hoarse. "Papa. Where exactly are we?"

The man crossed his arms over his chest. "Well, that is a great question, one that I've thought about for a long time. My best guess is that we are somewhere in between," he said.

Amy shrugged in confusion.

Papa nodded. "Not quite life, and not quite death. The universe holds many mysteries. This is one of them." He leaned toward her again. "So what can I do for you?"

The girl rose and picked up the dishes. She took them over to a sink and rinsed them off. Behind her, she heard him rise from his chair.

"You are avoiding the question," he said.

She turned and looked at him but didn't answer.

"Well, don't make me guess, Amy. I hate guessing. C'mon, out with it."

"I'm really not sure," she replied. She folded her hands and let them dangle in front of her. "This mission we are on. It's been a disaster. Dr. Greenland has a robot army that could destroy humanity; Lt. Ford and other Union soldiers have been kidnapped by terrorists. Yale shot Madison, who stayed behind with Dr. Greenland's other robots, and I have feelings for two different boys. All I want to do is go home."

Papa nodded. "That is a lot for a young girl to handle." He moved toward the door. "Let's get some fresh air. That helps clear the mind." He opened the door and held it for her.

They exited the home and sat in the rocking chairs. The noise of the other children became louder again.

Amy watched them and envied their unbridled happiness.

"They are so lucky," Amy said, "not a care in the world."

"Don't be so quick to judge," Papa replied. "Everyone has problems." He pointed to a brown-haired girl on a swing. "That is Judy. She has cancer. The doctors thought they had eradicated it, but it came back." He then pointed to a boy. "The lad next to her in the red shirt, that is Tommy. His parents are in the middle of a bitter divorce, and they use him to get back at each other." Papa nodded at another girl. "The blonde playing with the rubber ball, that is Morgan. Her step-father does things to her that no one should have to endure."

Tears welled up in Amy's eyes. "That's horrible. Do all of the kids have something terrible in their lives?"

Papa nodded.

Amy wiped her eyes. "Kind of makes me feel stupid for being so upset. They have real problems. Mine don't compare." She took a deep breath and slowly let it out.

"Don't sell yourself short, Amy," Papa said. "Your problems are real, and they are just as difficult as the others. No one goes through life unscathed. What defines us is how we face our problems." He stood and scratched his chin. "I did not handle my problems. I tried to run away from them, and that is why I am here."

Amy lifted herself out of her chair. "I need to solve my problems and not run away from them," she said. She looked at the caretaker, and he nodded back at her. "I get it." She leaned toward Papa and hugged him. "I'm ready to go back."

"Do you remember how?" Papa asked.

Somehow, she did. "Yes. I remember." She looked at the other children for a moment, taking a snapshot of the place before departing. She closed her eyes and let herself fall. A rush of adrenalin surged through her. All her cells seemed to vibrate.

Amy sat up in bed. She was in her quarters on the *Liberty Bell*. The girl rubbed her eyes, and the vibration in her cells ceased. She knew that it wasn't a dream. She had been there, wherever there was. Amy wondered if she would ever return to Papa's realm again. Part of her hoped that the answer was no.

Chapter Fifteen

The faces of Papa's children began to fade from Amy's memory, but she still felt sad for the troubled youngsters. The fantasy world they visited while they overcame their demons gave them a safe place to escape to, even if only for a little while. She realized how dangerous it would be if a child stayed there too long, but that was Papa's job, to usher them out when the time was right. Amy wondered if Papa's penance would ever end and would he be allowed to move on.

A knock on her door brought Amy back to her world. She rolled off the bed and hit the green button on the wall. The door slid open, and she found Corkland standing at attention. "Sorry to bother you, Amy," the Union soldier said. "But Yale asked me to bring you to the bridge. Our reinforcements have arrived." He took a step back and allowed the girl to exit her room.

She took the lead as they hurried to the bridge.

Yale rose from the captain's chair when she saw Amy enter. "The *Mount Vernon* just landed," Yale said. She peeked at a computer console and tried to fix her hair. The captain then walked past Amy and Corkland in route to the ship's exit.

They passed other Union soldiers, who fell in behind them to greet the new arrivals.

The late afternoon sun slid down the horizon as Yale and her crew approached the *Mount Vernon*.

The ship's main door opened, and a broad-shouldered young man with short, brown hair and green eyes departed, with two other soldiers behind him.

Amy saw that he was a captain, the same rank as Yale, and she wondered who would be in charge. She glanced at Yale and saw that her friend's eyes were wide open, and her face seemed a bit flushed. *Either she is attracted to this guy*, Amy thought, *or she is coming down with the flu.*

The officer approached Yale and saluted her. "Capt. John Tyler reporting, sir," he said. His right hand came down, and his arms flanked his midsection.

Yale returned the salute.

"Gen. Knox ordered us here to assist you with the rescue of your crew." He handed her a mini-com.

Yale read it and handed it back to him.

Tyler quickly introduced the two soldiers behind him, and Yale introduced Amy and Corkland. "The general's orders put you in charge of the operation," Tyler said. "How can we help you?"

Yale started walking toward the *Liberty Bell*, and Tyler followed her with the two crews behind them. "I have devised a strategy that I believe will work if we have the right number of soldiers. I take it Gen. Knox has provided us with the necessary number of troops?" Yale asked.

They entered the ship, and Yale marched toward the bridge.

"I am afraid there aren't as many of us as you requested," Tyler said.

Yale looked over at him but kept walking.

"It's getting more difficult to find soldiers we can spare for missions like this," Tyler said. He stopped to break the news, and Yale stopped as well. "There are only twenty-four of us here. No more are coming."

"Twenty-four?" Yale replied as her voice rose.

Tyler nodded.

"I requested twice that many." She shook her head in disgust. "Does the general know that we need an overwhelming force in order to save our people?"

Tyler nodded again.

"But the bureaucracy won't allow it. That's wonderful," she said.

They continued walking and soon entered the bridge.

Yale led Tyler to a monitor with a map on it. "This computer model is based on scans of the area and data that I entered from memory."

Tyler and his crew examined the model.

"I think we can surprise the terrorists by creating a diversion in the north part of the cave," she pointed to a spot on the monitor. "And then we enter the cave at the south and east." She pointed to those sections. "We can force them back and grab our people before they regroup."

Tyler stared at the screen. His eyes moved slightly as he studied the plan. Finally, he turned to face Yale. "This may sound crazy, but is there any way to enter from the top of the cave? That way, we can drop down on them and take out the terrorists before they can fire." He glanced at his men, who nodded in agreement, before looking at Yale.

Amy spoke up. "No, sir," she said. "I don't think we can." She stood straight and locked eyes with the young man.

He lowered his eyebrows, as if expecting this to be a joke.

Amy pointed to the model. "The top of cave is at least twenty-five feet thick," she said. "There is no way to cut through that without making a racket, and the falling rocks would endanger the prisoners."

"I agree," Yale said. She picked up a light pen and wrote on the image on the screen. "It's ambitious and quite clever, but it wouldn't work. We would be putting the lives of the hostages at risk." She put the pen down. "No, we need a surprise, coordinated attack from multiple sides in order for this to succeed."

Tyler took one step back. "I think you are correct," he said. "What do you have in mind for the diversion?" Tyler folded his hands in front of himself. He glanced at one of his men. "Gergan would be ideal for making a diversion."

His men nodded again.

Amy cleared her throat.

Yale laughed and put an arm around the young girl. "We have that covered, gentlemen," she said. "Right here, we have the best person for the job. Amy can cause more mayhem than anyone else in the Union."

Tyler raised his voice. "A child?" he asked. He glared at Yale. "You would put a child into the middle of a dangerous battle? What if she gets hurt?" He shook his head vehemently. "No, I will not allow a child to join in such a dangerous mission! Absolutely out of the question."

"Amy is no ordinary child, Capt. Tyler," Yale replied. She typed a command on the keyboard, and the story of Amy's rescue mission appeared on the screen. "She managed to steal the Union's best spacecraft and use it to rescue her father and others who would have died in the hands of the Crownaxians." Yale pointed to the screen for emphasis.

Tyler frowned. "Yes, I am aware of your exploits," he said

to Amy. "But I don't think you are a hero." He bent forward slightly and locked eyes with her. "You are a child who put many lives at risk by flying off like some space cowboy. From what I have learned about you, you lack discipline, you have no regard for authority, and you take too many risks. You are too reckless to be on this mission."

Amy took a deep breath. Part of her wanted to scream at this guy, while another wanted to curl up in the corner and cry. She kept herself in check. "I'm sorry you feel that way, Capt. Tyler," she said. She glanced at Yale. "But, as you said, Yale is in charge of this mission, not you." She turned to face her friend. "Capt. Brown, what are your orders for me?"

Yale smiled at her. "Your orders are to make as much noise as you can when the time is right." She glared at Tyler to drive home the point.

He graciously nodded at her.

"Good, I'm glad that is settled." Yale changed the image on the monitor back to the cave model. "Capt. Tyler, split your men into two teams, one for the south, and one for the east. I will be part of the north team, along with Amy and Private Corkland. We will keep radio communication open and try to push the terrorists back into the heart of the cave."

The meeting ended after Yale announced the time for the offensive. The operation would take place in two hours. The captain dismissed everyone, and she went back to her seat on the bridge.

Amy stayed on the bridge and sat in Lt. Ford's chair. The girl typed commands on the keyboard in front of her, and she listened for any terrorist chatter about the prisoners.

The radar screen lit up and beeped when a violent storm swept across the area. Heavy rain and intense winds shook the *Liberty Bell* as surprised crew members scrambled to their posts.

"How bad is it?" Yale asked Amy. The captain moved over

to Lt. Ford's seat. She looked at the radar screen and whistled. "Wow, this looks like a big one." She moved back to her seat and picked up the microphone for the ship's intercom.

"This is the captain speaking," Yale said. She cleared her throat before she continued. "A surprise storm just crept up from the west. Secure all stations. Security, please assist those who are still outside. Get them aboard immediately." She turned off the microphone. "Maybe we should get airborne," she said to Amy, "get above the storm."

The ship rocked again, nearly knocking Amy to the floor. "That sounds good to me," Amy replied as she straightened up. She typed in coordinates that would take the *Liberty Bell* above the storm. She looked over at Yale. "We are ready, sir," Amy said.

"Just another moment," Yale replied. "We are nearly finished loading the others." She held her right hand up, like a flag person standing in front of two drag racers. A minute later, she dropped her hand. "OK, everyone is on board. We are getting out of here".

Yale grabbed the yoke and pulled it back, causing the *Liberty Bell* to tilt upward. She then pushed the accelerator, and the craft roared into the darkening sky. On the radar, she watched the storm pound toward them. She also saw that the *Mount Vernon* was still on the surface. "Amy, ask the *Mount Vernon* if they need help."

Amy radioed the other ship. They responded that their engines were having trouble starting, but that they should be going at any moment.

Yale set an orbit for the ship and placed the craft on autopilot. "We are vulnerable up here," she said to Amy. "We need to keep an eye out for Crownaxian ships and rebel crafts that might rise from the surface." She rubbed her chin. "What is the status of the Sprint Drive? We may need it in a hurry."

Amy typed in a diagnostic command. She watched the monitor as the information appeared. "The Sprint Drive is fully charged and ready to use," Amy announced. She then checked other systems. "We have full lasers and missiles too, if we need them."

"Let's hope we don't while we are up here," Yale said. She moved closer to Amy and the monitor in front of the girl. "Where is the storm in relation to the cave?"

Amy typed more commands. She shook her head. "It's heading right for it, and the *Mount Vernon* is still on the ground." She looked up at Yale. "The ship should be OK, but will the cave protect our people from the storm?"

Yale didn't answer, which spoke volumes to Amy.

She closed her eyes for a moment and thought about Lt. Ford and the other Union personnel. Amy said a quick prayer for their safety.

A new alarm blared and startled Amy. She examined the radar and saw two ships heading toward the *Liberty Bell*. "Two incoming crafts, captain!" she yelled.

Yale rushed to her side and looked at the radar. She told Amy to turn on the ship's electrical shields.

"Done," Amy said. "I am hailing them, too," she added as she typed in the command.

Yale and Amy held their breaths for a moment.

"No response," Yale said. She picked up the microphone again. "Battle stations. Everyone to battle stations. This is not a drill." She sat in the captain's chair and secured herself in the seat.

Amy buckled herself in.

The two incoming space ships flew in a close formation and fired lasers at the *Liberty Bell*. The ship shook from the blast concussions. Yale steered the ship into a dive toward the planet.

The intruders followed, firing more shots.

The *Liberty Bell's* shields held, but each shot weakened them.

Yale turned the craft around and fired lasers back at them. The hits had little effect on the aggressors. "Try hailing them again," Yale ordered.

Amy did as she was told. "Still no response," she said. The viewscreen gave her a good look at the enemy crafts. They were rounded, gray ships with no clear markings. "They're not Crownaxians. Do the Su-Kanan have space fighters?"

"I don't know," Yale replied, gritting her teeth. "Remind me to ask Guinn the next time we see her."

The enemy crafts separated and tried to surround the *Liberty Bell*.

Yale shook her head. "Not gonna happen," she said. She glanced down at the controls and typed in the commands for the Sprint Drive. "Hold on!"

The *Liberty Bell* dashed between the two ships and shot out into the darkness of space.

The planet Janar and the enemy ships disappeared from the *Liberty Bell's* radar.

Yale let the engines run at full speed for thirty seconds before she turned off the drive. The ship slowed down, and Yale steered it back in the direction of Janar. "Damage report," she ordered.

Amy typed in commands, and data appeared on her screen. "No damages, captain," she replied. "The shields held, but they are now at eighty-three percent. I recommend that we try to avoid another fight like that for a while." She unbuckled and rose from her seat. "So now what?"

Yale shrugged. "I was hoping you would have some ideas."

Amy shook her head.

Yale typed commands on the keyboard. "Well, first I need

to contact Gen. Knox and let him know about the attack." Before she could send her message, however, a signal came through the Communications System. It was faint and crackled.

"*Liberty Bell*, this is *Mount Vernon*," the message said. "Are you there, *Liberty Bell*? This is *Mount Vernon*. We are still on the surface of Janar. Something happened to our thrusters, and we are unable to take off. I repeat, we cannot take off."

The signal crackled again before it was lost.

Yale picked up her microphone and told the Union ship to repeat the message, but they did not respond.

Yale stared straight ahead for a moment. The captain blinked her eyes and turned to Amy. "We have to go back. We need to help the *Mount Vernon*." Yale picked up the microphone again and addressed her crew. "This is the captain. Stay at your battle stations. We are going back to assist the *Mount Vernon*. We will utilize the Sprint Drive again in thirty seconds. Prepare for the run."

The captain and Amy returned to their seats and secured them.

Yale typed in the command, and the *Liberty Bell* darted forward. Yale steered the ship around some debris as they headed for their destination.

Another message from *Mount Vernon* came through. The ship was airborne and battling the two enemy crafts. The *Mount Vernon* asked for immediate assistance.

In less than a minute, the *Liberty Bell* was back above the planet Janar. Amy watched the *Mount Vernon* as she fought both invading ships.

The *Mount Vernon* spun, dove, and twisted as it tried to avoid the laser fire. Yale steered the *Liberty Bell* behind one invader and fired two missiles at it.

They both struck the back of the craft, and it exploded in a large fireball.

The *Mount Vernon* curled behind the other enemy craft and fired two missiles of its own.

The remaining aggressor exploded and sank into the planet's gravitational pull.

Yale sat back in the captain's chair. Her heavy breathing slowly normalized. She steered the ship down toward the planet's surface and landed it just outside the Command Center.

The *Mount Vernon* followed and landed nearby. Yale stormed off the ship, with Amy on her heels. The captain searched the center until she found Guinn.

The administrator was speaking to a doctor when Yale barged over to her. "Why the hell didn't you tell us that the Su-Kanan had space fighters?"

Guinn put a hand on the doctor's shoulder and asked to speak with him later. The doctor gave Yale an irritated look as he drifted away from the women. Guinn turned to Yale but didn't respond in time.

"You are putting my crew in danger when you withhold information," Yale said.

"I did not withhold anything," Guinn replied. She took a few steps away from a nearby huddle of medical personnel, and Yale followed her. "The truth is, we don't know that the attackers were Su-Kanan. And, if they were, we had no idea that they had acquired space ships. This would be the first time they've ever used them."

"They weren't Crownaxian," Amy said. "That's for sure. These ships were a different design and color. The Crownaxians haven't changed their ships."

Guinn nodded at the girl.

"Who else has access to space fighters and would want to attack the Union?" she asked.

Guinn shrugged. "I really don't know. The Su-Kanan are a powerful group. Maybe they've joined other terrorist cells that we aren't aware of." The administrator leaned closer to Yale and lowered her voice. "I am embarrassed to say this, but the Central Government doesn't have much data on terrorist activity. That kind of Intel is hard to get, and we aren't very good at acquiring it." She straightened up and spoke in a normal volume. "I have contacted the Central Government and asked for reinforcements to protect this command center. They should arrive in about three weeks." Guinn turned and hurried away from Yale and Amy.

The captain shook her head and followed Guinn.

"Three weeks?" Yale asked. "We don't have three weeks. Our people might be dead in three *hours*."

Guinn tried to ignore Yale, and she kept walking.

Yale finally grabbed her right arm and pulled her to a stop. "Are you listening to me?"

Guinn glared at the captain, and Yale let go of her. "I am doing the best I can, Yale," Guinn replied. "We have very limited resources on this planet, and our troops are spread thin, trying to locate and fight the Su-Kanan." She paused and took a breath. "There is nothing more I can do." The administrator walked away again and didn't stop until two doctors approached her.

"Looks like we are on our own," Amy said. She stood close to Yale.

"Not completely," Yale replied. "We still have Capt. Tyler and his crew." She turned and marched in the direction of the two Union ships.

Amy stayed behind her until they reached the *Mount Vernon*.

Two privates guarded the ship, and they snapped to attention when they saw Capt. Brown.

"At ease," Yale said.

The guards relaxed.

"Where is Capt. Tyler?" she asked.

"On the bridge, sir," one guard said. "He is waiting for you. Would you like me to guide you to him?"

Yale shook her head, and said that she knew the way.

"Very good, sir," the guard said. He stepped aside to let Yale and Amy board the ship.

The *Mount Vernon* was nearly the same length as the *Liberty Bell* but had fewer decks. It was constructed for battle, where the *Liberty Bell* was made for experimental flight. The *Mount Vernon* had a larger array of weapons, including more laser gun turrets, and more missiles.

Amy noticed a scent of engine lubricant on board the ship, and she wondered if there were a leak somewhere.

The crew saluted Yale as she walked toward the bridge, and she saluted them back.

Amy noticed the looks they were getting from some of the crew. She smiled and felt like a celebrity.

They strode to the entrance of the bridge and stopped.

Amy saw Capt. Tyler rise from his chair.

"Permission to enter the bridge," Yale said.

Tyler nodded. "Permission granted, Capt. Brown."

The women entered, and Tyler met them halfway across the room. He shook Yale's hand. "No need to stand on ceremony, Yale. Not under these circumstances."

Yale shook her head. "It's times like these when discipline and ceremony are needed most," she replied.

Tyler showed her to a seat, and Yale sat down.

Tyler sat in the captain's chair.

Amy remained standing.

"Are your men ready for the rescue?" Yale asked.

"They are, captain," he replied. "We await your order."

Yale glanced at Amy before looking back at Tyler. "My

crew is ready as well. I just hope we are not too late. The hostages are good people. The best. They deserve better than this." Yale looked away from Tyler, and Amy could tell that she was more worried than she was letting on.

The lives of Lt. Ford, and the others, were in Yale's hands, and Amy realized the pressure her friend was under. Amy turned away from the group, nodded her head, and said one more prayer, asking Him to help bring the hostages back unharmed.

Chapter Sixteen

Amy and Yale returned to the *Liberty Bell*. Yale went to the bridge, while Amy asked for permission to walk around the ship before they launched.

The young girl strode through the halls of the *Liberty Bell*, occasionally stopping and running her hands over some part of the ship. Her mind drifted back to her famous mission, and she suddenly missed Madison again. As much as she loved this ship, it wasn't the same without her robot friend.

She passed the mess hall and saw Ethan drinking a milkshake. He was alone at a table, and he looked depressed. She took a deep breath and slowly walked over to the table. "Is this seat taken?" she asked, pulling out a chair.

He looked up at her and smiled.

Amy sat down and tried to remain calm.

"Do you want something to eat or drink?" Ethan asked.

Amy shook her head.

The boy took another sip of his milkshake. "I saw Robinson about an hour ago," he said. "He's doing better. The doctor saved his foot, and his ankle was not that badly injured. He should be back on duty in a week."

"That's good to hear," Amy replied. She looked at his sad face. "How are you doing?" she asked.

He shrugged.

"I heard that you are not going on this mission," she said.

He nodded.

"I think that might be for the best. You and I have been in a lot of risky situations. We shouldn't push our luck," she said.

"But you are going, right?" he inquired. He finished his milkshake and rested the glass on the table. "Aren't you pushing your luck?"

Without a good answer, Amy just nodded.

"I understand," Ethan said. "You have a lot more experience than I do. I just worry."

Amy rose and pushed in her seat. "Do you want to take a walk with me?" she asked.

The boy's face brightened. "Sure, that'd be great." Ethan picked up his glass and carried it to disposal area. He turned and followed Amy out of the mess hall.

They walked quietly for a few minutes.

Amy continued to touch the smooth walls and other parts of the ship that caught her attention. She caught him watching her, and she laughed.

The duo came across a dark corridor, and Amy saw someone standing in the shadows ahead. The figure held something close to their right ear, and Amy faintly heard some words that were not recognizable. She and Ethan stopped and watched the figure pace back and forth. Whoever it was seemed agitated.

The figure finally stepped out of the dark with the item still in hand. It was Cole, and he looked guilty.

"Hey, Cole," Amy said.

The alien boy looked in her direction and smiled.

"What are you doing over there in the dark?" she asked.

The boy quickly tucked the device into his pocket. He took a few steps toward them and stopped. "I was just talking to someone who said they could help me locate my cousins. I haven't seen them in years, and I was hoping they made it to Earth."

"That so?" Ethan asked. "Any luck?" He stood close to Amy, and his fists were balled up tight.

Amy glanced at Ethan and wondered if she would have to break up a fight.

Cole shook his head. "I'm afraid not. I try to be positive, but these dead ends are frustrating. Not just for me, but for my parents, too." He sighed. "So, what are you two doing?"

"Just taking a walk," Amy said. The girl could hear her heart pounding. Some sweat dripped down from her forehead. Cole's beautiful smile and mysterious nature were getting to her. She slowly wiped her face and tried to sound calm. "I have to go soon," she said.

"Where are you going?" Cole asked. The alien boy moved closer to Amy and Ethan, so Ethan leaned in toward the girl. Cole crossed his arms in front of his chest. He looked like he was trying to intimidate Ethan. The device in his pocket lit up.

Amy pointed at the device. "Looks like someone is trying to get back to you."

Cole nodded with a smile, but he did not pick up the communicator.

"You can answer that if you want," Amy said. "We don't mind."

"It can wait," Cole replied. He kept his gaze on Amy.

She nervously glanced down at her feet.

"I am getting hungry," Cole said. "Do you have time to get

something to eat before you go? I'd love to have the company." He let his arms drop to his sides.

Amy shook her head. "I'm sorry, I can't eat right now. But maybe later?" Her voice cracked, and she thought she sounded like an eight-year-old. Her sweat continued to race down her, but she fought the urge to wipe it away. She used her left hand to gently push Ethan away from her.

He got the message and gave her some space.

"Yeah, later would be good," Cole said. He reached out and softly squeezed Amy's right hand. "Till then." Cole let go and quickly smirked at Ethan. The alien boy leisurely walked past them and disappeared into the darkness of the ship.

Amy and Ethan started walking again. "Well, that was creepy," the boy said.

Amy lowered her eyebrows.

"The way he was hiding in a dark corridor speaking to someone on his secret communicator. And he didn't answer when someone called back. He is hiding something. I just hope it's not dangerous."

The young girl didn't answer right away. Part of her was mad that Ethan was jealous again, but a bigger part wondered if his suspicions were warranted. Amy hated to admit it, but she still had feelings for them both, and that was a problem. She thought about Cole and smiled. He was mysterious, handsome, charming, and maybe a little dangerous. Ethan was his opposite: cute, smart, and lovable, but also a bit boring. If should could only combine the two.

The Union soldiers assembled outside the *Liberty Bell* and the *Mount Vernon* as darkness blanketed Janar.

Yale and Tyler held one last briefing, going over the details with their troops one more time.

Amy noticed that Guinn was not present, and that made

her wonder just how much support they were really getting from the Central Government.

Yale wrapped up the briefing by addressing all the Union soldiers. "I don't need to tell you how important this mission is." She slowly paced back and forth in front of the *Liberty Bell*. "The hostages' lives are in our hands. It is up to us alone to bring them home. Capt. Tyler's men might not know the names and faces of our friends, but they understand duty and obligation to the Union. They understand that all lives matter." She stopped and looked over the troops. "Good luck to you all, and may God be with us."

Capt. Tyler took a step forward. "Load up!" he ordered. "It's time to move out." He glanced at Yale and nodded.

The troops entered both ships in rows of two and marched to their posts. Those staying behind at the Command Center exited the *Liberty Bell*.

Tyler walked over to Yale. "Good luck, captain," he said.

They shook hands before parting for their ships.

Amy followed Yale toward the *Liberty Bell*. She stopped at the entrance when she saw Ethan and Cole.

Ethan stepped forward first. "I wish I could go with you," he said. "Just so I knew someone was watching your back."

Amy nodded and gave him a quick hug.

"Come back in one piece," Ethan said.

Cole politely offered his right hand, and Amy shook it. "I haven't known you very long, Amy," Cole said, "but I know you are one of the bravest people I've ever met. I wish I wasn't restricted to the Command Center." He leaned toward her, and they briefly hugged. "Take good care of yourself. I want to see you again."

The boys backed up as Amy entered the *Liberty Bell*.

She looked over her shoulder one more time at them and fought off tears. She took a deep breath and rushed aboard.

Once inside, she marched toward the bridge and found her seat next to Yale. Amy ran a brief systems check and told Yale that the ship was ready.

The *Liberty Bell* took off first, with the *Mount Vernon* behind them.

Amy watched the radar for enemy ships. She breathed a little easier when none appeared. She glanced at Yale and saw that the captain was piloting the craft with white knuckles. Amy hoped that no one else on the bridge could see how nervous their captain was. "It's a beautiful night," Amy said, trying to alleviate some of the tension.

Yale glanced at her and tried to smile. "It is," she replied. "Too bad we are not here for a nighttime stroll." The captain checked a reading on her monitor. "It must be nice having two suitors at the same time." Her smile grew. "Personally, I like Ethan more."

Amy's face reddened with embarrassment. She cleared her throat. "Well, Capt. Tyler appears to have eyes for you, sir," she replied. "And he is very handsome."

Yale looked over at Amy and nodded.

"Who knows. Maybe when this mission is over . . ."

"One step at a time, Amy," Yale said.

They both laughed before Yale regained her composure.

"We'll be at our landing point in a matter of minutes," she said. "Anything out there that we should be worried about?"

"No, sir," Amy replied as she checked the radar again. "No ships in the area, and nothing unusual on the ground." She typed a message and sent it to the *Mount Vernon*.

They immediately replied.

"Looks like all is well on the *Mount Vernon*, too," Amy said. The girl crossed her fingers. *So far, so good*, she thought.

The ships reached their landing point, and Yale began the

descent. The *Liberty Bell* suddenly began to shake. Lights flashed on the console in front of Amy.

She frantically typed a command into the system.

"What's going on, Amy?" Yale asked as she struggled to keep control of the ship.

Amy read the data on her monitor. "It looks like severe turbulence," she replied. "A windstorm just kicked up out of nowhere." She typed in more commands. "I'm trying to stabilize the thrusters." The shaking intensified. Amy had trouble keeping her hands on the keyboard. Her head began to ache, and she felt her stomach turn. She fought to keep from vomiting.

Her bleary eyes saw an urgent message from the *Mount Vernon*. They, too, were caught in the windstorm. The ships were dangerously close to each other. "We need to turn twenty degrees starboard, or the *Mount Vernon* is going to crash into us." She looked at Yale. "Captain?"

"Copy that," Yale replied. She fought with the yoke until she managed to make the adjustment.

The *Liberty Bell* moved away from the other ship but, now, they were hurling toward the planet's surface.

"We need reverse thrusters," Yale commanded.

"Working on it," Amy replied.

The wind kept the reverse thrusters from firing properly.

Amy diverted more fuel to them, in hopes of jump starting them. "C'mon, ignite," she mumbled. She watched the readings, but they didn't change. "C'mon, c'mon." She clenched her fists and tried to will the engines to respond.

One of them finally started, and the ship slowed down, but the other did not ignite.

"It's going to be a rough landing, captain," she said.

Yale nodded, and Amy picked up the ship's internal microphone. "All hands, brace for impact! All hands, brace for impact!" She let the microphone drop as she grabbed the handles beside her seat. She closed her eyes and lowered her head.

The *Liberty Bell* slammed against Janar's surface and bounced into the air. They hit the ground again, and the ship slid forward, turning clockwise into a violent skid. Several consoles on the bridge exploded, sending sparks and steam into the cabin.

Amy opened her eyes and saw that they were heading for a row of trees.

The ship sideswiped the trees, ripping them out of the ground before finally coming to a stop.

Amy got out of her seat and checked on Yale.

The captain leaned forward in her seat without moving.

Amy gently shook her friend. "Yale, are you OK?"

There was no response.

"Yale, wake up!" she yelled. Amy put her fingers on Yale's neck and felt her pulse. "I need a medic!" She turned and repeated her command. "I need a medic right now!"

A young woman with curly, blond hair rushed to the captain with a medical bag in her hands.

Amy watched her examine Yale.

The medic took Yale's pulse and checked her eyes.

"How is she?" Amy asked.

The medic didn't respond. Instead, she removed a device from the bag and measured the captain's breathing. The woman turned to face Amy. "She's unconscious, but alive and breathing. She probably has a concussion, but we won't know for sure until we check her out in sick bay."

Amy helped carry Yale to sick bay. The captain was placed on a table and nurses took readings, prepared an IV bag, and placed an oxygen mask over her face.

Other Union personnel dashed into the room, some pushing their way toward their captain.

Amy turned to face the crowd. "Everyone, listen. Listen." She put her hands up to hush the crowd. "The captain is OK for now. What she needs is quiet and rest. Go back to your stations and help anyone else who was injured. If they are seriously hurt, bring them here, but we must maintain order."

A frightened woman in a privates' uniform stepped forward. "If the captain is injured, and Lt. Ford is among the hostages, who is in charge?" she asked.

Those around her began mumbling amongst themselves, many asking the same question.

Amy raised both of her hands again. "Since I know this ship better than anyone else, I am assuming command of the *Liberty Bell*," she said.

Everyone became silent for a moment, and then the muttering returned. Amy whistled as loudly as she could, bringing silence back again. "This is not open for debate," she said. "Until Capt. Brown recovers, I will be the acting captain. Now, go back to your stations. Help the injured."

No one moved. Instead, they glanced around the room at each other.

"That's an order!" Amy shouted. Her conviction finally convinced the others to obey, and they scattered out of the room.

Amy sat down in a chair and started hyperventilating.

A nurse stepped over to her and put a hand on her back.

Another hustled over to the girl and quietly told her to relax.

The first nurse rubbed Amy's back and gave her a bag to breathe into. After a few minutes, Amy's breathing normalized.

The second nurse handed the girl a glass of water.

Amy slowly drank it.

Amy put the glass down on a table and stood up. She spoke to the nurses. "Thank you for helping me."

They both nodded.

"Now, do me a favor. Go through the ship and make sure the injured are getting help. I don't know how long these folks will continue to listen to me."

The nurses said they understood, and they left the room and headed in different directions to help those in need.

Amy drank more water and she turned to see Cap. Tyler enter sick bay with two of his soldiers. "We just heard about Yale," he said to Amy. "How is she doing?"

Before Amy could answer, one of the nurses filled him in on Yale's condition.

After the nurse finished, Tyler stepped toward the injured captain. He gently lifted her right hand and kissed it. He placed the hand back down and turned to Amy. "Who is in charge here?" he asked.

Amy pushed her shoulders back. "I am, Capt. Tyler," she said.

Tyler shook his head. "Another joke, I presume."

Amy stood firmly in place and looked the man in the eyes.

Tyler placed a hand on Amy's left shoulder. "You are a child," he said. "I know that Yale let you get away with a lot, but I will not." He looked past her to his men. "Inform the crew that I will take over while Capt. Brown is indisposed."

"You can't do that," Amy said.

Tyler asked why not.

"Because Union regulations do not allow a captain to lead more than one ship at a time, to avoid splitting his attention," she replied.

Again he looked to his men, and one of them said that she

was correct. "Fine, but I am not leaving a little girl in charge of a Union ship."

"A ship I know better than you or anyone else." She paused to let that sink in. "As I informed the crew, I am in charge until Capt. Brown returns. They listened to me, and if you want to avoid a civil conflict between our crews, you need to listen to me, too."

Tyler took a deep breath. "Fine, child, you are in charge of this ship. But, if I give you an order, whether I'm on the *Mount Vernon* or the *Liberty Bell*, I expect you to follow it." He glared at her, and she nodded. "Good. The first thing we need to do is postpone the rescue attempt," Tyler said.

"With respect," Amy said, "we shouldn't do that. The hostages' lives are in danger every minute they are there, and we are already close enough to help them." She glanced at Yale before continuing. "We must move forward with the plan. Time is running out."

Tyler did not look convinced. "No," he said. "We must wait until our injured are healed and the captain is healthy. Then, we can proceed."

Amy started to speak, but a faint voice from Yale's bed cut her off.

"No, Tyler," the voice said. "We will proceed with our plans." She tried to sit up, but a nurse kept the captain laying down. She looked at Amy and Tyler. "We will not wait. The rescue plan remains the same, and we will launch at the same time." She ignored the nurse and forced herself into a sitting position.

Yale looked at Tyler. "And that's an order."

Chapter Seventeen

Repair crews worked frantically to get the *Liberty Bell* back together. The ship sustained damages to nearly every section and did not have propulsion, weapons, or shields. The *Mount Vernon* faired better, with only minor damage to the hull. Though both crews suffered numerous injuries, neither had any casualties. Capt. Tyler oversaw the repairs, and mixed crew members from both ships to maximize their talents.

The spacecrafts landed further away from the cave than was planned. That meant a longer walk before they started their rescue attempt.

Yale, still a bit dizzy, insisted on leading her team in their part of the mission.

Amy and Tyler both tried to talk her out of it, but her stubbornness won out.

A nurse gave Yale some medications to help with the pain and the dizziness, and the captain began to look steady on her feet.

Amy checked her personal supplies and felt a tinge of sadness when she saw the communicator that Madison had given her. She stuffed it into her pocket and hoped that she would see her robot friend again.

Yale and Tyler called the mission team together for one last briefing.

Amy stood near her captain and kept a close watch on her.

Yale raised her hands to quiet the troops. "I know this mission has gotten off to a terrible start," she said. "But don't let that wreck your focus. We need to band together and do our jobs to the best of our abilities. The lives of our friends and fellow soldiers are squarely in our hands. We cannot fail them." She paused and looked over the team. "We will not fail them."

The troops cheered and clapped their hands.

"You all know what you need to do. Now, let's do it." She stepped back and the soldiers cheered again.

Tyler gathered his squad and gave them last minute instructions.

Yale's smaller team met with her, and she started the march toward the cave.

Amy made sure that she was always within a few feet of Yale.

Tyler's team marched behind them and provided cover.

Amy heard Yale as she struggled to breathe, but she did not want to embarrass her leader, so she kept quiet.

The nighttime air was thick with humidity, and Janar's bugs seemed hungry as they landed on the soldiers' skins. The path to the cave took them through thick bushes and tall grasses. That was good for cover, but rough on the feet and hands, as the soldiers had to push aside the vegetation to move through it. The original plan called for a twenty-minute walk to the cave but, now, they were facing an hour-long march to their destination.

No one spoke during the arduous trek.

Yale led the way using a lighted compass, but the rest of the crew moved on without illumination. They all relied on the person in front of them to guide them.

Amy kept an eye out, as best she could, for traps like the one Robinson stepped into. She saw that Yale was slowing down a bit, and she wondered if her captain had the physical strength to complete the mission. She knew that Yale would not quit, so she took it upon herself to make sure that the captain did not push herself too hard.

The team was nearly halfway to the cave when something moved in the thick grass to their right.

Yale stopped and put up a hand.

Amy did the same, and the silent message was soon received by the entire team.

They stood still for what seemed like hours, until the creature rushed past the front of the line.

Another creature quickly followed, and Amy and Yale got a glimpse of it. It was a human, and he was running at breakneck speed.

Amy turned to Corkland, who had been behind her. "It could be one of the hostage-takers," she said.

Corkland nodded and turned on the light that was mounted on his laser rifle. He took off after the intruder, and Amy followed him.

She pushed her way through the lanky grass and tried to keep up with Corkland. Their prey was fast and elusive. Amy wondered if Corkland could still see them. Hoping he hadn't lost them, Amy kept up her pursuit. Her heart pounded, and her lungs screamed out for more air, but she refused to stop.

Amy heard a laser blast followed by a squeal. Another laser blast soon followed. Amy trailed the split-second illumination and stopped when she found Corkland pointing his rifle at one of the runners.

On the ground lay a motionless man in a tattered green uniform. Next to him sat a smaller human wearing a white shirt and green shorts. It was a little boy.

Corkland's hands shook as he kept his rifle pointed at the child. He glanced at Amy before looking back at his prey.

Without a word, Amy leaned down and felt for the man's pulse. There was none. She slowly rose. "He's dead," she softly said.

The little boy began to cry.

Amy moved toward him, when Corkland told her to stop.

"He may be wired," Corkland said. "He could blow us all up."

Amy nodded but eased her way toward the boy.

His eyes widened.

She put her hands out to show that she meant no harm.

Corkland kept his weapon pointed at the boy. "Amy, stop!" he yelled.

The girl ignored him and gently reached for the captive. She slipped her hands under his arms and pulled him toward her.

The boy put his head on her right shoulder and wrapped his arms around her. His entire body shook.

Amy looked over at Corkland, and he finally lowered his weapon. "He's a baby," Amy said. "I'd guess he's about four-years-old. He is no harm to us. Let's take him back to the team."

Corkland nodded.

"You go first," Amy said. "Use the light on your rifle."

"What about him?" Corkland asked, pointing to the dead man.

"There's nothing we can do for him now," Amy replied. "His people will find him eventually. They will deal with him."

Amy carried the boy and followed Corkland.

It took some time, but they finally reached the rescue team.

Amy brought the boy to Yale, and she filled her in on the details of the encounter.

Everyone crowded in to see the child.

The boy had stopped crying, but his body continued to shake. He reached out for Amy, and she took him into her arms again.

"What are we going to do with him?" Corkland asked. He looked at Yale before glancing at Amy.

His question started mumbled conversations among the team.

"We can't take him with us," Corkland said, "but we can't let him go."

"We could tie him up and gag him," one soldier said.

Some in the group agreed with him, while others did not. A debate started, and the soldiers' voices began to rise.

Yale raised her hands and quieted the group. "We don't have time for this. We are already way behind on this mission. If we don't hurry, we will lose the darkness." She took the child from Amy and held him in her arms. "He cannot get to the cave before we do. I don't even think he knows where it is on his own. We will give him some rations then let him go."

Some team members voiced their disagreement with her decision.

The captain lifted her hands again. "This is not up for debate. I have made my decision, and that is what we are going to do."

No one objected this time.

"Does anyone have any food or water on them?" she asked. "If you do, give it to Amy."

Amy followed her captain's orders and collected some dried food bars and water from the team.

Yale handed the child to her, and Amy carried him away from the group.

Capt. Tyler followed her. "The captain has made her decision," Tyler said, to quiet any further dissention.

Amy hugged the boy and eased him to the ground, telling him that he will be all right. She kissed the top of his head and stepped away from the child.

Tyler nodded at Amy as she walked past him.

Amy stopped when she saw his expression change. She took a step toward him, but she was too late.

Without a word, Tyler pulled a laser pistol from his holster and shot the boy in the chest.

The blast knocked the boy off his feet, and he landed on his back. A water bottle and some food bars scattered around his body.

"No!" Amy screamed as she rushed to the boy. She lifted his limp body and saw the round hole in his chest. The boy's eyes were still open, but his head tilted back like a rag doll. She hugged him tightly before resting the body on the ground. She turned and faced Tyler. "Why the hell did you do that?"

Yale darted over to Tyler and grabbed him. She shook his shoulders. "Are you insane?"

Tyler didn't answer her.

"I decided that we were going to release him. You defied a direct order. Why? Why?" She shook him again.

Tyler grabbed Yale's hands and pried them off him.

Corkland quickly aimed his rifle at Tyler.

Several of Tyler's men countered by aiming their rifles at Corkland.

"Everyone, stop!" Amy yelled.

Some of Tyler's men shifted between aiming at Corkland and aiming at Amy.

"Lower your weapons," Amy said.

No one did.

"Think about our mission," she resumed. "We can't save our people if we turn on each other like this."

Tyler waved his hand at his men, and they finally lowered their rifles.

Yale nodded at Corkland, and he did the same. Yale faced Tyler again. "We do not murder innocent people. When this is over, you will face a court martial."

"That's fine," Tyler replied. "Just remember that the mission comes first, and me and my men will do anything necessary to complete the mission." He paused and looked into her eyes. "Will you?" He stormed past her and his men followed him.

Amy approached Yale and put an arm around her.

Yale hugged Amy for a moment before she turned and marched toward the front of the line, where she resumed her command.

The troops tensely followed Yale as they renewed their march toward the cave.

The darkness began to wither as Janar's sun peeked up over the horizon.

Yale pushed the pace, and Amy worried that she was going run herself into the ground. The captain's face was pale and drenched with sweat. Her breathing was labored, and her legs appeared ready to give out.

The cave finally came into sight.

Yale stopped, and the team gathered around her. She bent

over and put her hands on her knees for a moment before she straightened up and spoke softly. "Tyler, take your team that way," she said, pointing to the northwest direction. "Once you are in position, send up a silent flare. Then, we will start the commotion on the south side. That will be your signal to start your advance." She looked at the troops' faces. "Any questions?"

No one spoke.

Yale dismissed Tyler's team. Once they were out of earshot, she approached Amy. "We need to keep an eye on Tyler. He is liable to take a shot at you, or me, during the fighting. A man facing a court martial is not to be trusted."

"I agree," Amy said. She glanced over at Corkland. "None of us on our team is safe." She took Yale by the arm and moved a few steps away from the rest of their team. "What about Corkland? Can we trust that he won't shoot Tyler first?"

Yale shook her head. "No." She turned and marched toward Corkland, and Amy followed her. Yale put hand on Corkland's shoulder. "Are you ready, Tom?"

The private nodded as he checked his laser rifle.

"About what happened before," Yale said. "I appreciate the fact that you had my back. Just keep in mind who the real enemy is, OK?"

Corkland looked into Yale's eyes. "I understand what you are saying, captain," he replied. "I'm not looking to start trouble with the other crew, but I will fire on anyone who threatens you, or this team. No matter who they are."

Yale and her team reached the south side of the cave as the last of the darkness faded. The captain removed the silver disks from her tactical backpack and handed them to Corkland and Amy.

The team waited for the flare. Several more minutes passed before the silent signal rose into the blue sky.

Yale activated her disk and put on the ground.

Amy and Corkland did the same.

The disks sat about fifty yards away from the cave, close enough for those inside to hear them. Yale and her team hid in the tall grass.

Seconds later, the disks started firing loud bursts that sounded like laser fire and bomb explosions. The commotion lasted for four minutes.

Amy covered her ears, and she noticed that Corkland had his laser rifle in his hand.

The noisemakers finally ceased and were replaced with a creepy calmness. There were not footsteps, no crying women or children, no bloody soldiers trying to surrender.

Amy and Corkland looked at Yale. "Where are they?"

Yale didn't respond. Instead, she walked past her team, toward the southern opening of the cave.

Amy and Corkland slowly followed her. They stopped at the mouth of the cave. The captain ordered them to stay behind her as she took a few steps into the cave.

The ground suddenly shook. The team pressed their hands against the rock walls to keep their balance. Rocks rained down on them.

Corkland grabbed Amy and Yale and dragged them out of the crumbling cave. They landed on the ground with a thud and scrambled back to the tall grass to hide.

Amy put her hand on her chest as her heart pounded.

"Is everyone alright?" Yale asked.

Amy and Corkland said that they were.

Yale crawled to the edge of the tall grass and looked at the cave. "Damn," she said. "It didn't work." She opened a hand-held communicator and spoke into it. "Tyler, can you hear me? It's Capt. Yale Brown. Can you hear me?" She repeated her words over and over again, but there was no response from Tyler, or anyone else.

"We need to go to the north side to see what's happened," she ordered.

Her teammates nodded in agreement.

"Corkland, do you have a spare laser pistol?" she asked.

The private nodded, pulled it out of his backpack, and handed it to Yale.

"Thank you," she said. Yale turned and gave it to Amy. "Don't make me regret this."

"I won't, captain," Amy replied. She looked over the weapon as Corkland pointed out the key components of the pistol. She nodded and kept the shooter in her left hand as the team hustled to get to the north side of the cave. The pistol was surprisingly heavy compared to others that she had held, and she had a little trouble holding on to it.

The team reached the north entrance of the cave. They dropped to the ground behind thick trees and fired their weapons at the rebels.

Amy saw that Tyler's fighters were pinned down near the cave opening. There was no sign of Capt. Tyler. Amy ducked a laser blast that burst just over her head. She took a deep breath and stood, firing at the enemy. She hit a rebel soldier in the right leg, and he fell backward with a scream.

More rebels appeared and unleashed a firestorm of ammunition.

Amy dropped to the ground again and covered her head. She felt the heat of the laser blasts as they exploded around her. She peeked through her arms and saw that some rebels were advancing toward them. Amy raised her heavy pistol and fired again, but she missed her target. She shifted around the tree to get a better shot. Amy fired, hitting one rebel in the shoulder.

He fell to the ground, and one of his men dragged him back inside the cave.

Yale crawled forward from her position and fired her weapon as she moved.

The rebels focused on her, as three soldiers aimed and fired at the captain.

She rolled toward some tall grass and hid inside.

The rebels continued their advance in defense of the cave. Some used multi-fire laser rifles to ferret out the intruders.

The deafening sound of laser blasts was disorienting, and Amy had trouble locating Yale and Corkland.

The private then appeared on Amy's right side, shooting and dodging laser hits. He pushed his luck too far, and one shot hit him square in the chest. He fell back as his weapon dropped from his hands.

Amy screamed, and the rebels focused on her position.

"Fall back!" Yale commanded. "Fall back!" She waved her arms to get the Union troops' attention.

Either they couldn't hear her, or they were ignoring her orders, as Tyler's men stayed put and kept fighting.

One by one, they fell to the ground as the rebels pushed back the attackers.

Yale and Amy were soon surrounded, and the captain ordered Amy to stop firing. Yale laid her weapon on the ground. "Amy, it's over!" she screamed. "It's over!"

A rebel soldier kicked away Yale's weapon, while another pushed her head into the ground and pulled the captain's arms back.

Yale's hands were bound behind her. The captain's chin smashed against the rigid ground and started bleeding. She was pulled to her feet and two rebels stayed behind her and marched her toward the cave.

Two other shooters grabbed Amy from behind and knocked her pistol out of her hands.

One soldier grabbed Amy's shoulders and pushed her face-first into the dirt.

Amy spit out soil and blood as she struggled against her attackers. Her hands were also bound before she was hoisted to her feet and made to walk to the cave entrance. Amy saw Yale and shook her head as she fought off tears. Corkland was nowhere in sight.

The rebel soldiers led their captives into the heart of the cave. The dark cavern reeked of urine and stale air.

In the faint light, Amy saw that Yale was ahead of her and straining to stay on her feet. The young girl fought to break free, and one rebel turned and slapped her across the face. Amy dropped her head and wept as they continued to force her forward. She closed her eyes and thought of her parents. All she wanted at that moment was to be safe in their home on Paldor.

The new hostages entered the center of the cave.

Amy saw bodies strewn across the cave floor, and she recognized some of the fallen Union soldiers. Her head turned from side to side as she tried to locate Lt. Ford and the other abductees.

The march stopped, and Yale was pushed to the floor.

Amy was thrust down beside her. The girl rolled onto her side and forced herself to sit up. She spit out more dirt and blood and fought to catch her breath.

The laser fire soon ceased as more Union fighters were dragged into the center of the room. The moans of the injured echoed off the cave walls. Some of the rebels began pulling the corpses by their legs to the edges of the cave. The bodies left red trail marks behind them.

Amy and Yale looked at each other, and Amy saw something in Yale's eyes that she had never seen before: defeat.

One rebel in a dirty, but medaled, coat stood in front of everyone. He raised his right hand, and the rebel soldiers quieted. "These are the collaborators of the Central Government," he said, pointing to the Union fighters.

The rebels booed and hissed until the speaker raised his hand again. "They are the oppressors who want to keep us from ruling ourselves."

Again, the boos poured out.

"But we have shown them the might and the determination of the Su-Kanan," he said.

The crowd cheered and whistled.

The speaker raised both of his hands over his head and he shook his tightened fists.

The rebel crowd settled as the speaker lowered his arms.

"We have done what no one else before has been able to do. We have pushed the Central Government to the brink of disaster. We have shown that the will of the people cannot be denied. Let us remember this day as we continue our efforts to reshape Janar into a world of peace and prosperity for everyone."

More cheers from the rebel fighters.

"And we should never forget the help of our benefactor, the one true ally we have in this fight for our freedom."

The speaker moved to the side to allow his guest to occupy center stage.

Amy's eyes widened when she saw a bejeweled Crownaxian walk toward the crowd with four Crownaxian guards on either side of him.

The figure towered over his hosts as he stood in his purple overcoat.

Amy had never seen his face before, but she had no doubt who he was.

Amy rose, with her hands still bound behind her, and she slowly walked toward the frightening figure.

His guards quickly moved to stop her, but their leader put up a hand and waved them off.

The young girl stopped in front of him and stared into his eyes, into the very embodiment of evil.

Amy Sutter stood face to face with Drelk.

Chapter Eighteen

The Crownaxian emperor smiled at his visitor. He lowered his eyes into a squint as he examined the human girl. His head shook ever so slightly. "For someone so small, you have great courage," he said.

Amy remained quiet but continued to stare him down.

"I have heard stories about the bravery of humans," Drelk said. "I remember a story about one girl in particular. She stole a heavily guarded ship and flew into my planet's territory. Somehow, she managed to escape my fighters, and she abducted several human subjects."

"More like rescued them," Amy said. For some reason, she couldn't stop glaring into the Crownaxian's eyes. She seemed almost drawn to this dark figure. She struggled against her restraints again. Amy glanced at Yale, who shook her head in an attempt to warn the girl not to go too far. "I know who you are," she said.

Drelk took a step toward her. "Then you have me at a disadvantage, child." The ruler looked more closely at her. "But maybe not. Maybe I do know who you are, too." He laughed again. "Yes, I think I do. Some of my people call you the Paldor Pest, while the less enlightened call you the Hope of Humanity." He paused and pressed his lips together. "You are that girl, aren't you? You are Amy Sutter."

"In the flesh," Amy replied. She paused and let a smile emerge. "You are a lot uglier than I imagined."

Several people gasped at her audacity.

One of Drelk's guards drew a laser pistol and pointed it at her.

Drelk glared at the guard, who immediately put the weapon away.

"I am surprised to see you this far from Crownaxian space," Amy said. "Travar always said that you liked to rule from a distance."

Drelk sighed. "Travar. Now that is a name I have not heard in a long time."

Amy thought she saw a twinge of regret in the leader's face. "He was a good friend and an excellent leader before he turned on me. Before he betrayed me." He punched his left hand with his right fist. "He died a traitor!"

"No," Amy said. "He died a hero."

More gasps came from the crowd, but Drelk did not try to stop her.

"He was killed while trying to help the Crownaxian people rid themselves of you. You are a warmonger. You don't care about your people. You only care about how much power you have." The girl took a breath. "We had monsters like you on my planet once, but they died off and were replaced by great men and women who knew that freedom was a right for everyone. That justice was more important than power."

Drelk nodded and placed his hands on his hips. "Yes, I am familiar with your home planet's history. You call them monsters, but I call them visionaries. They saw the terrible shape your world was in, and they knew that strong leadership was needed. Prophetic men like Stalin, Hitler, Gaddafi, and Trump. They knew that salvation could only be delivered by a firm hand. They were gods."

Amy shook her head. "No, they were delusional men with insane ideas, and they all perished at the hands of justice." She fidgeted in a vain attempt to free her hands. "Someday, you will experience the same fate. One day, your people will rise up against you, and you will suffer, as all dictators ultimately do. I just hope I am there to see that day."

Drelk's face reddened. He slowly turned to his guards. "Lock her up," he said. "And see that nothing happens to her. I want this one to die last."

Two guards rushed toward Amy and grabbed her by the arms.

They dragged her away from the others, but Amy kept her eyes on Drelk for as long as she could. She didn't make a sound as she memorized every feature of his face. She didn't want to forget a single thing about her nemesis.

The Crownaxian guards searched her and found the communicator that Madison had given her. They seized it and dragged Amy to darker section of the cave. They pushed her into a makeshift cell and pressed a button on a control panel. An orange forcefield covered the doorway as the girl fell to the floor.

One guard pressed another button on the panel, and Amy's hand restraints fell off her.

Amy rubbed her sore wrists as the guards turned and left. The girl walked around the room, feeling the walls with her hands. She guessed that the room was about twelve feet long and ten feet wide. Some light managed to enter from the cracks in the walls, but it only provided the illumination of about three candles. It was humid inside the room, and it smelled like old garbage. Amy was thankful that she was the only person in the cell and that, so far, she had not come upon any creepy critters.

She searched the room for nearly an hour before she sat down against the wall across from the forcefield. It was hard to breathe in the stuffy room. Amy wiped streams of sweat from her forehead. She tried to sit very still and listen to the sounds from the other sections of the cave. It was too quiet. Amy bit her lip and worried about the other Union personnel.

Amy closed her eyes. In the distance, she thought she heard a rhythmical tapping. She couldn't make it out clearly at first, but soon it became more distinct. It was a combination of long and short taps that reminded her of Earth's old Morse code.

The girl snapped her eyes open as she realized that it was Morse code and the message continued on a loop. She looked down at the dirt and started writing with a finger what she heard. The dots and dashes soon became a clear message from the sender. Amy sat back and sighed as she read the communication: *Welcome to your final resting place.*

Amy found a small stone and tapped it against the wall. She drummed out a message of her own. *Who are you?* she sent. Amy listened as the original message stopped repeating itself. Instead of a response, there was only silence. Amy resent her message but, again, there was only silence. *Where are you?* she sent. She sat back against the wall, listening for a reply.

A few minutes passed before she heard tapping again. She recorded the message. *I am close by.* Amy was about to respond when she felt something crawl over her right hand. She pulled her hand back and saw a four-inch long brown insect with tiny legs inching across the floor. It lifted its head for a moment before continuing on its journey. Amy lifted the stone and aimed at the intruder, but she stopped. She watched it slip inside a hole in a wall and disappear.

The girl took a deep breath and let it out. She wiped the dirt on the floor, looking for any other bugs, but she didn't find any. Amy rephrased her first question. *What is your name?* she asked.

A minute passed before the answer arrived. *Chase* was the single word answer. Then came another message. *How did you wind up here?*

Amy laughed out loud, even though she knew it wasn't funny. *Long story,* she replied. She let that sit for a moment before adding to it. *How do I get out of here?* she asked.

A much longer silence than before resulted. It lingered for nearly twenty minutes. Amy began to think that her new friend would not, or could not, answer.

Then came just two words: *You can't.*

Amy was about to ask why when another message quickly followed. *No more for now.*

Amy tossed the stone onto the floor. She sat back against the wall, dejected. The orange forcefield emitted a low buzzing sound that Amy hadn't noticed before. In the quiet of the room, the buzzing became thunderous, and Amy covered her ears with her hands. She lowered her head until her chin touched the top of her chest.

When Amy looked up again, she was no longer in the cave. Instead, she was stumbling through a wooded area populated with colossal redwood trees. A yellow sun blazed above her, and her shirt and long pants were soaked with sweat. At first, she thought she was back in Papa's realm, but something in the air felt different. There was no sound of children playing, nor the smell of the carnival food. No, wherever she was, it wasn't there.

Something in her told her to run. She sprinted forward,

fighting to keep her balance on the uneven ground. Amy thought she heard the heavy breathing of someone, or something, that was behind her. It grew louder as she pushed herself to keep moving forward. She was running so frantically that she had to use her hands to keep her from falling down. Whatever was pursing her was gaining on her, and it was hungry.

Amy came to a clearing, and she saw a purple house across a meadow. She ran toward the house and refused to look behind her. The flat ground made it easier to run, and the heavy breathing finally began to fade. Still, she knew that stopping was not an option. Instead, she kicked into a higher gear and rushed forward with all her might.

The girl was nearly at the house when the front door opened, and two Crownaxian soldiers appeared with laser rifles in their hands. They fired at her, and Amy dropped to the ground to avoid getting hit. The predator behind her closed in, and Amy desperately searched for a place to hide. She crawled toward a hollow log and ducked inside of it.

She curled up into a fetal position and held her breath.

Something lifted the log and began to shake it.

Amy pressed the palms of her hands against the wood inside to steady herself.

A screeching howl tore through the log and into Amy's ears. The log slammed against the ground, and Amy smacked her head against the splintering wood.

Blood poured from a gash in her head. Amy became dizzy and had trouble keeping her eyes open. She couldn't hear her pursuer anymore, and she hoped that it was gone. Too scared to leave the log, Amy kept very still and prayed for help. She did her best to keep the tears from escaping her eyes.

Shaking and hungry, Amy eased herself out of the broken log. The sunlight was gone, and only a few stars shone in the sky. The girl limped toward the house, in hopes of finding shelter and safety from the predator. She staggered up the steps of the porch and put her right hand on the doorknob. It turned, and the front door opened with a creak. She shook her head. *Of course, it had to be a creaky door*, she thought.

Amy closed the door behind her. There were candles lit throughout the slender hallway ahead of her, so she picked one up and carefully moved forward. Unlike the cave, the air in the home smelled sweet, like a baking apple pie. To her left, she saw an empty dining room, where an antique wooden table sat with four wooden chairs around it. To her right, there was a living room, complete with two couches, a reclining chair, and a large-screen television mounted on a wall. Amy entered that room and sat on one of the couches.

The cushions were soft and supportive, so Amy leaned back and rested her aching body. She felt the stress leave her. Her eyes grew heavy as the couch cradled her head. She blinked a few times and allowed herself to fall asleep. Amy smiled as her breathing slowed, and she felt the joyful wave of sleep coming upon her. Suddenly, the front door slammed open, snapping Amy to her feet. She heard the familiar breathing of the predator. Amy looked around for a place to hide, but the monster entered the room and found her. Amy felt her chest tighten. Before her stood Drelk with a laser pistol in his right hand.

"Welcome to your final resting place," he said.

Amy lifted her head from her arms and looked around. The house was gone, and she was back in the dark cave cell. She rubbed her eyes and realized that she had never left. The realistic nightmare left her sweaty and exhausted. She had no idea what time it was or how long she had been in the cell. Amy felt her stomach grumble.

She found the stone and tapped a message to Chase, asking what time it was.

There was no reply.

She sat still again and tried to listen for any sounds from outside the cell. Amy couldn't hear anything helpful. She rose and moved toward the orange forcefield. To test it, she found another, smaller stone and threw it at the forcefield. The stone was incinerated upon impact.

The girl fell to the floor when she heard the familiar tapping again.

Chase told her that it was late at night and that dinner was arriving. The food came at odd times, never the same each day, so it was hard to judge when it would arrive. He told her to eat, no matter how bad it looked.

A few minutes later, a small opening in the forcefield emerged, and a round bowl of something slid through. It was followed by a bottle with water in it.

Amy grabbed her dinner and sat back down. The bowl was filled with stale bread and rotting fruit. It smelled rancid, but she was too hungry to care about that. She rapidly ate her meal, but slowly drank the water. She wanted to make the water last, so she limited herself to drinking only half of it. Amy put the empty bowl near the bottom of the forcefield.

She poured a small amount of water onto her hands and wiped her face and hands with it. The girl then carefully put the bottle in a far corner of the room, so she wouldn't knock it over by accident. She sat down against the wall opposite the forcefield again, and she tried to think of what to do next. Amy knew that it was her responsibility to try to escape, but she realized that there weren't many options available to her.

Amy used the feeding schedule to keep track of time. Based on the number of meals she ate, assuming it was twice a day, three full days past before a pair of Crownaxian guards appeared at the door.

One turned off the forcefield, while the other tossed a person into the room.

The stranger landed hard on the floor as the guards turned the gate back on.

Amy retreated to her favorite corner and watched the newcomer rise to their feet.

The new prisoner cursed the guards and turned to face Amy.

The astronaut's face lit up as she recognized Private Corkland's face. Amy rose and rushed toward him, but he told her stop.

"Don't touch me, Amy," he said with full-blown fear in his voice. "I've been contaminated with some kind of virus."

Amy stepped back with a look of horror. "It's not airborne," Corkland said, "so you should be fine as long, as you don't touch me."

The young man kept his distance from Amy. "What is going on? Why would the rebels infect you?" She sat back against her wall.

Corkland rubbed his eyes and found a seat as far away from Amy as space would allow. His movements were slow, and he looked like he was struggling to move his arms and legs.

"The Crownaxians are running things out there," he said, "Not the Su-Kanan." He took a deep breath, which made him cough. He covered his mouth with his hands and, when he pulled them back, Amy noticed blood on them. He wiped his hands on his pants. "The Crows have executed nearly half of the prisoners," he continued. "They have some of their scientists with them, and they are conducting experiments on the other half."

Amy covered her mouth in shock. "What about Yale and Lt. Ford?" Her hands began to shake. "Are they still alive?"

Corkland shrugged. "I don't know," he replied. "They keep us separated throughout the cave. I haven't seen Capt. Brown in days." He lowered his voice. "I thought that you were dead; I'm glad to see that I was wrong."

Amy smiled. "I thought the same of you," she replied. "I am glad I was wrong, too." She wiped some tears from her eyes. "Do we have an escape plan? How the hell do we get out of here?" She folded her hands together and laid them on her lap.

"I was hoping that you could tell me that," Corkland said. He rose and moved toward the forcefield. He put his right hand up to the gate.

Amy warned him not to do that.

He nodded and pulled his hand back. Corkland sat back down in his spot. "Have they questioned you yet?" he asked, trying to make himself comfortable on the floor.

Amy shook her head. "No, I've been just sitting in here waiting." She nervously tapped her feet. "Have they questioned you?"

The private nodded. "Yes, for hours at a time." He slowly blinked his eyes. "They told me that they won't give me the antidote until I give them the information they want." He punched his left hand with his right fist. "Bastards."

"What did they ask you?" Amy asked.

Corkland grimaced. "They wanted to know our troop deployments in this sector of space," he said. "They asked me what our battle plans are for defeating the Crows." He turned his hands upward. "I told them that I am only a private. I don't know that stuff. But they didn't believe me." He sighed. "So, they shot this stuff into my arm."

Amy gulped some air. "How long do you . . . have?" she

asked. The words barely made it out of her mouth. She stared at Corkland's face. Though he was nearly ten years older than she was, Amy realized that he was still a young man. A man with his whole life ahead of him, or maybe not.

Corkland rubbed his stubby chin. "They told me that I should start to see symptoms in a few hours," he said. "Like coughing, dizziness, breathing problems, and abdominal pain." He took a breath. "Then, my organs would shut down. I would have thirty-six hours at most." He turned away from Amy as a few tears rolled down his face. "I don't want to die," he said, "not like this."

"God, I wish I could help you," Amy said.

He looked at her again and nodded.

Amy then heard the tapping of her unseen friend. She listened closely and wrote his message in the dirt. It said that he was feeling ill, which was why she hadn't heard from him in so long.

Corkland looked at what she wrote. "What's going on?" he asked. He kept his distance but still tried to make out the message.

Amy slowly erased it. "It's from another prisoner here." Amy tapped back, saying she hoped he felt better. She glanced over at Corkland and saw his confused expression. "It's Morse code," she said.

He nodded, but still seemed unsure.

"You do know Morse code, don't you?" she asked. "It's still taught to all Union soldiers."

Corkland bashfully smiled. "Yeah, I never really got the hang of it," he said. He suddenly leaned back against the wall and grimaced in pain. His breathing was labored. "What you said before about helping me. You meant it, right?"

"Yes, I did," she replied. "But what can I do?"

Before Corkland could answer, Chase sent her another

message, asking her how she was doing.

She signaled back about Corkland and his dilemma.

Chase quickly responded that she needed to be careful. She tapped back, asking why.

Corkland coughed and more blood landed on his hands. "Well, if you know anything at all, please tell me," he said. He took several deep breaths. "I need to tell them something to get that antidote." The private inhaled deeply, trying to catch his breath.

Chase signaled back. *The Su-Kanan are tricky people*, said the message. *They will try anything to get information that they can share with the Crows*.

Amy quickly erased that message and stared coldly at Corkland.

"Please," the private said. "Anything you can tell me. It could save my life." His face whitened, and his words came slowly out of his mouth. "Please, tell me something."

Amy nodded. "I might have something for you," she said. She eased her right hand toward the stone and slowly picked it up. In one quick motion, she threw the stone at Corkland's chest. It passed through his body and bounced off the wall behind him.

Corkland looked at her with fear in his eyes. He started to speak, but no sound came from his mouth. His image flickered before completely disappearing.

Amy rose and walked over to where he had been. She waved her hands through the air and felt nothing. She knew that Chase was right. "Damn," she said. "It was a hologram."

The forcefield suddenly dropped, and two Crownaxian guards rushed in with laser rifles pointed at her. Behind them stood their supreme leader, Drelk.

He sighed and shook his head. "Amy Sutter," he said. "You are too smart for your own good."

Chapter Nineteen

The chains around Madison's arms and legs were five feet long and attached to a wall behind him. He fought to break out of them for the first sixteen hours that he was locked in his cell, until he realized the futility of his efforts. The robot spent that next two days trying to conserve his limited energy. He passed the time remembering Emily from the Link-Up and imagining what life would be like if he were human and she were real.

He dreamed of a log cabin by a lake, where he and Emily would grow their own food and raise their children. They would grow old together maintaining their home, fishing at the lake, swimming in the water, and teaching their children the beauty of nature. The war with the Crownaxains would end, and humanity would experience peace and prosperity while continuing to explore the stars. His friend, Amy Sutter, would visit from time to time, sharing her wondrous space adventures with Madison's children.

The pain and stiffness Madison felt in his arms and legs made him wish Dr. Greenland hadn't given him such sensitive receptors in his metallic body. He wondered what Greenland had in mind for him. Was he to be disassembled and rebuilt? Or did his creator plan to leave him in this dark, empty room for the rest of his existence? Madison wasn't sure which would be a worse fate. He just wished he were back on the *Liberty Bell* with his friends.

The door to his cell opened for the first time in days, and Madison opened his eyes to see who was there. One of Greenland's men entered. Madison thought his name was Dalon, but he couldn't be sure. His fatigue and low battery power were affecting his memory. The man quietly walked over to the robot and checked the chains. Satisfied with the results, the man took out a small transmitter and spoke into it. "This is Dalon," the man said, confirming his identity. "The robot is secure. Tell Dr. Greenland that he is clear to enter the room." Dalon heard a response and replied. "Copy that," he said.

Dr. Greenland entered the room with two other hench-men, one of whom carried a small black bag in his left hand.

Dalon moved to the back of the room and stood watch.

Greenland stopped a few feet in front of Madison. The inventor had a sad expression. He shook his head as he looked at his creation. "How did it come to this?" Greenland asked. "Where did I go wrong?" He crossed his arms over his chest.

Madison shrugged. "I do not have an answer for you, Dr. Greenland. All my programs are running perfectly. Perhaps the fault lies in your expectations." The robot pulled his right arm forward to illustrate his bondage. "Please remove these chains. They are most uncomfortable." He lowered his right arm and the chain rolled back again.

"How do I know you won't attack me the way you attacked Lincoln?" Greenland asked. He shook his head again. "No, you will remain locked up for the time being, until I am sure that you are not a danger to me or anyone else." He nodded at one of the men beside him.

The man removed a tool that looked like an electric drill from the bag in his hands, and he moved toward Madison. The man then drilled a hole in the back of Madison's head and attached a bolt to it.

"What are you doing, Dr. Greenland?" Madison asked.

The man with the drill finished his work, closed his bag, and returned to Greenland's side.

Madison detected a new signal emitting from the bolt. It was a low frequency sound that pulsated every thirty seconds. Madison found it extremely annoying.

Greenland smiled. "You have just been fitted with a tracking device," he said. "In the unlikely event that you escape from here, I will be able to find you immediately." The scientist paused. "If I am unable to retrieve you, the tracker also contains a high-yield explosive powerful enough to blow up a space ship. Like, say, the *Liberty Bell*."

Madison shook his head. "I will not try to escape. You have my word on that."

They stared at each other for a moment.

"I chose to stay here to work with you, and to learn more about the other robots." He paused and noticed that Greenland did not seem to believe him. "How is Lincoln?"

The inventor stormed forward and grabbed Madison by the throat. "You do not get to say his name!" he shouted. He pushed the robot's head back and it slammed against the wall. "You nearly killed him when you attacked him. He is severely damaged. I don't know if I can save him."

Dalon and the other men rushed toward the scientist. "Dr. Greenland," Dalon said. "Remember the bomb in his head. One hit like that, and this whole building could go up."

Greenland let go of Madison and returned to where he had been standing.

Madison felt some ringing in his ears. That sensation soon passed. "No, Dr. Greenland," he replied. "You are wrong. I did not attack Lincoln. He attacked me. I was just defending myself."

Greenland snarled at the robot. "And were you just defending yourself when you spread gun powder all over the room? If my men hadn't arrived, you would have destroyed all my robots. Then where would I be?"

"Without an army," Madison replied. The robot stared into his maker's eyes.

They widened in anger and recognition.

"Yes, I know that you have an army that you plan to use against the Union. I'm just not sure how," Madison said, "or when."

Greenland shrugged. "OK," he said. "Why not?" The scientist glanced at Dalon, who shook his head. Greenland faced Madison again. "There is nothing you can do to stop me." He moved closer to his creation. "Yes, I do have an army, and I will use them against the Union. Those fools laughed at me when I proposed the idea of robot soldiers. Now they will see for themselves how wrong there were."

"Dr. Greenland, you are a scientist," Madison said. "You are not a killer. You have a responsibility to aid Mankind, not destroy it. This isn't you."

"You know nothing about me," Greenland said. He turned and moved away from the robot. After a few steps, he turned back to face him again. "I did have fancy ideals once. But, when no one believes in you, when no one gives you a chance to prove what you can do, those ideals fall by the wayside."

"Do you even know how to launch such an attack?" Madison asked.

Greenland smiled. "I don't have to. I have allied myself with someone who has lots of experience in military operations, someone who hates the Union just as much as I do. It is the perfect partnership." He leaned forward and lowered his voice. "I am going to sell my robots to Drelk and the Crownaxians." He stepped back and smiled. "It's the perfect plan."

"Perfect for the Crownaxians, but not for you," Madison replied.

The scientist squinted and moved toward Madison again. He stopped just a foot away from the shackled robot. "What do you mean? What am I missing? I will make lots of money, and my detractors will get what they've got coming to them. It is perfect."

Madison shook his head. "No." He let the word linger, and he could see the irritation growing on his builder's face.

Greenland's breathing increased, and sweat formed on his forehead.

"You are missing the most obvious part," Madison said. "Frankly, I'm surprised you haven't realized it."

"And what is that?" Greenland asked. His lower lip shook.

The others in the room inched forward to hear what the robot would say.

"Drelk is an evil dictator," Madison said. "He rose to power by taking what he wanted and killing anyone who got in his way. He won't pay you anything for the robots. He will just steal them from you and kill you and all of your men." He shook his head again. "You made a deal with the devil, and you won't live to see those who doubted you get what they deserve."

Greenland's face turned red. His entire body shook.

The other men backed up, expecting the scientist to lash out violently. Instead, a creepy smile came across his face. "Nice try, Madison," the inventor said. "Trying to build doubt in my mind and force a wedge between me and my business partner." He shook his head. "But it didn't work. I know what kind of person Drelk is, and that is why all my robots have the same destruction bolt on them as you do. Drelk knows this. He won't double cross me."

Greenland turned and left the room without another word.

His men followed him, the last shutting the door behind him.

Madison was alone again. He spoke quietly to no one. "Ah, Dr. Greenland. You cannot see the forest for the trees. And that will be your downfall."

The robot started rubbing the back of his head against the wall. Madison knew he had to be precise. If he put too much pressure on his head, the explosive would ignite. He closed his eyes and pictured the bolt in his mind. He imagined its size, shape, and composition. Madison took his time, slowly grinding the metal down. Hours passed, and the sensors in his head detected pain equivalent to a human migraine.

Madison felt the wobbly bolt rattle against his head. He slowed down, careful not to let the bolt fall to the ground. He opened both of his hands and held them behind his back. Slowly, he continued his operation. He titled his head, and felt the bolt slip off. He caught the bolt in his right hand and closed his fingers around it.

The robot moved both of his hands to his front. He looked down at the bolt and saw the explosive device. Madison laughed when he saw that Greenland had packed it with gunpowder. He wondered why his maker was so obsessed with such an old-fashioned weapon. The robot also saw that Greenland was lying. There was enough explosive to blow off Madison's head, but not enough to do any more damage.

Madison slowly and carefully dumped some of the powder onto the floor. He brushed away the fallen powder with his right foot. The robot kept a small amount in the device. He moved his arms together, and he squatted until his arm chains overlapped with each other and his leg chains. Madison quickly rubbed the exposed powder against the chains. Soon there was a spark, followed by a small explosion that broke the chains apart.

Madison shook off the damaged chains. He sunk to the ground and leaned against the wall. The explosion was not very loud, and he doubted that Greenland's men heard it. Since no one came rushing in, he knew that he was right. He sat on the floor for a moment, trying to figure out his next move. Madison knew that he could not allow Greenland to sell Drelk the robots, but he wasn't sure what he could do to stop it. He looked around the room and saw an electrical outlet in one wall. The robot forced himself up and stumbled toward it. He sat down again and connected to the outlet for some much-needed power.

An hour passed before Madison felt recharged and rejuvenated. He disconnected from the outlet and stood up. The stiffness in his arms and legs was gone and his mind cleared. The robot quietly ripped the door from its hinges and lowered it to the floor. He took a cautious step outside and saw no one around. Madison crept through the hallway until he found an exit. He slipped outside the building and felt a tranquil breeze touch his face.

Madison rushed to the enormous warehouse and forced his way inside. Like before, it was dark, and there was no movement in the room. Madison only turned on the emergency lights, and he examined the still robots. He found the bolts on the back of their heads that Greenland had mentioned. Though individually limited, if they were all set off at the same time, they could bring down a building.

Madison knew that this would be the best way to get rid of them all at the same time.

However, when Madison looked at their motionless faces, he knew that he could not destroy them this time. He wondered what had caused his change of heart. Perhaps it was the time spent in the Link-Up. Maybe they, too, dreamt of being human and living out normal lives. Whatever it was, Madison realized that they were innocent, and he could not eliminate them.

Madison wandered around the room, trying to find a solution. He touched their metallic arms and felt a connection to them that he hadn't expected. Soon, he came across the repair shop in one corner of the room. There he saw the remnants of Lincoln. The robot had been disassembled in an attempt to fix him. Without thinking, Madison picked up some tools and began putting the robot back together. He didn't know if Lincoln would function the same as he had before, but something compelled him to try.

Madison worked frantically on the damaged robot. The parts soon became a whole entity, and Madison polished and oiled the final product. He opened the back of Lincoln's head and found the small keypad on the right side. Madison typed in a series of codes before shutting the covering. He took a step back and waited as the robot rebooted.

Slowly, Lincoln sat up on the table and blinked his eyes. He turned his head from side to side before settling his eyes on Madison. "Who are you?" Lincoln asked. He looked down at his hands before Madison could answer. He lifted his hands to his face and studied them with sincere fascination. "What are these?" he asked, turning his hands at the wrists.

Madison smiled and spoke slowly. "Those are your hands," he said, as he softly touched Lincoln's fingers.

Lincoln repeated the last word as he studied his appendages.

"They help you touch, grab, and pick up things." Madison demonstrated by picking up a screw driver. He handed it to Lincoln, who gratefully accepted it.

Lincoln put it down and picked it up again.

The duo spent the next half-hour playing with the tools.

Madison watched Lincoln closely, and he thought he saw flashes of recognition on his friend's face.

Soon, Lincoln grew bored with the games and he began to ask questions. He wanted to know who he was, why he existed and what they were doing in the large, dark room.

Madison did his best to answer them.

Lincoln finally hopped off the work bench and landed solidly on his feet. He turned to look at Madison, when his eyes suddenly widened. "I know who you are," Lincoln said. "You attacked me." His voice sounded like a frightened child's. "Why do you want to hurt me?" He backed away from Madison before the older robot could answer.

"I don't want to hurt you," Madison replied. He spoke in a calming tone. "I want you to help me prevent Dr. Greenland from hurting millions of people. But, first, we have to protect you from him." Madison pointed to the back of his own head. "Reach back to this point on your head."

Lincoln didn't move.

"Trust me, this is for your own good."

Lincoln reached back with his right hand and touched his head. "Feel that circular bump back there?" Madison asked.

Lincoln nodded. "That is a tracking bolt with an explosive in it. Dr. Greenland installed that on you and the others to control you," said Madison. "I want to remove it from you, and I want you to help me remove it from the others, too."

Lincoln dropped his hands to his sides. "But Dr. Greenland

loves us. He said we have a great destiny. Why would he put explosives on us?" He shook his head. "It doesn't make sense." He took a step forward and put his hands on Madison's shoulders. "Please, help me understand," he said.

"He lied to you, Lincoln," Madison said. "He lied to everyone. There is no great destiny for you, or me, or them," he said, pointing toward the other, motionless robots. "Dr. Greenland simply wants to sell us to the Crownaxians so they can destroy humanity. We cannot let that happen. Too many lives are at stake."

Lincoln nodded slowly. "Get this thing off of me, and we will remove it from the others." He turned around and stood still as Madison carefully began taking the bolt off. He was pleased that Lincoln finally believed him, and that Lincoln was there to help him with the enormous task ahead of them.

Chapter Twenty

The food schedule changed. It only arrived once a day, which threw off Amy's internal calendar for a while. Drelk and the guards questioned her for four hours after she discovered Corkland's hologram, but that was days ago, and she hadn't had any visitors since.

Amy refocused her escape plan. She realized that her best chance was to recover the communicator that the guards had taken from her, but that would not be easy. She didn't know where it was, or if it was still in one piece. Amy thought about bribing one of the guards, but she had nothing to offer them.

The messages from Chase had stopped, and she wondered if he were still alive. She hoped that, when she found her way out of this cell, that she would get the chance to search for him, but the caves were long and intricate, and finding him would take considerable luck. Amy began to suffer from cabin fever as the hours crawled by. That and her fear for her friends' safety made it difficult to sleep. When she did drop off, she often found herself immersed in nightmares.

Amy was drawing a map in the dirt with the stone when the forcefield dropped, and two Crownaxian guards entered the cell. Amy slipped the stone into her pocket.

One of the guards grabbed Amy by the shoulders and pulled her to her feet.

"What the hell?" she asked. She fired a punch at the guard that grabbed her, and it landed on the soldier's shoulder. She pulled her hand back in pain.

The guard laughed at her before shoving her out the cell door.

The guards marched Amy through the dark passages of the cave, and the girl darted her eyes, hoping to catch a glimpse of something useful. They entered a room illuminated with electric torches and one guard thrust the girl into a chair. The guards then backed away from her.

Amy saw another chair beside hers, and a larger one in front of her.

Two more Crownaxian guards entered with another prisoner.

Amy blinked her eyes a few times to clear her vision. Her heart raced as she recognized Yale's face.

The captain wobbled as she moved, and she had fresh bruises on her cheeks and forehead.

The new guards roughly planted Yale into the seat beside Amy's.

The young girl put her arms around her friend. "Yale," she said breathlessly. "It's so good to see you. I didn't know if you were still alive."

Yale struggled to speak. "It's good to see you too, Amy." Her breathing was labored, and she had trouble holding her head still. "Remember, tell them nothing," said Yale. "No matter what happens. The Union comes first. Always." She rested her head on Amy's right shoulder, and the girl snuggled close to her.

Amy looked up as another Crownaxian entered. She clenched her fists when she saw Drelk sit down in the chair in front of them.

"A very touching reunion," the dictator said. He looked at one of his soldiers. "It warms the heart, doesn't it?"

The soldier nodded in agreement.

Drelk then addressed the prisoners. "I hope you find your accommodations to your liking."

"They suck," Amy replied. She laughed. "I'm surprised that you are still here. I didn't think you could stand these primitive conditions."

Drelk smiled, but Amy sensed that she was pissing him off.

"Unless there is a palace around here that I'm not aware of, I find it hard to imagine you bunking with your pals in this putrid cave."

Drelk leaned back in his chair. "You certainly do have a lot of spirit for someone in your situation, child. You think you've had it rough here? Look at your captain. You have been spared the adult inquisition. But, if you insist on rattling my cage, I will forget that you are so young the next time you are questioned."

Amy realized that it was time to back off. Instead of a smartass remark, she quietly nodded at the Crownaxian leader.

"That's better," Drelk said. "I know you are both wondering why you are here. It is quite simple really. I have observed you quite closely since your capture, and I am impressed with what I've seen. Few species are as resilient as humans are, and you have proven to be exceptional, even by those standards."

Drelk removed something from his cloak and he held it out

228

in front of him. He spoke directly to Amy. "I believe this belongs to you, child."

Amy nodded again as she saw the communicator that Madison had given her. He carefully placed the device on one of the arms on his chair. "What would you do to get this back?"

Amy felt Yale's hand cautiously squeeze her right leg. "What did you have in mind?" Amy asked. She stared into Drelk's eyes, trying to read his face.

His expression remained neutral as he stared back at her. His body was still, and he looked relaxed and in total control.

"Have you been communicating with someone else in the cave?" he asked Amy.

The girl shrugged and tried to hide her anxiety.

"I believe you have, using an old Earth messaging system." He paused and pretended to be remembering. "Oh, yes. Morse code, I believe. Very quaint."

Amy shook her head. "I have no idea what you are talking about."

"Don't you?" he asked. Drelk motioned to one of his guards and, a moment later, another prisoner was brought into the room.

Amy didn't recognize the older man, but she knew it was probably Chase.

The guard dumped the prisoner in front of Drelk. "Let me introduce you to your pen pal, as it were," Drelk said. "This is Commander Charles Abbott, but his friends call him Chase. He was a Union captain, like Yale."

Drelk rose from his seat and stood over Chase, who was too frightened and weak to stand up. "This man has caused us considerable trouble over the years. But not anymore." Drelk reached into his cloak again and pulled out a laser pistol.

Before Amy could react, the dictator shot Chase in the head. His body slammed to the floor.

Amy tried to stand, but Yale wrapped her left arm around her and held her in her chair. Amy's chin shook in anger and fear. The girl whispered. "I'll kill you someday." She felt Yale's arm tighten around her again. The youngster sat back and bit her lip.

"I'm sorry, did you say something?" Drelk asked.

Amy shook her head.

"Good, I wouldn't want to miss a single quip from your wonderful mind." He sat down in his chair as two Crownaxian guards dragged away Chase's body. "Now, where were we? Oh, yes. You two are remarkable people, and I pride myself on working with only the best. And that is what I am offering you." He paused for a moment. "I want both of you to join me."

Amy raised her eyebrows. "Join you?"

Drelk nodded.

"In what way?"

"In every way," he said. "You and Yale will become two of my military advisors. Not only are you both clever and courageous, but you also have inside information about the Union. You know their strategies, the way they react, and their troop locations. That information is invaluable to me."

Amy felt the rage build up inside her. She clenched her fists and took a deep breath. "And what if we decide to decline your generous offer?" she asked. Again, she felt Yale's hand squeeze her leg. Amy forced a smile. "Just suppose," she added.

Drelk leaned forward in his chair. "Then I would have to kill you both."

Amy laughed loudly. She slowly rose to her feet and continued laughing. She bent over and giggled so hard that she had to fight to catch her breath. She stumbled forward, shaking her head and pointing at Drelk.

The dictator looked confused by her reaction.

The girl finally composed herself and she was two steps closer to Drelk. "Wow, you really know how to negotiate, don't you?" she asked. She took another step forward.

The guards moved toward Amy, with their weapons raised.

She addressed them. "Easy, fellas. I'm not armed, remember?" The girl looked back at Drelk. "So, let me get this straight. To stay alive, all we have to do is betray all the people we love and everything we stand for. Is that right?"

Drelk didn't respond.

"'Cause I gotta tell you, that is a lot to ask." She slowly moved in a tight circle in front of Drelk.

Amy looked back at Yale, who shook her head. The girl carefully slipped her right hand into her pocket and felt the stone in it. She continued to circle until she faced Drelk again. She was two steps away from him. Amy ran her thumb over the edge of the stone that she had sharpened while in captivity. "OK," she said. "You've got a deal. Spare our lives and the lives of everyone in my crew, and I will join you."

Drelk lowered his eyebrows. "Just like that?" he asked. He stared at her, and she knew he was trying to read her. She nodded slightly but kept the rest of her body still.

"Somehow, I don't believe you," he said. "Prove it to me."

Amy shrugged. "How do I do that?"

Drelk smiled. "Use that stone you've got hidden in your right pocket and kill Capt. Yale Brown with it," he ordered.

Amy's face whitened.

"Yes, I know about the stone," he said. The bulge in your pocket gave it away. Perhaps you thought of using it to kill me?" He shook his head and laughed. "Foolish girl. That plan never had a chance."

Amy froze, not sure of what to do. She was too far away to rush Drelk. She smiled again. "You are too smart for me," she said. Amy crept back to her seat. She stopped in front of Yale. "I'm sorry, but I don't want to die." Amy whipped the stone out of her pocket and struck Yale on the forehead.

The young girl did her best to make it look good. She kept her fingers around the stone to absorb the blow.

Yale instinctively played along, falling back in her chair with a scream. The captain grabbed Amy's hands and pushed the girl backward.

Amy fell onto the floor and Yale pounced on her.

They wrestled on the floor, exchanging fake punches.

Yale got to her feet and pulled Amy toward her. She punched the girl in the midsection and threw her across the room.

Amy landed at the feet of the dictator.

The guards moved to protect Drelk, but he told them to stay back. He was clearly enjoying the bout.

Yale rushed at Amy, and the girls grabbed each other by their shoulders. The tussle continued at Drelk's feet, and he laughed at the spectacle.

Amy let go of Yale and stood up. The young girl quickly fired the stone at Drelk. It struck the leader in the forehead, drawing blood. In the confusion, Amy grabbed the communicator and stuffed it into her pocket.

The guards descended on the girls as Drelk leaned forward in his chair and moaned.

Amy and Yale fought for their lives, punching at kicking at the guards.

Yale seized a pistol from one guard and shot him in the chest. She shot at the other guards and took two more down.

Amy grabbed a pistol from a fallen guard and fired at the remaining Crownaxians. The girl aimed at Drelk and fired, but he dove to the floor and fired back. His shot knocked the pistol out of Amy's hands.

The dictator took aim at Yale and fired.

The laser blast caught Yale in the back. She dropped to the floor, and her weapon slipped away from her.

Amy dove for it, but another guard got to it first. Before he could fire, Amy kicked him in groin. He dropped to the floor.

Amy kicked his head, knocking him out.

Drelk tried to shoot at Amy, but his pistol was empty. With no guards to protect him, Drelk raced toward the nearest exit and disappeared.

Amy rushed over to Yale. She pulled her friend into her arms. The limp body laid heavily against the girl. Amy checked for a pulse but did not find one. The girl lifted Yale and carried her over her right shoulder like a fireman. She stumbled toward an exit and hurried through the dark hallway. Amy's shoulder ached, and her legs burned, but she continued to carry her fallen friend. The girl weaved through the intricate tunnels until she found her way out of the caves.

Once outside, Amy found a rock structure to hide behind. She eased Yale's body to the ground and checked her again. Yale was not breathing, and she still had no pulse. The laser blast left a hole in her back that was visible through her clothing.

Amy shook her head and wept as she accepted the fact that her friend was gone.

Amy took the communicator out of her pocket and sent a message to Madison. At first, there was no reply, so she sent it again. Amy resent the message two more times before her robot friend responded. She gave Madison her coordinates and filled him in on the situation. He told her to stay where she was, and he would come and get her.

Amy carefully gathered some foliage, and she covered Yale's body.

Four vulture-like birds circled over them, squawking hungerly to each other.

Amy kept a careful watch and did not let anything near Yale's body. She kicked at a rodent that got too close, and she threw rocks at the birds above her. Amy bent down on one knee and said a prayer, asking God to guide Yale's soul to her next destination.

Soon, a cavalcade of land vehicles approached Amy's hiding spot. The vehicles stopped and circled around her. Surprisingly, the occupants were all robots. There were nearly 200 in all.

The girl smiled when she saw Madison exit the first transport. She rushed over to him and hugged him tightly. "You have no idea how happy I am to see you," she said.

Madison smiled back at her. "I am glad to see you too," he replied. He paused, and his smiled faded. "I am sorry about Yale. Where is she?"

Amy took him to Yale's body. He checked her vital signs and shook his head. He motioned toward another robot. "Get a blanket to wrap her in and put her into the first transport," he ordered.

That robot followed Madison's order, and Yale's body was moved.

"We still have to rescue the hostages," Amy said to Madison. "Lt. Ford and the others are still in the cave." Amy nodded toward the other robots. "Will they help us?"

Madison said that they would, but they needed a plan.

Amy shook her head. "At this point, all we can do is storm the cave and bring back whomever we can."

Madison organized the robots into two teams. He would lead the first team in the initial attack, and Lincoln would lead the second team in the follow-up assault. Madison told Amy to stay behind with Yale, as the girl had done enough fighting.

Amy was too tired and too sad to object. She sat in the transport beside the covered body as the robots launched their mission.

Chapter Twenty-One

Madison commanded the first wave of robots, 100 armed and well-programmed fighting machines. Their leader downloaded the names and faces of all the hostages.

The secret soldiers stormed the cave front and blasted their way past the outer guards. They met little resistance, and Madison guided them deeper into the cave. Only then did the terrorists make a stand and force the rescuers to halt their advance.

Dodging laser fire, Madison used his communicator to contact Lincoln. He ordered the second group to enter the cave and provide backup.

The combined force of the robots was too much for the terrorists.

Madison and Lincoln advanced their teams to the heart of the cave, where fierce fighting led to some of the terrorists fleeing, while the others finally surrendered. Madison organized the release of the prisoners, while Lincoln rounded up the fighters who had given up.

Outside the cave, Amy sat in the first transport, next to the body of Capt. Yale Brown. Amy watched the robots exit the cave with the survivors and the captured terrorists. She hopped out of the vehicle when she spotted Lt. Telsa Ford as she walked next to Madison. Amy ran to Lt. Ford and hugged her tightly. "I'm so glad you are OK," Amy said.

"Thank you, Amy," Lt. Ford replied. Her voice was understandably weak, and her face was pale and tight. "I'm happy to see you, too." The officer's expression saddened. "Madison told me about Yale." She shook her head. "I'm so sorry. I know you two were close."

They hugged again as Amy began to weep.

Madison ordered two of his robots to organize the distribution of first aid to the prisoners. The injured were treated in a triage fashion, with the most serious aided first. Madison told Lincoln to have a squad of robots guard the terrorists. The robot leader asked Lt. Ford what should be done with them.

"We will hold them until the Central Government can take them into custody," Lt. Ford said. "Until then, they are to be treated with dignity and respect. Give them whatever food, water, or medical help they need."

"I understand," Madison replied. He relayed the orders to Lincoln, who informed the other robots.

The security squad kept their laser rifles at their sides as other robots treated the wounded and gave them provisions.

The beaten rebels cooperated and waited for the authorities.

Amy helped the wounded Union prisoners get food, water, and treatment. Her sadness turned to anger every time she caught of glimpse of the terrorists on their side of the camp. Some of them laughed while they ate, which made the young girl furious. She approached Lt. Ford as the officer was speaking to someone on a communicator.

"Thank you, director," Lt. Ford said. "We look forward to your arrival." She turned off the device and rubbed her eyes. "I finally got a hold of Director Guinn," she said as she saw Amy. "The Central Government is sending a security team to take the rebels off of our hands." The woman put a hand on Amy's right shoulder. "How are you holding up?"

Amy shrugged. "I'm OK." She paused and looked over her shoulder. "It just seems odd that we are giving those animals our supplies." She looked back at Lt. Ford. "They kidnapped you and the others, and killed many of our people. Why are we being so nice to them?"

"Because that is our job," Lt. Ford replied. "There are rules for treating captured enemy soldiers." She put an arm around Amy. "They may be animals, but we are not." She dropped her arm from Amy's shoulder. "Make sure you get something to eat. You need it."

The Central Government troops arrive two hours later.

Madison and Lt. Ford helped oversee the transfer of the rebel fighters.

They were handcuffed and bound at the legs before they were loaded into CG transports. The Union prisoners were checked out by CG medical staff before they were escorted to vehicles that would take them back to the *Liberty Bell* and the *Mount Vernon*.

As a final measure, two CG aircraft flew overhead and fired missiles at the empty caves, obliterating them.

Madison and Lincoln approached Lt. Ford as the Union personnel prepared to leave.

Lt. Ford was signing paperwork for a CG official. She completed the task and the official departed.

"Lt. Ford," Madison said. "We have a matter of great importance to discuss."

Amy wandered over to the group to find out what was going on.

Lt. Ford smiled at the robots. "What can I do for you?"

"Lincoln and the other robots do not want to go back to Dr. Greenland," Madison said. "And I am sure you know that would not be in the Union's best interest."

Lt. Ford said she agreed.

"They want to come with us," Madison continued. "They want to join the Union."

"They are asking for asylum?" Amy asked.

Everyone glanced at the girl for a moment.

"That is correct," Madison replied, looking back at Lt. Ford. "Can we do that for them?"

Lt. Ford titled her head. "Asylum for robots?" she asked. "I don't know if that has ever been done before. But, why not?" She shook Lincoln's hand. "I don't have the authority to offi-cially grant anything, but you and the others are welcome to come back with us." She turned to face Madison. "I will contact Gen. Knox when we get to the ship and recommend it. He would be able to make it official."

"Thank you, lieutenant," Lincoln said. "I will tell the others." He turned and walked away from the group.

Amy watched him share the news with his fellow robots.

Many of them smiled and shook his hand.

Amy playfully slapped Madison on his right shoulder. "It looks like you won't be the only robot in the Union anymore," she said.

He nodded.

"They will need a leader, someone to show them what life is like in the Union."

"I think they already have their leader," Madison said. He continued to watch the other robots. "But, if he needs help, I would gladly assist him."

Lt. Ford cleared her throat. "It's time to get going. Madison, you are in charge of the robots while they are with us. Get them to their vehicles. I want to get off this planet as soon as we can."

Amy insisted on riding next to Yale's body on the transport back to the *Liberty Bell*.

A CG doctor injected the body with a chemical that would slow down its degeneration.

The girl wondered where Yale's funeral would be held and who would deliver the eulogy. She wasn't prepared to do that, but she hoped that she would get the chance to say a few words of her own.

The *Liberty Bell* glistened in the sunlight as the transports approached it. The vehicles stopped, and Amy watched as Union soldiers departed the ship.

Four soldiers lifted and carried Yale's body on a stretcher and respectfully brought it aboard the craft.

Amy followed them as they carefully stored the body in a casket with a refrigeration system. The soldiers left, but Amy stood in front of the casket and placed her hand on it. She knelt and said a quiet prayer before turning and leaving her friend in peace.

Ethan was waiting for Amy as she entered the hallway. His eyes were wet, and his face was red. He gently stepped toward her and hugged her.

Neither spoke for a moment. They just held each other.

Amy buried her face in his shoulder. Then it all came out. She wept and hugged him tighter, and he cried, too.

Amy finally pulled back. "I can't believe she's really gone." She turned and kicked a nearby pillar. She faced Ethan again. "It's not fair. It's just not fair." The girl shook her head. "Why did it have to be Yale? She was a good person. She was young and smart and beautiful. Why did it have to be her?"

Ethan pressed his lips together. "I don't know," he softly said. "She was a great person, and it's not fair." He paused and glanced at the floor before looking back at Amy. "But I am glad that it wasn't you. I don't know what I'd do if I lost you."

Amy wrapped her arms around him again. She kissed his right cheek. All her doubts about Ethan vanished. "I love you," she whispered.

He repeated it back to her, and she could feel the tension in his body fade.

———

Amy reported to the bridge with Ethan behind her. They were both composed, and Amy approached Lt. Ford as the officer sat in the captain's chair.

At first, Amy didn't like to see Lt. Ford in that seat, but she quickly realized that she was the logical replacement. Amy sat in the co-pilot's seat, while Ethan remained standing behind her.

Lt. Ford wore a headset, and she spoke into the microphone. "Yes, Gen. Knox, I am sending you the casualty report. Regrettably, both Capt. Yale Brown and Capt. John Tyler were killed during the mission. I have assumed command of the *Liberty Bell*, and Lt. Monroe is taking charge of the *Mount Vernon*. We await your orders." She listened and nodded several times before she responded. "I understand. I will inform Lt. Monroe that we are to return to Paldor immediately."

Amy sat back in her chair and let out a deep breath. They were finally going home. She looked over her shoulder at Ethan, and she forced a smile.

He smiled back and sat down in a chair behind her.

Amy listened as Lt. Ford shared the information with the other ship.

Lt. Ford then addressed her own crew over the communications system, informing them of their new orders.

Amy closed her eyes and thought of her parents. She had never missed them more than she did at that moment.

The preparations for take-off were delayed, as the crew of the *Mount Vernon* worked on final repairs to their ship.

Amy became restless, so she rose from her seat and decided to take a walk.

Ethan silently followed her.

The couple strolled through the corridors, and some of the Union soldiers offered Amy their condolences.

She politely listened to their words and tried not to break down again. She realized their good intentions and she thanked them for their support.

Amy led Ethan to what she knew would be a less traveled part of the ship. She needed to get away from the others for a while. She reached out for Ethan's hand as they entered a dark passage. He wrapped his fingers around hers and remained quiet. "Tell me it's going to get better," she said.

He hugged her. "It will get better. You just need time."

She nodded as she pulled back. She was about to thank him when she heard something further down the hallway. "Was it that?" she asked.

Ethan shrugged.

Amy turned from him and marched toward the sound of a voice.

The couple made a right turn, and Amy saw a figure leaning against a bulkhead.

The figure took a step toward them, and Amy saw that it was Cole.

The alien boy smiled at Amy and Ethan. "Hello, Amy," he said. "It's good to see you again." He kept his arms by his sides and Amy thought she saw something in his right hand. "What are you two doing down here?"

"I could ask the same of you," Amy replied. "You seem to like to hide out in dark places."

The boy shrugged and causally slipped something into his right pocket.

"Who are you talking too?" Amy asked.

Cole laughed. "I wasn't talking to anyone. I was singing." He laughed again, a nervous sound that barely made it out of his mouth. "When I'm alone, I like to sing. My parents say I don't have a great voice, so I've learned to avoid an audience."

Amy lowered her eyebrows. "Funny, it didn't sound like singing."

"Then I guess my parents are right," Cole said. His expression changed. "I am really sorry to hear about Capt. Brown. I know you two were close. If you need someone to talk to, I'd be happy to listen."

"She has someone to talk to," Ethan said, a little too harshly.

Cole nodded. "I see. Well, my parents might be getting worried about me. I should head back to our room." He took a step toward the couple and stopped. "Do you know where we are going?"

"We've been ordered back to Paldor," Amy replied. She touched Ethan's shoulder. "That's the planet Ethan and I live on, and I can't wait to get back." She dropped her arm to her side. "Once we are there, I can ask Gen. Knox what the Union can do for you and your family. Maybe you can even join the Union."

"That would be wonderful," Cole said. "Maybe we can finally reach Earth. I know my parents would love to settle there." He smiled again before walking past them toward his quarters. He sang lightly as he disappeared into the darkness.

Ethan was about to say something, but Amy cut him off with the wave of her right hand.

They stood still for a full minute before the girl dropped her arm. "Something's not right," she said. "He was clearly talking to someone. But who?"

"One of his relatives, like before?" Ethan asked. The boy crossed his arms over his chest.

"But why hide it?" Amy asked. "No, he's up to something." She looked at Ethan, and his expression changed. "I know, you tried to tell me before, but I didn't listen. I'm listening now." She grabbed his right hand. "C'mon, we are going back to the bridge."

Lt. Ford was talking to another officer when Amy and Ethan approached her.

The junior officer departed, and Amy rushed up to Lt. Ford. "Lieutenant, we have a problem," Amy said.

Lt. Ford raised her eyebrows in concern.

"It's about Cole and his family."

"The aliens we rescued on our way to Janar?" Lt. Ford asked.

"Yes," Amy said. "Something is going on with Cole." The girl went on in great detail about the boy's odd behavior.

Ethan added his story about the blue light.

Lt. Ford listened intently, but her expression showed her doubt.

"I know this sounds crazy," Amy said. "But this is all true. I think we should keep him, and his family, confined to their quarters until we get home."

Lt. Ford shook her head. "We are not out here to make enemies. And, frankly, we need all the help we can get to defeat the Crownaxians. I don't want to start an interplanetary incident with a new species based on your suspicions."

Amy looked down at the floor.

"Bring me something solid, and I will honor your request." Lt. Ford turned and sat down in the captain's chair.

Amy pulled Ethan aside. "Once we get off the ground, it will take us at least a full day to get home, so it is up to you and me to keep an eye on Cole."

"If we could get our hands on his communicator," Ethan said, "we might be able to find the evidence we need." The boy shrugged. "But how do we do that without his knowledge?"

Amy smiled. "I guess we will have to do it Watergate style."

"What's Watergate?" Ethan asked.

Amy rolled her eyes. "You really need to brush up on your 20th Century history." She lightly kissed his right cheek. "Follow me. I have an idea." She turned and walked out of the room.

Ethan hesitated before going after her.

Chapter Twenty-Two

Amy sat at a table in the mess hall, drinking a vanilla milkshake. It was her third drink in the past hour, and her stomach was getting bloated. Beside her sat her partner in crime.

Ethan kept nodding off, and he shook his head each time he came close to succumbing to sleep. He wrapped his hands around a hot cup of tea. Their long day should have ended hours ago, but their new mission extended late into the night.

"Does he ever sleep?" Ethan asked. He raised the cup to his lips and drank some of the sweet tea. He put the cup down and rubbed his tired eyes. "We've been watching him for hours, and he hasn't touched his communicator. Maybe we are wrong."

Amy shook her head. "No, we're not wrong, and we will prove it tonight. He is getting tired. It won't be long now." She finished her milkshake and pushed the glass away from her. She wished that Cole would hurry up and go to bed. *The Liberty Bell* and the *Mount Vernon* were only a few hours away from Paldor, so they needed their evidence now.

"Can't we just take it from him now?" Ethan asked. He yawned and stretched his arms over his head. "The two of us could take him by surprise."

"Not if he has those powers," Amy said. She folded her hands and watched their prey. Cole sat alone at a table across the room. He was playing a video game on a different device. Amy could hear the sound effects in the nearly empty room. "And Lt. Ford told us not to create a political incident. Mugging him would qualify as one."

The alien boy continued to play with his game for another half-hour before he finally turned it off.

Amy tapped Ethan on the shoulder, and they watched Cole rise and exit the room. The duo quickly followed but were careful enough to keep their distance.

Cole went straight to his quarters and closed the door behind him.

Amy and Ethan waited in the hallway outside the room.

Amy heard Cole talking to his parents. The sound was muffled by the door, but Amy overheard three different voices inside.

Ethan stood next to her, nervously rubbing his hands together.

Amy whispered to Ethan, "We'll give them a half-hour, then we'll go in."

Ethan nodded and sat down on the soft carpet.

The young girl shook Ethan's shoulder and woke him up thirty minutes later. She pressed her forefinger to her lips. "Shhh." She helped the boy to his feet. "It's time." Amy removed an electronic skeleton key and swiped it over the door lock. The door quietly popped open, and Amy led Ethan inside.

The room was understandably dark, and the kids had to

feel their way around until their eyes adjusted to the low level of light.

Amy eased forward, trying not to bump into things.

Ethan was right behind her. She could hear his heavy breathing.

They cleared the living room and moved toward the smaller bedroom.

Amy opened the door. She saw Cole sleeping in his bed.

The intruders split up, quietly searching the room for the communicator. Amy checked a nearby bureau, while Ethan went through the pockets of several pants.

Amy slowly opened drawers but did not see the device.

They rummaged through the room for fifteen minutes, but neither of them found it.

They retreated to the living room and closed Cole's bedroom door. They huddled together and tried not to make noise. "Any ideas?" Amy asked.

Ethan shrugged.

"It has to be in his room. He would want it close by, and he wouldn't take the chance that someone else could find it." She snapped her fingers. "What if it is under his pillow?"

"Could be," Ethan replied. "Then how would we get it?"

"I don't know, but we have to look. C'mon." She turned and walked back toward the bedroom door. She quietly opened it, and the duo returned to the room. Amy tip-toed toward the bed, with Ethan a stride behind her.

Amy went toward the right side of the bed and she pointed the left side.

Ethan nodded and carefully stepped around to the opposite side.

Cole snored as he lay, facing Amy's direction.

Ethan went first. He gently lifted an edge the pillow and

peeked underneath. Ethan shook his head and eased the pillow back down.

Amy nodded. She took a slow, deep breath and let it quietly escape her. The girl lifted a small portion of the pillow and moved closer to it. Amy smiled as she saw something thin and metallic under the cushion. She looked up at her cohort and smiled.

Suddenly, the alien boy's body shook, and he turned over in his sleep.

The abrupt movement startled Amy, and she nearly let out a shriek.

The intruders froze in place, and Amy felt her heart racing. She concentrated on her breathing until it returned to normal.

Cole was now facing Ethan.

Amy waved Ethan away from that side of the bed.

The boy backed up slowly, and he quietly strode over to his friend.

Amy leaned toward Ethan and whispered into his ear. "You lift up the pillow, and I will grab the device."

Ethan nodded and leaned toward the pillow. He looked over his shoulder at Amy.

She whispered again. "Now."

Ethan cautiously lifted the pillow, and Amy grabbed the metallic object. "Got it," she whispered. She pointed toward the bedroom door. "Go."

Ethan moved swiftly toward the door, with Amy behind him. They were nearly there when a voice stopped them dead in their tracks.

"Looking for this?" the voice asked.

The youngsters turned and stared back at the bed.

Cole sat up against the headboard holding the communicator.

Confused, Amy glanced at the object in her hand and saw that it was a game console.

Cole pushed his covers off his legs and rose to his feet. "I was wondering when you would show up."

Ethan flashed a smile and charged at the alien boy.

Cole reflexively waved his right hand, and a blue light appeared around him.

Ethan bounced off the light and crashed onto the floor beside the bed.

Amy was stunned by what she saw. She took an angry step toward Cole, but he waved his hand again, and an invisible force pushed her backward and she slammed against the bedroom door.

Amy tried to stand up, but her head hurt, and the room appeared to spin around her. She squinted and saw Cole approaching her. "Ethan," she called out. In her haze, she couldn't see her friend.

Cole finally reached her, and he pulled her to her feet.

Amy blinked but still had trouble seeing clearly. "What kind of monster are you?" she asked Cole.

"The kind that is going to be very rich," he replied. He kept both of his hands on her shoulders. "Now, I'm afraid that you two are about to become victims of a tragic accident." He pulled his right arm back to strike her, when a wooden chair crashed against his back. Cole sank to the ground, and Amy saw Ethan standing before her with pieces of broken wood in his hands.

———

Lt. Ford paced in front of Amy and Ethan as they sat in chairs in the chilly brig.

Behind them, Cole lay unconscious in a bed inside a cell. A laser shield hummed as it kept the alien boy locked inside.

Cole's parents sat in two chairs on the other side of the room, answering questions from security officers.

Amy could hear them as they proclaimed their innocence.

Madison entered the brig with Cole's communicator in his right hand. He marched toward Lt. Ford and handed her the device. "I have analyzed the data on this device," he said.

Amy and Ethan sat up in their chairs.

"Although the data was encrypted, I was able to decipher it," the robot continued. "There are hundreds of messages from Cole to the Crownaxian leader Drelk. The boy was providing reports on our activities. The communications began before we even rescued him and his parents from their ship."

Lt. Ford scanned the unencrypted data on the device as she listened. She shook her head and handed the device to another security officer. "Arrest them," he told the officer. "Put the parents in separate cells so they can't work on their stories. They may be innocent, but we can't take that chance. We will let the courts decided when we get back to Paldor."

The security officer approached his peers and shared the order. Cole's parents were read their rights before they were escorted to separate cells.

Lt. Ford turned toward Amy and Ethan as they rose from their seats. "I guess I owe you both an apology. You were right."

Amy shook her head. "None needed. You were right to demand evidence. I'm just glad that we were able to get it." The girl yawned and stretched her arms over her head. "How long until we reach Paldor?"

"We are about six hours away," Lt. Ford said. She started walking, and Amy and Ethan followed her. "I'm going to return to the bridge and send Gen. Knox a report on all of this." She sighed. "I can't believe that boy was a spy."

"He must have sabotaged the *Adams* as part of his plan," Ethan said. "He put a lot of lives at risk to get aboard the *Liberty Bell*, including his own."

"I guess greed is a universal trait," Amy added.

The trio walked through the ship and entered the bridge.

Lt. Ford sat down in the captain's chair.

Amy rested in the copilot's seat beside her, while Ethan remained standing behind them.

Lt. Ford smiled at the young girl. "You look like a natural in that seat, Amy."

Amy returned the smile and thanked her.

"What you say we make it official for the rest of the trip?" Lt. Ford asked.

"Sounds good to me," Amy replied. She looked over her shoulder at Ethan, and he smiled at her.

The boy found a nearby seat and sat down.

"And my first official act will be to order us something to drink," she said. "Coffee, captain?" she asked Lt. Ford.

"That'd be good," Lt. Ford said. "Make mine with two sugars, no cream."

"Got it," Amy replied. She spun in her seat and faced Ethan. "Wanna milkshake?" she asked him.

He nodded.

"Me too," she said. She spun back around and hit a button on the console in front of her. "Madison, please contact the bridge," she announced over the loud speaker.

The robot replied, and Amy politely relayed their drink order to him.

He acknowledged and said he would be there in a few minutes.

Amy sat back in her seat and admired the stars as the ship

passed them. She heard Lt. Ford typing out her report to Gen. Knox. Amy closed her eyes and shuddered as she thought about the loss of Capt. Yale Brown.

Madison entered the bridge empty-handed and rushed up to Lt. Ford. "Lieutenant, I have urgent news," he said.

Amy sat up and asked him where their drinks were.

He ignored her. "I was going over the last pieces of data that Cole sent to Drelk," he said. "The boy said that the tracking device is in place. The Crownaxians know where we are and where we are going."

Lt. Ford turned to her console and typed in a command. "I'm scanning the ship for any foreign devices," she said.

Amy rose from her seat and stood beside Lt. Ford.

A minute later, an image blinked on the screen.

"It's in the mess hall, under table six," Lt. Ford said. "Madison, get in there and destroy that thing."

An alarm suddenly blared.

Amy rushed to her seat and looked at the radar. She saw six objects on the screen. Amy typed in a command, and the screen zoomed in on the objects. She turned to face Lt. Ford. "We have six Crownaxian ships heading toward us!"

Lt. Ford quickly turned on the ship's loudspeaker again. "Battle stations," she ordered. "Battle stations. This is not a drill." She turned off the loudspeaker and addressed Amy. "Raise our shields, and power up the weapons."

Amy immediately did so.

Lt. Ford contacted the *Mount Vernon*. "This is Lt. Ford of the *Liberty Bell*. We have enemy ships approaching. Prepare for battle."

A voice from their sister ship responded. "Yes, we see them, too, *Liberty Bell*. We will follow your lead."

Lt. Ford sent an encrypted message to the *Mount Vernon* with an attack plan.

They acknowledged receipt of it.

"How long until they are in firing range?" Lt. Ford asked.

Amy typed in another command. "Two minutes and twelve seconds," she said. She looked at her leader. "We could lose them by using the Sprint Drive," she suggested. Amy remembered the code for the propulsion system and she prepared to type it in.

"That won't help the *Mount Vernon*," Lt. Ford replied. "It hasn't been installed on their ship yet." She typed in more commands. "Our weapons systems are armed. We are outnumbered 3 to 1, so the Crows have more missiles than we do. We need to make every shot count." She glanced at her copilot. "Are you ready?" she asked Amy.

Amy swallowed hard. "Yes, captain," she said. "I am."

The Crownaxian ships split into two groups of three ships each. They immediately circled around both Union crafts and fired their laser cannons.

Lt. Ford steered the *Liberty Bell* at one Crownaxian ship and fired all lasers. She followed up with one missile. That first Crownaxian ship took on heavy damage and pulled back.

Lt. Ford initiated the Sprint Drive as the other two crafts fired at them.

The *Liberty Bell* scurried off into space before Lt. Ford turned the ship around and rushed back to the battle. They came up behind another Crownaxian ship, and they fired laser cannons and another missile at it. That ship exploded on impact.

Lt. Ford ignored the third ship in the group and instead moved toward the *Mount Vernon*. The sister ship fought valiantly and managed to destroy one of its attackers, but the craft was taking a beating.

Lt. Ford headed directly toward one enemy ship and fired all lasers and one missile. The *Mount Vernon* aimed at the same

Crownaxian ship and fired a missile at it. That craft exploded, leaving just two active enemy crafts and one disabled ship. Lt. Ford wiped her sweaty hands on her lap and prepared to finish the battle.

However, the Crownaxian ship behind the *Liberty Bell* closed in quickly on them. It fired two missiles, and both hit their marks. The *Liberty Bell* shook violently and began to spin downward toward a small moon.

Amy looked over at Lt. Ford and saw the officer's body leaning on the yoke. Amy rushed to her and pulled her off the controller.

Lt. Ford's eyes were closed, and she wasn't moving.

"We need a medic!" Amy yelled. She put both hands on the yoke and pulled it back with all her strength.

Ethan and Madison lifted Lt. Ford out of the chair and gently laid her on the floor as a medic approached them.

Amy sat in the captain's chair and steered the *Liberty Bell* out of the dive and back toward the battle.

The two active Crownaxian ships fired on the *Mount Vernon*. Smoke poured out of several areas of the Union craft, and Amy knew the ship would not last might longer. Amy fired two missiles at the nearest enemy craft and it exploded. "Yeah!" Amy yelled as she slapped the terminal in front of her. "Die, you bastards!" she screamed.

Amy glanced over her shoulder at Lt. Ford. She was still not moving, as the medic performed CPR. "How is she doing?" Amy asked.

Madison came over and sat in the copilot's seat and said that she was in dire straits.

Amy pressed her lips together and focused on the battle again. "Let's end this."

The *Liberty Bell* flew between the *Mount Vernon* and the last active enemy ship.

Amy turned toward the craft and fired a missile at it. The projectile hit its target but did not destroy it. "Damn," Amy said. She looked at the weapons inventory and saw that she had only one missile left. Amy shook her head. She steered toward that enemy ship and fired laser cannons until the craft finally exploded.

A message came from the last Crownaxian craft, which had been crippled early in the battle.

"They want to surrender," Madison said. "With no conditions," he added. "Shall we send security teams to the docking ports?" he asked Amy.

Amy didn't respond. Instead, she stared at the Crownaxian ship. It looked as bad as the *Mount Vernon*, with smoke spilling out from the back. Amy thought about her incarceration in the cave and the murder of her best friend.

Madison said they were waiting for instructions.

"They want instructions?" Amy asked through gritted teeth.

Madison said, "Yes."

"Tell them to go to hell!" Amy exclaimed. She pressed the firing button, and the last missile zoomed across the silence of space until it struck the Crownaxian ship. It obliterated the craft in a brilliant display of light that made Amy smile.

She turned to face Madison.

Ethan slowly walked up behind the robot and placed his hands on the back of the copilot chair.

"They had surrendered," Madison said. "They were no longer a threat. Why did you do that?"

"They killed Yale," Amy replied. "And countless other people. They deserved to die. All of them." She looked up at Ethan. "Do you have something to say?" she asked.

The boy spoke softly. "There were eighteen Crownaxains on that ship," Ethan said. "They didn't have to die." He shook his head. "They didn't have to die." The boy turned and slowly sat down in his seat. He dropped his head into his hands.

Amy rose and addressed everyone on the bridge. "Listen up," she said. "Until we reach Paldor, I am the captain of the *Liberty Bell*. What I say goes. Understand?"

No one spoke, but several crewman nodded. "We are going to repair our ship and the *Mount Vernon*, and then we are going home." She looked at Madison. "You are in charge of repairs. Find out what the other ship needs and take a team over there."

The robot stood up and left the bridge.

Amy sat down in the captain's seat. Her hands shook, and her mouth was dry. Ethan's words echoed in her mind. She shook her head. *This is war and, in war, bad things happen*, she thought. *Much worse is yet to come.*

Epilogue

Amy sat between her parents with her hands folded in her lap. She had trouble focusing on the speaker, as she kept blinking her tear-filled eyes.

Gen. Knox's booming voice detailed the tragically short life of Capt. Yale Brown. He spoke about her childhood on Earth, her years of service in the Union, and her inspirational leadership as an officer. The general also recalled the first time he met Yale, and how she immediately impressed him with her poise, intelligence, and compassion. He finished by saluting her casket, which was covered with the Union flag.

Two Union fighter jets flew overhead and released fireworks over the crowd.

Amy watched the casket as it was lowered into the ground in Paldor's lone cemetery for military personnel. She rose slowly, along with the 200 other mourners, as a Union band played a solemn ballad for the dead. The ceremony ended with Gen. Knox presenting Yale's parents with a folded Union flag.

Yale's mother accepted it as Yale's father shook the general's hand.

Amy followed her parents as they moved toward the reception line. She looked around but did not see Ethan anywhere. The boy hadn't spoken to her since the last battle. The crews of the *Liberty Bell* and the *Mount Vernon* received a hero's welcome just four days ago. Amy, and most of the others, spent nearly two days in debriefings with senior Union officials. The young girl struggled emotionally while recalling the details of her imprisonment and the murder of Yale Brown. She was assigned a counselor and her first session was scheduled for the next day.

The Sutter family made it to the front of the line, and Clayton shook the general's hand. "A very moving speech, Gen. Knox," Clayton said.

Knox thanked him.

"You remember my wife, Pam," Clayton said.

The doctor put her hand on the general's shoulder and praised his speech, before moving beside her husband. "And my daughter, Amy."

Gen. Knox smiled. "I don't think you need any introduction, my dear," he said to Amy.

She politely shook hands with the military leader.

"How are adjusting to home life?" he asked.

Amy forced a smile. "It's good to be home," she said. She wrapped an arm around her mother. The girl looked at Gen. Knox. "General, I just wanted to say . . ." her voice trailed off. Her thoughts were a jumbled mess and had been since she got home. "I mean . . ."

The general nodded. "I understand," he said. He leaned closer to her. "I miss her, too. She was a wonderful person, and we will never forget her." He inched back and glanced at Amy's parents before looking at the girl again. "I have some news for you," he said. "Lincoln and the other robots have been accepted by the Union."

Amy's face lit up. "That's wonderful. They will be great additions to the Union." For a moment, she worried about their exploitation. "Will they all be soldiers, or will they have options?"

The general smiled. "The robots were given choices. Most of the them selected the military, but others chose civilian positions." He crossed his arms over his chest. "I think they will all be happy with their new lives."

"Whatever happened to Dr. Greenland?" Clayton asked.

The general cleared his throat. "Dr. Greenland and his men were arrested. They will be charged with treason. Probably spend the rest of their lives in prison."

A soldier approached the general and whispered something to him. The soldier then handed him a small box.

"This is for you, young lady," Gen. Knox said to Amy.

She tilted her head in surprise. The general opened the box, and Amy saw a circular gold medal attached to a dark green ribbon. Amy took the medal out of the box and held it up for her parents to see.

"It's the Medal of Courage," Gen. Knox said, "for your service during your mission."

"I don't know what to say, general. It's beautiful." She gently ran a finger over the medal. "Thank you, sir." She stared at it as her parents guided her away from the general so he could speak to the other mourners.

The Sutter family stopped at Yale Brown's gravesite.

Amy read the words on the tombstone. *Here lies a brave soldier who gave her all for the Union.* Amy wept again, and felt shivers run through her body.

Her mother put a supportive hand on her left shoulder.

Amy said a brief, silent prayer before she bent down and

draped the gold medal over the tombstone. She whispered a secret message to her friend.

"I will make him pay for your death," she said.

Amy rose and walked away from the gravesite.

Her parents quickly followed her.

Amy clenched both of her hands into tight fists as she remembered Drelk's face. She had a new mission now, and she silently vowed that nothing would keep her from fulfilling her promise.

About the Author

Steven Donahue was a copywriter for TV Guide magazine for 14 years. His first novel, *Amanda Rio*, was originally published in 2004. He released three novels in 2013: *The Manila Strangler* (Rainstorm Press), *Amy the Astronaut and the Flight for Freedom* (Hydra Publications), and *Comet and Cupid's Christmas Adventure* (Createspace). His fifth novel, *Chasing Bigfoot* (Createspace) was published in 2014, and his short story *Grit* was also included in the anthology *Hero's Best Friend* by Seventh Star Press in 2014. In 2015, he published his sixth book, *Where Freedom Rings: A Tale of the Underground Railroad* (Createspace). In 2017, he released his seventh book, Solahütte (Createspace). Donahue lives in Pennsylvania with his wife Dawn, and a home filled with pets.

www.ingramcontent.com/pod-product-compliance
Lightning Source LLC
Chambersburg PA
CBHW052040240626
47153CB00006B/2167